LIFELINES

A NOVEL
ELEANOR BERTIN

Published by Leaf & Blade Publishing, Big Valley, Canada

Welcome to

THE MOSAIC COLLECTION

We are sisters, a beautiful mosaic united by the love of God through the blood of Christ.

Each month The Mosaic Collection releases one faith-based novel or anthology exploring our theme, Family by His Design, and sharing stories that feature diverse, God-designed families. All are contemporary stories ranging from mystery and women's fiction to comedic and literary fiction. We hope you'll join our Mosaic family as we explore together what truly defines a family.

If you're like us, loneliness and suffering have touched your life in ways you never imagined; but Dear One, while you may feel alone in your suffering—whatever it is—you are never alone!

Subscribe to *Grace & Glory*, the official newsletter of The Mosaic Collection, to receive monthly encouragement from Mosaic authors, as well as timely updates about events, new releases, and giveaways.

Learn more about The Mosaic Collection at
www.mosaiccollectionbooks.com

Join our Reader Community, too!
www.facebook.com/groups/TheMosaicCollection

Books in

THE MOSAIC COLLECTION

When Mountains Sing by Stacy Monson
Unbound by Eleanor Bertin
The Red Journal by Deb Elkink
A Beautiful Mess by Brenda S. Anderson
Hope is Born: A Mosaic Christmas Anthology
More Than Enough by Lorna Seilstad
The Road to Happenstance by Janice L. Dick
This Side of Yesterday by Angela D. Meyer
Lost Down Deep by Sara Davison
The Mischief Thief by Johnnie Alexander
Before Summer's End: A Mosaic Summer Anthology
Tethered by Eleanor Bertin
Calm Before the Storm by Janice L. Dick
Heart Restoration by Regina Rudd Merrick
Pieces of Granite by Brenda S. Anderson
Watercolors by Lorna Seilstad
A Star Will Rise: A Mosaic Christmas Anthology II
Eye of the Storm by Janice L. Dick
Lifelines by Eleanor Bertin

Learn more at www.mosaiccollectionbooks.com/books

Für meine Mutti, die wahre Anna, and for Timothy, my own Jesse.

CHAPTER 1

—————————~⌇~—————————

Covered but not at rest or ease of mind,
They sat them down to weep; nor only tears
Rained at their eyes, but high winds worse within
Began to rise, high passions, anger, hate,
Mistrust, suspicion, discord, and shook sore
Their inward state of mind, calm region once
And full of peace, now tossed and turbulent.
—John Milton, Paradise Lost, Book IX

Dr. Robert Q.M. Fielding stood poised to ring his neighbour's doorbell, rejecting the irrational but persistent notion that this simple senior woman held the key to his vexing personal dilemma. The prickly branch of overgrown rose bush that scraped his face annoyed him. So did the wasp that worried past his ears and the grating screech of hinges as he opened her screen door. He blew pent-up air out of tight lips, pffpllpff. Most of all, he was annoyed with himself. That he should have accepted a dinner—scratch that, *supper*—invitation to her home this evening was simply preposterous. That cursed inability of his to think fast on his feet too often got him into uncomfortable spots like this. Yet here he stood at her door.

He should have seen it coming. The mid-August day he had moved in, there she was at his door looking up at him over her glasses and proffering a couple of still-warm cinnamon buns. Her cheery waves or

1

greetings the last few days when he came home after work. Attempts at long-distance conversation from her back deck when he was mowing his grass. Then her handicapped twenty-something son, Jesse, brought him some cookies he had baked himself.

The day she had asked him a simple question he'd been unable to answer about the oscillation of her new lawn sprinkler, he was annoyed for hours. First, with himself for finding that a PhD in biology hadn't sufficed to solve an elementary plumbing problem, but worse and more puzzling, with the odd and unaccustomed feeling of guilt his curt response had brought him.

So when Jesse came to his door last week with an invitation card written carefully crooked and wearing a smile carelessly wide, Robert Fielding surprised himself and said, "Yes, I'll come." And he knew precisely why he'd accepted. Anything was better than sitting at home waiting for the call that never came.

Yet now as he waited for the sound of her step he grimaced at the thought of an evening with this simple woman and her son. He was momentarily relieved at the tangle of branches that screened him from the street as a car drove by. What if someone from the college should see him in this tired neighbourhood? But he'd rung the bell.

"Come in, come in." Anna Fawcett beamed her guileless face directly up at him as she opened the door. It was a door identical to his own in this subdivision of sameness. But the contrast between the interior of her home and his spare and blank rooms struck him. Aromas yeasty and savoury rushed at him. So did the overwhelming sense of colour and life when he entered her small world.

"Jesse will be here in a minute. He's just pulling the buns out of the oven," she said, leading him through the living room toward the dining table. "He does so love the chance to bake for someone. Why don't you have a seat? We'll be right with you."

She scurried out to the kitchen and Robert gravitated toward the stretch of bookcases along one wall of the room. He scanned the surprising range and contrast of titles: Sun Tzu's *The Art of War* next to *Charity and Its Fruits* by one Jonathan Edwards, a complete set of the works of Charles Dickens, Isaac Watts' *Logic*, Rousseau, Austen, Dawkins, and here, a wad of *Calvin & Hobbes* cartoon books. Martin Luther, philosopher Anthony Flew—

Anna's stock had just risen in Robert's estimation when Jesse entered from the kitchen carrying a basket of golden dinner rolls in one hand and a salad in the other. Robert made his way to a table set for three on a worn-smooth yellow cloth. Anna followed her son with two steaming dishes and urged her guest to sit down.

"I hope you're hungry, Robert," she said as she took her place at the end of the table.

Jesse sat across from him, a smile splitting the freckles as he reached first for his mother's hand and then Robert's.

"If you don't mind the time it takes, Jesse likes to ask the blessing." She bowed her head.

Feeling awkward, Robert kept his glance down as he held Jesse's dry, plump hand, catching about half of the earnest prayer.

"Thank you for books I got yesserday, for Chrissmas... gerbils... Lego... Thank you that Caleb passed his 'zams... help Passer Tom not be sad an' lonely for Alice anymore... Thank you that Misser Fie'ding is here and for this good food," Jesse intoned. Then very distinctly, "In Jesus' name, amen!" With relief, Robert pulled back his hand and his opinions.

"Jesse has a heart of thanksgiving," Anna said as she offered Robert the salad. "To fill you in a little, Caleb is my grandson and those exams he passed were Grade Nine finals—back in June." She winked at him, then sobered. "Our pastor, Tom Townsend, just lost his wife Alice in May after a long fight with cancer. I'm afraid he's going to be sad and lonely for quite some time. And she was a dear friend of mine, so we'll miss her, too, won't we, son?"

She turned to Jesse and heaved a great sigh, stroking his sturdy arm. The young man squeezed his eyes shut tightly, but a large droplet escaped despite his effort.

Robert sat suspended in the long uncomfortable pause that followed until Anna checked his plate and brightened.

"Pass our guest the goulash, Jesse. And maybe after supper you can show Mr. Fielding your gerbil. I'll bet he has some of his own at work."

Her son swiped away the tears and dutifully passed the meat dish in a china bowl with an old-fashioned pattern vaguely familiar to Robert.

Jesse's almond eyes widened. "You do?"

"Just lab rats and mice." Robert directed his answer to Anna, uncomfortable with the disabled man's open-mouthed gaze.

"Whaddaya do wif 'em?"

"Well, we... uh... we—" Robert turned to look deeply into the young man's eyes, wondering what to tell him. What would he understand?

With a twinkly glance at her guest, Anna told Jesse, "Sometimes they give mice medicine to see if it helps them get better when they're sick. If it works on mice then it might help people, too."

Medical research reduced to its simplistic roots. Although the description wasn't entirely applicable to Robert's vocation, it was enough.

"Thass good then right?" Jesse asked him intently.

Robert scrutinized his young neighbour, not having considered the moral value of his work in a long time.

"I hope so," he said.

"Could I see your rass and mice sometime, Misser Fie'ding?"

Robert observed with distaste the unappetizing bolus of brown-mottled food rolling around inside Jesse's mouth. He averted his eyes quickly and looked toward Anna for a clue as to how to answer. She simply smiled.

"You could do that," he answered.

"Mom, when c'we go?"

"When I can work it out with Mr. Fielding and he's not too busy." Anna patted Jesse's arm and then leaned toward him, whispering, "Chew with your mouth closed."

Jesse busied himself with the noodles and beef, rolling his eyes and giving exaggerated attention to keeping his lips together.

Robert was so focused on the morsels of tender beef and pearl onions for a time that Anna's voice beside him gave him a jolt.

"When you moved in a few weeks ago, were you new to Red Deer?" she asked.

"No," he said, finishing his mouthful. To divert the conversation from the recent past as much as to keep from sounding abrupt, he added, "This will be my eighth year here. I teach biology at the college."

"The study of life," Anna said, setting down her fork to pass Jesse the butter. "Now that must be fascinating to teach. There are so many moral and ethical implications that go along with what we believe about how life began."

"Yes, I suppose so."

With the current turmoil in his life, Robert had no desire to embark on a discussion of morals, whatever Anna meant. Thankfully, she let that trail die. He floundered for a safer topic of conversation and remembered her library across the room.

"Your books, Mrs. Fawcett," he said, buttering a warm bun. "It's quite an eclectic collection. You seem educated. What's your degree in?"

Anna's eyebrows rose. "Hmmm. No degree, just a lot of curiosity," she said. Her laugh tinkled along with the silverware at the table. "My husband and I had five children—I used to tell people we were Mr. and

Mrs. Fawcett and our five little squirts." She ducked her head and looked at him sideways.

Robert stared, realizing some response was required of him. "Ah, I see. You're making a little joke."

Anna cocked an eyebrow, then chuckled. "My children usually groan, too, when they hear that one for the umpteenth time. Anyway, each one of them has unique interests and talents. Gerry and I always tried to keep up with them enough to know what fascinated them. I've always wished I'd had the opportunity to become a nurse myself." She looked off into some distant corner of disappointment. "So it was important to me to learn on my own by reading whatever I could lay my hands on and teaching our children to do the same. After all, what is education really? Isn't it just learning to learn? Just using literacy and research skills to pursue a love of knowledge?"

Robert thought of the freight of student loan debt he'd acquired simply pursuing a love of knowledge. He gave a taut smile. "I don't think that definition would go over very well with my department head. There does need to be an extensive body of knowledge passed on to the student, you know." He savoured a forkful of the meaty potage.

"Yes, of course. But don't you think relationship between teacher and student is a prerequisite? No amount of pounding will permeate an unwilling mind. You teach, so you must know the value of knowing your students so that you can tailor that body of knowledge to their needs."

"That may be true of young children, but the students I teach are there voluntarily so there's no pounding involved. I wouldn't be up to it." Robert scooped up the last of the rich gravy with the remainder of his bun. Philosophy of education was more conversation than he'd expected this evening. "It's certainly a topic that deserves some thought." He glanced at his watch. "But I have a lecture to review tonight so I should probably get going."

"There's an awful lot of goulash left here. Would you like another helping?" Anna asked.

Robert found the offer irresistible and accepted another plateful. "It's the best dinner I've had in a long time, Mrs. Fawcett," he told her, his appreciation real.

"I'll bet you're too tired to cook a full meal after a long day's work. And you probably don't have time in the morning to throw something into the crockpot, do you?"

"My—" He cleared his throat. "No, I never think of it then. I usually just grab fast food or something from the deli on the way home."

"Tell you what, Robert, why not have supper with us once or twice a week? I'm cooking anyway and one more mouth won't make any more work. In fact, since my oldest kids are grown up and away, Jesse and I would enjoy the company."

There it was. More down-home neighbourliness than he knew what to do with. But how could he refuse?

"Oh, I appreciate the offer and your fine cooking—"

"Great. Then we'll expect you Tuesdays and Thursdays, all right?" She beamed at him.

Robert sank his teeth into a tender fresh roll, relishing its airy warmth, and was helpless to do anything but nod.

Jesse knows he has to help clear the table. He doesn't really want to. It's only fun if he makes a story out of it. He slides Mrs. Salt and Mr. Pepper together. Then, one by one, he walks them to the end of the table nearest the kitchen doorway. At the end of the table, he takes them two at a time and bounces them gingerly through the air to the kitchen. He does the same with the salad dressing bottles. And the stacks of plates. And the cups.

Mom presses the phone to her ear with her shoulder as she puts the food away.

"Marlene?" Jesse hears his mother say on his way back to the living room, "it's Anna... Oh, okay, I won't keep you but I'm wondering if you have any books on biology or microbiology? I need anything you can get me... Sounds great! Love you. Thanks."

She hangs up the phone and comes to the window where Jesse is watching their neighbour. Mr. Fielding gets to his own door in just a few long strides. His shirt hangs loosely from his bony shoulders and his shaggy brown hair needs a trim.

"I wonder what he was about to say earlier this evening," Mom says. "'My *wife* used to use a crockpot?' There's no evidence of anyone else living there. But he did wear a wedding ring."

"'Poor li'l bug on the wall,'" Jesse starts to sing. "'No one t' love 'im at all. No one t' wash his clo'es—'"

"Tsk tsk, Jesse!" Mom smiles and musses his buzzcut. Jesse strokes it down quickly.

CHAPTER 2

Long my imprisoned spirit lay, Fast bound in sin and nature's night
Thine eye diffused a quick'ning ray, I woke, the dungeon flamed
with light: My chains fell off, my heart was free, I rose, went forth
and followed Thee.
—Charles Wesley, "And Can It Be that I Should Gain?"

Her snowy hair dripping like a sunny late winter day, the woman beside Amelia Ashton rearranged her cape and settled herself in one of a row of dated green vinyl stylist chairs. Behind them, another row of the chairs was equipped with 60s dryer hoods. As her cape settled, a poof of air pushed up a strong whiff of perm solution, beginning the day's queasiness in Amelia's stomach. Added to that, her feet dangled uncomfortably, unable to quite reach the rung of the chair. Her stylist answered a cell phone.

"Hair Today Salon, Brooke speaking," bubbled the multi-pierced, two-tone-haired Brooke. "Oh, hey Jen! How's it going?"

Phone clenched between her chin and shoulder, Brooke began to separate Amelia's dark hair into sections.

"How's Mallory?... Aww... No way. She's not thirteen already?... She did? Awesome! What a cool birthday present!... Oh no! Not good! But she's still got the ring in it?... Hasn't it formed a scab or whatnot?... Whaddaya mean 'pus'? Is it yellow or green?"

Too much information! Where did they pick up this girl? Her belly roiling, Amelia glanced up at the mirror above a long counter in front of her. Her lips were turning green, a gruesome contrast to her café au lait complexion. The *café* was from her Indian mother, the *lait* from her Anglo-Canadian father.

An older woman in the next chair was watching her, a sympathetic lift to her brow. Their eyes, mirror-met, exchanged grimaces.

Undaunted by the queasy drama beneath her hands, Brooke babbled on. "More than just a few drops? That doesn't sound normal, a big gush like that..."

Violent stomach lurch!

"Where'd she get it done?... When I got mine done, they gave a whole spiel about their safety procedures and whatnot. Was she taking good care of it?... Yeah, but all that pus and whatnot—that's no good!... Since the nostril skin is so tender, it might have pierced through a cyst or whatnot..."

Keep the breakfast down, just keep the breakfast down... Amelia's fingers moved faster and faster, tightly pleating the hem of her barber's cape.

"Mine seeped a little but nothing like that! That's just awful! She'll have to get it checked."

Staring at her reflection, Amelia could see the colour had drained from her lips. She noticed her neighbour in the next chair looking at her, concerned.

The woman told Amelia in a stage whisper, "I used to whine to my mother about cold trickles down my back when she was putting up my hair in rags for the Sunday morning ringlets."

It was all Amelia could do to try and smile at the woman in response.

Please don't make me talk. If I open my mouth I'm going to puke!

Oblivious to Amelia's silence, the older woman asked if Amelia came to this salon regularly.

Swallowing hard and willing her stomach to stay put, she said, "Oh, it's my first time here. I used to go to Club Ritz before—well... things change, you know?"

She looked away as her stylist returned to work.

"I know that place. Quite exclusive isn't it?" the woman said, addressing Amelia's reflection. "I'm Anna Fawcett and I've been having Marlene here," she looked up at her stylist, "do my hair for—is it thirty-two years now?"

Marlene nodded with a smile.

"Some things never change," Anna added, grinning at her fellow patron. "We've known each other since Grade One, then both moved away until each of us got married. Turns out Marlene and her husband farmed just five miles down the road from us. That was nearly forty years ago. They moved around a bit more and then we both ended up retiring here in Red Deer. And your name, dear?"

"Amelia."

"I'm just a couple of blocks up the street and around the corner from here. Do you live nearby?"

"Just a few blocks away," Amelia said, not offering another opening.

Both freed at the same time, they almost collided at the till. Amelia could feel Anna's eyes on her as she winced at the total and made careful calculation for a tip. And watching, too, as she put on her jacket, her long chunky-knit sweater covering the hips of her slim jeans.

Once outside, Amelia gulped the cool fresh air eagerly, relieved at how it settled her insides.

She heard footsteps behind her and noticed the older woman catching up. Together, they walked into the stiff west wind for half a block without speaking.

"So much for the style. 'Hair Today' and gone tomorrow. Seems like I could have saved my money and gone without the blow-dry." Anna turned to Amelia and gave a wry smile as her white hair whipped flat against her cheek.

Amelia smiled. "Maybe I should have."

"Things a little tight for you, too?"

She felt her smile vanish. "Yeah."

"I turn in here," Anna said. "Are you going much farther?"

"About two more blocks." Amelia kept walking. "Bye."

"Wait, Amelia," Anna said. "It's almost noon and I've got hot homemade soup simmering here. Why don't you stop in for lunch?"

Amelia looked into the smiling blue eyes of the older woman. It occurred to her that she'd like to have crinkles around her eyes like that someday. Here was one who over the years had earned a face worth having. There was compassion at the corners of the mouth and unflinching truthfulness around the eyes. She surprised herself by accepting the invitation.

"Just hang your jacket on the hook and come on into the kitchen. I left Jesse with the job of taking the cookies out of the oven. We'll see if he did what I asked." And she scurried into the next room.

A kaleidoscope of quilts, books, plants, needlework on the coffee table, a small pet cage in one corner, and an age-darkened upright piano filled the room. Amelia read the story the house told of its people. It was a busy room, with little cohesion in the décor, but the palpable safety of it enveloped her. Above the door to the kitchen was a brown wood-look plaque: *Casting all your care upon Him, for He cares for you.* She took in the wall of photos covering what appeared to be a lengthy family history. A large family evidently. She had just narrowed her search for Anna's wedding picture to an early 1970s portrait of a bride with dark-rimmed glasses and a groom with hefty sideburns when the Jesse Anna had mentioned came through the kitchen door with her.

Not the meek, greying husband she'd assumed; what met Amelia's eyes made her grasp the sideboard to steady herself. It was all there in person, the small ears and slanted eyes, the rounded body and flat upper lip so familiar from her recent research.

But he was reaching out his hand and smiling and asking her something she couldn't quite understand or even hear for the blood pounding in her ears.

"Amelia, aren't you well? Come over here dear, and sit down." Anna guided her to a chair at the dining room table.

The phone warbled just then, and Anna hurried over to a small paper-packed desk in one corner of the kitchen to answer it. While Amelia sat, willing calm into her mind and body, she watched Jesse bring a third bowl, glass, and spoon to the table. Then he filled all three glasses with water, carefully holding the glass jug with both stubby hands. Amelia could hear Anna's voice drop with murmured concern as she listened to her caller.

"But Tina, remember what we've talked about before... He loves you with an everlasting love. That means he never stops loving you and it's not something you earn."

Advice to the lovelorn, Amelia surmised. *Never stops loving you? Right. This old lady is a relic of a bygone age.*

"...No, no, you mustn't think that way..." and Amelia saw her reach for a book covered in floral cloth. "'He remembers that we are dust.'"

Dust? What or who is she talking about?

As Jesse slid a basket of freckled buns onto the table, the topmost one rolled off and fell on the floor. He picked it up and was about to put it back in the basket but catching Amelia's eye, he put it on the small plate opposite her instead. Quickly he looked away and a smile crinkled the corners of his eyes. He passed her the basket, and she took a bun. Then, taking another bun, he put it on the third plate and, glancing through the door into the kitchen, switched the two plates back and forth, back and forth, until even Amelia had forgotten which was the offending bun. Grinning now, his tiny teeth barely showing, he patted both buns, sat down, and folded his hands to wait for lunch.

Amelia felt his smile light her own face and its warmth caught and spread through her. That one revelation of mischief and humour gave her a curious pleasure. Unexpectedly, a seed of hope had just sprouted in her.

Anna hurried to the table at last, soup pot in hand.

"Most inelegant to serve from a pot, a lady we visit at the Sunset Seniors' Lodge tells me. But I wasn't expecting company and I'm just lazy enough to want to avoid washing any more dishes than necessary." She sat down, breathless, and added in a poor parody of Scottish brogue, "'No pots on Mrs. Cochrrrrane's table and only Limoges china, if you please.' But I'm sorry for the delay. A dear friend is struggling with the weight of the world on her shoulders these days."

She surprised Amelia by reaching for her hand and asking a blessing.

When Anna raised her head, Amelia, unaccustomed to the practice, blurted, "Do you think you can help?"

"Help? Oh, you mean my friend?" Anna ladled soup. "I once read a study somewhere that showed depressed people recover at about the same rate by having therapy as they do if only a friend listens. So I figure I'm the friend." Her eyes twinkled as they gazed into Amelia's. "And besides, I'm always happy to save a friend a bundle of money!"

Jesse held a hand to his mouth as giggles fought to emerge while he watched his mother bite into her bun.

"What's up with you?" Anna asked, a suspicious smile lifting one eyebrow. "What have you been up to?"

Amelia watched the two of them, marvelling. Jesse's face was turning red and he appeared to be about to hyperventilate. She explained the Trick of the Fallen Bun and Anna laughed.

"But maybe yours is the bad one, Jesse." his mother said.

Jesse's smile morphed into a slight frown as he gravely brushed his bun with his hand.

"Amelia," Anna said as she spooned her soup, "you seemed to be feeling ill just as we came in the house. All better now?"

Embarrassed, Amelia assured her the dizziness had passed.

"If you don't mind my asking, dear," Anna said, her eyebrows raised. "I think I recognize the signs after five pregnancies of my own."

Amelia nodded, hoping the mere fact of pregnancy was explanation enough for her vertigo. How could she ever explain to the mother of a son with Down syndrome her own turmoil and angst at the sight of him?

"How far along are you?" Anna asked.

"Just past twelve weeks."

"So you're due in..." Anna's eyes rolled upward, calculating. "March?"

"That's right." Amelia enjoyed her buttered roll and the soup. Her appetite these days alarmed her.

"Spring is a lovely time to have a baby. By the time you're recovered and the baby is old enough to enjoy it, the milder weather has come and you can spend time outside. My oldest was a February baby."

"I hadn't thought of that," Amelia said. "The way I've been feeling, it's hard to imagine an actual baby. All I've been aware of is a lot of nausea and just being so tired all the time." *And not having a husband anymore.* And all too soon no home, she could have added, if the figures in her chequing account today were to be trusted.

"No baby movements yet? No little flutterings?" Anna glanced at Amelia's empty bowl with a questioning look.

"Yes to the soup, but no, no movement yet."

Anna passed Amelia's bowl to Jesse, who ladled some of the steaming creamy soup into it. "I always loved those little kicks. They made it all worthwhile. I suppose you're working full-time?"

"Yes, I teach English at Clearbrook High. It's everything I can do some days to keep my breakfast down and face a class of bored and mouthy fifteen-year-olds."

"Ah yes, class warfare," Anna commented knowingly. "But at least you can have the evening to rest. Hopefully, your husband helps with supper. This is your first baby?"

Amelia struggled to answer. "Yes, it's the first... and my husband isn't with me anymore."

"Oh, I'm so sorry dear," Anna said, her warm hand immediately on Amelia's arm. "I know just what you're going through. My husband Gerry passed away four and a half years ago. You've been widowed recently then?"

"No, no, he's not dead! I just—we're actually separated."

Jesse was staring at her. She wished she'd thought quicker to evade the question. Inexplicably, her cheeks were flaming.

"Well then, there's hope isn't there?" Anna said.

Amelia told her most emphatically there was not.

"But surely this is the most exciting stage of life and marriage you could possibly be in. Why wouldn't the two of you want to enjoy it together?"

"He's never wanted children," Amelia felt compelled to explain. "I'd always agreed with him until... well, I was surprised by how much I wanted this baby." Her voice faltered. "But he thought my age made it too risky—"

And then the fountains of the deep erupted. Never far from the surface these days, they spilled in great torrents down Amelia's face. She doubled over in an agony of weeping into the older woman's lap. Anna stroked Amelia's hair making soothing sounds.

"Jesse," Anna whispered. "Go get a clean washcloth and wet it with warm water."

Between sobs, Amelia heard a chair scrape the floor and Jesse went off to his task.

"I'm sorry, I just—" Amelia tried to gain control and still more sobs came. Wrenched from her depths, they left her limp and empty.

"Now Amelia, listen," Anna began, lifting Amelia's face to look into her eyes. Gently wiping away the tears and ravaged make-up, the older woman told her something, the details of which would become clearer as time went on. But this dear simple woman's hand on her face washed Amelia in such a wave of compassion that she knew it was her turning point, the climax of her life. Everything else would be denouement. What was empty was filled, the lost found, the spoiled restored.

Somehow, she left Anna's small home that day with the ineffable sense that her burden had been divided and shared, if not altogether eliminated. She was not alone and never would be.

"Oh baby, my baby! I can show you the way now," she breathed as she walked home late that fall afternoon. The chilly wind swirled leaves to bury summer's dying blooms in flowerbeds. But nothing could bury the budding peace she knew she now kept within her forever.

CHAPTER 3

―――――*ɑ*――――

First Moloch, horrid King, besmeared with blood Of
human sacrifice, and parents' tears Though, for the noise
of drums and timbrels lov'd
Their children's cries unheard that passed through fire.
—John Milton, *Paradise Lost, Book I*

Waiting for Dr. Baldwyn, chair of the Pure and Applied Sciences faculty, Robert and the other professors and staff were mostly subdued. There was a certain anti-climax each year at the end of the first week of classes. Further, rumours of provincial funding cuts to education were making even the most job-secure skittish. Seven years ago, when he had gotten the job at this small central Alberta college, Robert's father had warned him that the western province's volatile oil-based economy could mean career instability. The old man had pressured him to hold out for Dalhousie where he'd studied for his undergrad degree, closer to home in Halifax. There, Marlowe Fielding had business interests and claimed to have some pull. But his father had no idea of the competition for jobs at the larger universities and Robert had accepted the first job offer he'd received when he finally graduated with his doctorate. He felt far safer in a smaller pond. Besides, the three years he'd spent working in the family business at his father's insistence prior to beginning his PhD, had made Robert more than ready to put a continent of distance between them.

Farewell to Nova Scotia. He hadn't regretted leaving "the sea-bound coast," though occasionally he missed those spectacular Atlantic sunrises.

As he and his colleagues waited to hear the reason for the meeting, the conference room was filled with their scattered polite murmurs. Then the door opened. Thirty-three heads swivelled expectantly to— Jamie McCoy. A barely audible release of breath went around the room. McCoy breezed past the row of empty chairs around the perimeter of the room with his usual charming banter. Finally, he claimed the last vacant seat at the end of the long mahogany table. Was he truly unaware that it was reserved for the department head? Or did he consider himself on the same level?

Robert was sitting beside Sarah-Mae Ballard, the lush-bodied blonde administrative assistant for the science department. They had started work on the same day, and since then had fallen into the scatheless ease of parallel lives. At first their main commonality had been hockey and a friendly rivalry between her pet Calgary Flames and his loyalty to the Montreal Canadiens, but gradually she had begun to confide in him the vagaries of her roller-coaster love life. Her thirtieth birthday in January had been a particular nadir for her, having been rejected by yet another deadbeat boyfriend, and Robert had, as usual, been both her coffee partner and dumping ground. In her view, he surmised, he was safely married and "way older," as she'd once termed it, though in fact she was only eight years his junior. It certainly hadn't been his sagacious advice on her predicaments that kept her coming back to him, since he'd had none to offer.

Now they both sat listening to McCoy pontificate on the latest from the scientific journal *Philosophical Transactions*. Robert elbowed Sarah-Mae. He suspected she had come to be in awe of McCoy, a self-assured prof whose boyish enthusiasm and clear-eyed good looks had been captivating students and faculty alike. McCoy had arrived from

Australia as an exchange professor in bioethics at the beginning of the winter semester last year. One day last spring, Robert had seen on Baldwyn's desk a student's evaluation of the new prof. Apparently trendy dress and an Aussie accent were worth two or three extra points on the ratings scale in the eyes of the female student population. He had to admit he found the guy compelling. But recently, Robert had begun to hate the fact that by comparison, he himself was a slow-witted clod, a plodding bore. Every news piece Robert had heard, McCoy knew more about it. Every avenue of research, McCoy was on top of it. He could make even the most edgy scientific conjecture plausible. Didn't the guy ever sleep? Worst of all, he was actually likeable, with his willingness to talk to anyone and that quirky down-under habit of adding the "-zza" suffix to everyone's name. With a smirk, Robert anticipated the day McCoy called the dean "Balzza". It was astounding, though, how everyone seemed to defer to the newcomer. And of course, the terms of the exchange program meant McCoy had no worries about provincial education budget slashing.

While they continued to wait, the staff bastion of tenure and academic wisdom herself, Dr. Walli Slootenberg, captured everyone's attention by asking McCoy's opinion on a recent case of wrongful birth that had been in the news.

"What we've really got in that case," McCoy began, leaning forward in his chair with his elbows on the table, "is a woman who is thinking in a logically consistent way. Because she was not offered prenatal screening of any sort, she's saddled with a handicapped infant that's going to be a drain on her emotionally, financially, physically—just in every way for the rest of her life. She probably planned to have two or three children and now this one is getting in the way of the ones she's always hoped for. If the disabled one is dispatched, won't that mean there will be another human being who would not otherwise have existed? One who will offer a valuable contribution to the world?" McCoy asked. "And let's not forget that Canada has no restrictions on abortion at any time during a pregnancy. So what's the difference?"

This line of reasoning made perfect sense to Robert, but he was aware of some in the room shifting in their seats. Predictably, his friend Phil Thiessen, the wavy-haired math prof, started to protest. But the Aussie plunged ahead.

"So yeah, what's the difference if a woman aborts and tries again for the child she's always dreamed of or if she asks the hospital staff to withhold life support after birth for the same reason? My mentor, Dr. Saeger, has argued that infanticide is ethical on the same grounds that abortion is. Even a viable fetus can't be considered truly human, since it isn't a rational, self-aware person with desires and plans." McCoy emphasized each of these points on his fingers. "So it shouldn't have the same rights as a human who does have such qualities."

Robert found himself wondering what his neighbour Anna would say to that. He could picture the unassuming woman asking one of her innocent questions—

The sudden backward shove of Sarah-Mae's chair next to him jerked everyone's attention her way.

"Then by that criteria, *you* are not human every night when you're asleep!" she screamed and rushed toward the door.

Robert caught her chair before it toppled back and was about to go after her when Baldwyn came in. Sarah-Mae charged past the big man whose forehead furrowed deeply as he watched her flee.

"Anyone care to provide an explanation?" Baldwyn glowered at the group from under heavy sandy eyebrows. Only stunned silence answered him.

Finding his accustomed chair at the end of the table occupied, the bulky man frowned and took Sarah-Mae's place beside Robert. He opened the folder his young assistant had left on the table.

Baldwyn's announcement, when he finally made it, was met with a singular lack of enthusiasm, even consternation. In an attempt to meet government cutbacks, administration had decided to appoint a task team to review course offerings and shortlist those drawing the fewest students. In effect, it would heighten the contest for popularity amongst professors, a domain in which Robert already felt he was losing ground. He could feel the eyes of the others mentally weighing each other's value, and he could barely wait for the meeting to adjourn.

From the midst of the murmuring that followed, Robert left the meeting room intent on finding Sarah-Mae. Passing through the flow of other professors clotted in the doorway, he caught Dr. Slootenberg's return to the earlier conversation as she gushed over McCoy's "detached analysis" and "evident compassion for women".

Robert found Sarah-Mae at her computer in the reception area of the Science office cluster, pounding the keys as if they were an enemy's teeth.

"Do you want to talk about it?"

She gave one quick shake of her head. Sniffed hard.

Robert started toward his own office, but at an inarticulate sound from her he turned back in surprise. "What did you call me?"

"Oh, not you!" She was fuming again, her face hidden by her hair, fingers flying across the keyboard.

"Why don't we go for coffee," he suddenly suggested. "I don't have a class until 11:30. C'mon."

They found a corner booth in the Student Centre, the student radio station's heavy metal throbbing from the speakers. It provided a good cover and Robert wondered how many sorrows and dilemmas had been poured out and absorbed under it.

"So tell me," Robert said.

"I just can't stand him!" Sarah-Mae surprised him with her

vehemence, her perfect features twisted in hate. "You think I was taken in by all his clever talk and that knowledgeable way he has. And I guess I was. In fact, we kind of had a thing going through the summer." She snorted. "A thing *growing,* you might say."

She sucked air through her teeth viciously. She paused and stared at Robert, daring him to decipher her meaning.

"So on Saturday morning I went to the clinic downtown and got rid of it," she finished. "Just like he told me I should."

She gazed at Robert fiercely, red-eyed and bitter. He flinched under that stare.

"Yeah. That's right. I killed my baby. And he can sit there just talking it up and never even glance my way. No recognition that I've just been through hell. Yeah, I killed *his* baby! You know, the kind that's a human being but that we can 'dispatch,' as he calls it, for survival of the fittest?"

She glared silently at Robert for what seemed a long time. Accusingly, the idea that there were moral implications to his view on origins flashed into his mind. He had never felt so inadequate, empty of answers. "So why do I feel like *I'm* the one who's not fit to survive?" The despair in her eyes frightened Robert.

He had long striven for logical consistency, Robert reminded himself as he drove home late that afternoon. Was he the only one who tried to live in a way consistent with his beliefs? He'd often wondered. Of course, there was Anna. If early impressions were correct, she evidently did. Always alert to inconsistencies in others, he admitted they were harder to spot in his own life. But he tried. And he prided himself on the belief that he would freely abandon any ideas contradictory to his basic principles. New information, in keeping with the tenets of good science, had to be evaluated and either incorporated into the body of evidence in favour of a belief, or discarded.

He shifted down for a yellow light on Taylor Drive. His neighbour's suggestion that there was a connection between one's view about the origins of life and ethical issues had unsettled him, distracting him from the worry of competing to maintain his course load and the ever-present pressure to gain tenure. The prospect of rethinking the beliefs he shared with McCoy about abortion, however, touched something deep, something tender within him.

It gave him as bottomless a sensation as if he'd jumped off this very bridge into the languid autumn river below.

Yet Sarah-Mae's words, her anguish, haunted him. Notwithstanding his gallantry toward her, he somehow felt a sense of responsibility for her torment.

As far as he knew, all of the Science faculty, and probably most of the Humanities profs, held a pro-choice view. Well, that may have been an overstatement. What was it Phil had been about to say? Come to think of it, he'd never heard much from Dr. Baldwyn on the topic either. Of course, as much as they all revered Dr. Baldwyn, it wasn't like Robert had spent much time chewing the fat with him in the staff lounge. The thought of revisiting his views on the topic made his stomach clench. He couldn't be wrong on that score. He couldn't!

Abruptly his mind flailed for some safer current of thought. But all he came up with was another pressing problem that yesterday's mail had turned up.

Hot rage surged through him as he considered last month's Visa statement. His foot grew heavier on the accelerator. Was his wife purposely trying to ruin him? Uttering her name had always flooded him with emotion, and now more than ever. But whether on purpose or not, purchase after expense after impulse buy lay in stark print on that page. He'd been sure that leaving her on her own would have brought her to her senses right quick. There had to be an end to it! For years he'd been cleaning up the messes, juggling their accounts to keep current, chunk down his student debt, pay extra on the mortgage, save for retirement, and still try to do some investing, and there was no logical reason, with their ample combined income, that they should have had money stress, yet in recent years it seemed he always had to play the bad guy, curtailing her spending. She never seemed to have any concept of their obligations, yet hurt feelings abounded if he asked her for an accounting. He shuddered to think of how she'd scramble her money matters without him.

Perhaps he should make a move toward selling the house. His wife wouldn't like moving, especially as things were now, but it was that simple. Simple, but difficult. Robert had never been one to get attached to a building, yet it had been their first home and he had more than money invested in it.

No! He was not about to rehash the whole conflict that had precipitated his leaving her so abruptly in mid-summer. That last explosive confrontation over her betrayal, his unplanned, fast and furious departure... His stomach churned at the mere thought of all the confusion.

Just breathe. Consider the next logical financial step.

Robert noticed an RCMP cruiser driving in the opposite direction and quickly checked his speed. No need to add a speeding ticket to the burden.

Once again, he considered doing the stock-trading his brother had suggested. Some quick income could pay off the duplex where he now lived, and at least the rent on the adjoining unit would be all profit. But the risk. Muscles at the base of his head tightened at the thought of that much risk. He'd have to start with something simple. Getting his wife's name off his Visa card could be the first step. Then he'd contact a realtor for an appraisal on the house.

As he pulled into his driveway, Robert let out a long breath and reached up to crack his neck joints both ways. Worries trampled the carefully honed calm of his mind. What if his classes were cut? What if he ended up with only half-time teaching? And then his loans were called in? Or his remaining tenant next door moved out and he couldn't find another renter? If he were tenured, these government cutbacks wouldn't faze him. Then too, why oh why couldn't he make headway on his research paper? Because of all the stress his wife caused him, that was why.

The decision to take concrete action toward separation after all these years of marriage had to have been the right choice. But it had more than just his neck taut with tension. He got out of the car, slowly probing in his pocket for the key to his solitary life.

CHAPTER 4

There are two things for which animals are to be envied: they know nothing of future evils, or of what people *say about them.*
—Voltaire, *Letter*, 1739

Rubbing sleep from his eyes, Robert hurried to his side door, hearing the rising pitch of hysterics even before he opened it. A tall, strongly built woman stood on his step, braying.

"If it's your dog over at my place you'd better get him out of my yard right now!"

She was all angles and straight edges, from her blunt-cut hair to her square-toed shoes. Square-tipped nose, square shoulders, square frame. Red-faced and breathing hard, she clamped together the front edges of her rumpled grey sweat jacket with one hand.

"I've had to chase my cats into the house and keep that animal away from them at the same time. I finally got my babies all safe inside but I can't get rid of your stupid dog! I'm telling you, I had to fight so hard for my right to have a fence built and the whole point was to keep out the neighbourhood dogs. They knock over my bird feeders and dig up my vegetables and leave their crap all over. And that guy from city hall had the nerve to tell me I should just," in a sing-song voice, "'have some patience with my neighbours.'"

Robert could feel the old calm descending on him in the face of this raging barrage. It had served him well against his father's blustering.

"I don't believe we've met?" His tone was clipped as he offered his hand. "I'm Dr. Robert Fielding."

The woman's square jaw sagged as she paused mid-rant, then meekly shook his hand. Once again, his credentials hadn't let him down, he noticed, gratified.

"I'm Joan Klug." She straightened her dishevelled iron-grey hair with sturdy fingers. "From two doors over." She cleared her throat. "You'll have to get used to me. You've met Anna, I'm sure. Always the first in the neighbourhood to greet newcomers. She isn't home right now—always off gallivanting who knows where when she promised to come help me with my project. She told me someone had finally moved in here so I figured that must be your dog. Come and get him." And she turned on her heel abruptly toward her home.

"It's not my dog..." Robert called after her, then muttered, "but perhaps I can help."

He grabbed his jacket off the hook to follow her. He would at least try to get the animal out of her yard, and from there it could wander back to wherever it had come from.

Peering over Joan's gate, a midsized auburn dog on hind legs with black-tipped ears and tail gazed at him eagerly. Robert had always wanted a dog. To his father, pets were a "dead investment." To his wife, a perpetual sneezing fit. But living by himself now, Robert let himself consider taking in the animal.

"A gentledog in reduced circumstances, I see," Robert murmured as he moved to pet the fuzzy head.

"Don't touch him!" Joan squawked, having stopped short of her fence. "See? He's baring his teeth. He looks like he has rabies!"

Robert saw the dog's lips crinkled back from white teeth, but he also noted the tail-plume waving fervently.

"He's just smiling, aren't you, boy?" Much leaping up and bunting of Robert's hand ensued. He heard a distinct "tsk" from his neighbour, presumably affronted that anyone could admire a representative of the canine race. After he had opened the gate to let him out, the animal trotted down the street, looking back repeatedly.

He should call the dog back, but of course he had heard the jingle of dog tags on the leather collar. Yet he needed a friend. A nice, uncritical friend who wasn't smarter than Robert, who couldn't spend his money willy-nilly, and who might encourage him to get down to writing with a friendly wag of the tail.

It was out of the question obviously. There would be dog food to buy and possibly vet bills... No, it couldn't be. But he'd liked that canine smile.

CHAPTER 5

---~~---

Sanctity in ministers is a loud call to sinners to repent, and when allied with holy cheerfulness it becomes wondrously attractive.
—Charles Spurgeon, *Lectures to My Students, Volume One*

On the last Saturday in September, when Robert arrived at Anna's she was ready with the clippers and a vinyl cape depicting a cartoon primate labelled *Curious George*. Twice each week now, Robert anticipated a hot supper of comfort food with the side helping of thought-provoking conversation he'd come to expect. So when he'd mentioned his shaggy hair on Thursday, he gladly accepted Anna's offer to "lower his ears," as she put it. Robert cared little what he sported on the top of his head and had always found the whole procedure a waste of time and money. It had usually been his wife's insistence that brought him under the scissors. But now he'd rather pay Anna the twenty dollars and save himself the hassle of going downtown.

Robert meekly suffered the indignity of the monkey cape, feeling foolish as he sat on a low stool in her kitchen, knees against his chest.

"Jesse's upstairs taking a shower. I thought I might as well buzz him today, too," she said, gently running a comb through Robert's hair. He winced as she ran into some snarls. "Sorry, I'm pulling. My goodness, this is a heavy crop of hay—and these tangles!"

"I'm used to it," he said. "But don't cut it as short as Jesse's, all right?"

"I think I can civilize you."

She turned on the clippers and began shearing. The hum and vibration dropped brown clumps of fur soundlessly onto the floor around him.

"Tell me about your classes. What do you teach?" she asked.

Gratified for an audience and a favourite topic, Robert launched into his course load. "I teach two first-year courses, Introduction to Cell Biology and another one on evolutionary biology, as well as a second-year Biology and Technology course. Then I conduct three different labs each week, and somehow I've got to keep up my own research by publishing something every year."

"That's quite a load for one semester isn't it?"

"One of those courses is spread over two semesters, so the weekly hours end up being fewer. But yes, it keeps me busy."

"So how are your classes going this year? Chin down."

He lowered his chin, bringing him face to face with the cape's riot of curious little monkey clones dressed as firefighter, baker, and train engineer. "Not bad at all. Each year gets a little easier as I know the lectures better. I only have to study up on any revisions there may be in the new edition of the text. And, of course, anything I might like to add that I think illustrates the material to make it more memorable."

"Sounds like the mark of a good teacher to me. Tilt to your right."

He tilted his head to the right. "I enjoy teaching."

"Perhaps you had some memorable teachers in your time?"

"Hmmm. I suppose I did. One prof during my undergrad biology courses in particular..."

"What was it about him—or her—that stood out?"

"Dr. Dawes... Jack Dawes was—"

"Really? Like the bird?" Anna turned off the clippers and threw back her head, laughing. "I love pun names!"

"I suppose it was a pun; I really hadn't thought of it at the time,"

Robert said, adding, "but he didn't use one when he wrote."

She looked down at him in mid-chuckle, then pressed his shoulder with the back of her hand. "Oh, pun name—" More squeaky laughter.

He couldn't resist. "You're crowing, Mrs. Fawcett."

This sent Anna off into another gale of giggles. "So he didn't use a... nom de plume?"

"No, but he did have an uncanny knack for giving a bird's-eye view of any subject."

"Oh, ho ho ho!"

"That one was unintended!" Robert said, grinning in spite of himself. "Really."

"All right then," Anna settled down and resumed with the clippers, each stroke punctuated by a series of fading giggles. "Tilt to your left. So what was it about Dr. Dawes that made him memorable?"

"I remember something he often said that's stayed with me ever since. Must have been one of my first-year labs. He told us: 'Whenever you observe a biological organism or mechanism, ask yourself how it would have evolved to become as it is.'"

"Really? That doesn't sound very... uh... scientific to me."

"What? Why would you think that?" The temerity of his uneducated neighbour taking on the brilliant Dr. Dawes amused Robert.

"Well, I thought scientists were supposed to be rather a blank slate, so to speak, in order to follow the evidence wherever it leads."

"Of course, scientific inquiry follows the evidence wherever it leads. But no one is truly a blank slate. Some prior knowledge is a given. It's what leads a scientist to propose a hypothesis."

The clippers buzzed close to his left ear. "Hmm... I suppose a question like your professor's does narrow the possibility to only evolutionary conclusions, though."

"Naturally."

"I wonder then if it truly can be called scientific inquiry if no alternatives are investigated?"

"Alternatives?" Robert frowned. The clipper buzzed around his right ear.

"Alternatives to random chance evolution."

"There's no evidence to provide any solid alternatives to evolution. We consider some things to be settled fact. It would make the practice of science incredibly cumbersome to have to reinvestigate the established laws of nature—say, gravity, for example—before carrying on with a new line of inquiry."

"Like reinventing the wheel, you mean."

"Exactly." Robert was pleased she seemed to understand, but he was becoming alarmed at the forest of hair on the floor around him. Anna rattled her hand around in a worn yellow box, then switched the clipper's guide to begin lightening the load on the top of his head.

"Tell me, Robert. Do you have a Christian background at all?"

Her harmless question took him by surprise, and for a few moments he pondered how to respond. "No, I haven't. I believe my grandmother was a church-goer, but I never accompanied her."

The hum of the clippers was the only sound for a time.

"When I was in high school," Robert added, "there was a student religious group that held meetings at noon once a week. I got to know the staff leader—Doug, I remember his name was. He and I used to have some good discussions and he actually offered me thoughtful answers to some of my questions. But he didn't come around anymore when the school made a rule that the club had to meet off school grounds. And he got caught in possession of drugs not long afterwards. Which, for me, destroyed any credibility he'd had. So much for all his talk about morals. Anyway, once I got to university, I was reinforced in my understanding of how naturalism is the best explanation for how everything came to be. I found that science had

33

the answers to all my questions."

"*All* your questions?"

Robert hesitated for a moment. "I'd say so, yes."

"Did your conversion to evolutionary science better suit the direction you wanted to go in life?"

Disturbed, Robert cleared his throat. "I wouldn't say it was a *conversion*. I was convinced by overwhelming fact. And it had nothing to do with any direction I wanted to go in life. Facts are just facts." Then, guessing what Anna may have been hinting at, he added, "The facts of the world around us, with all of its evil and suffering, support randomness more than they do some benevolent creator. After all, no one can sit beside a dying child and still believe in God."

"Bertrand Russell, right?" Anna asked.

She was sharp, he had to admit. He thought of her library and realized he'd underestimated her. It was careless of him to use a quote without being sure of its source.

"Uh, it may have been him who said that. I can't exactly remember where I read it."

Anna stopped the razor. "I wonder how many bedsides of dying children Mr. Russell ever sat beside. And if he did, I wonder what he would have said... 'Too bad about your luck'?" She had put some distance between them and at the sharp tone in her voice Robert turned to look up at her.

"What hope would *he* have had to offer? 'Tough beans, kid, now you can make room for someone who's a little fitter'?"

She stared out the window, her mouth gathered in a grim line. He sat awkwardly below her, uncomfortable.

At last she turned back to him and sighed. "There are many eyes through which we can look at facts, wouldn't you agree? As a scientist, I mean?"

"Yes, I suppose so," he said, more out of eagerness to move to a safer topic than actual agreement. The idea of more than one way of viewing facts carried with it doubt, and Robert far preferred certainty.

Anna took scissors and made a few last snips. "There, I think that's done. You can check the mirror in the powder room." She carefully whisked his neck with a small scratchy brush and removed the juvenile cape from around his shoulders.

He stepped into the half-bath beside the rear entry and, closing the door of the tiny room, examined Anna's workmanship. She'd given him a classic 1960s look. The resemblance to his father's high school graduation photo was uncanny. But he could work with it. Robert glanced around the sink for a comb and, finding none, opened the medicine cabinet. No comb there either. It would have to wait until he got home. At least it felt better around his neck and ears.

As he closed the cabinet, a small, yellowed news clipping taped to the inside of the door fluttered, catching his eye. He leaned in to read the tiny print.

Breathes there the proper
And timorous guest
Who never once peeked in the medicine chest?

"What?" The catch inherent in commenting to Anna about the message made Robert chuckle.

When he came out, he said, "I have to confess—"

"You peeked?" Anna laughed, looking up from the dustpan into which she was sweeping hair.

Smiling a little sheepishly, he said, "I was looking for a comb."

"I've had that clipping for years. I even moved it here from our home on the farm. It was originally meant to foil snoopy visitors. Though I fear the subtlety may have been lost on them."

Robert was unsure how to broach the delicate matter of payment. "I owe you for the haircut."

"Nonsense, Robert. I'm glad to help, even though I only know one style." She glanced up at him with a sly lift of one eyebrow. "As my husband used to say, 'The only difference between a good haircut and a bad one is two weeks.'"

Grinning, he said, "Can I do anything for you then?"

"Well now, there is something... I'm having a load of firewood delivered next week. Jesse can stack it, but it will need to be split—"

"Consider it done."

CHAPTER 6

No condemnation now I dread,
I am my Lord's and He is mine...
—Charles Wesley, "And Can It Be That I Should Gain?"

Amelia was sitting on the grey velvet chaise by her living room window after dinner, folding and refolding her purse strap in one hand, racking her brain for more ways to pay off her debts, when Anna's seafoam green car crept up the driveway. She pulled her blue leather boots up over the legs of her white jeans, checked her makeup in the mosaic entry mirror, and dashed out the door.

"I wasn't sure what to wear," she said as she adjusted the seatbelt. "I've never been to a Bible study before."

"You look lovely, as always, dear," Anna said as she backed out the driveway and drove slowly down the street. "Nice scarf. I've never been able to wear those clear bright colours myself. I picture your closet looking a bit like a crayon box."

Amelia grinned at her. "I'm glad this top is as long as it is. I've had to leave the button on these jeans undone and I don't think I'll be able to wear them much longer." Sniffing, she asked, "What smells so good?"

"Apple pie air freshener. My daughter-in-law sent it. Said it reminded her of my house." Anna stopped for a red light and glanced at Amelia. "Why? Haven't you eaten?"

"Yes, but I'm always ready for the next meal." She gave a wry smile. "So, tell me what to expect. Who goes to a Bible study in the middle of the week? Is it like a lecture class with a single teacher? Or more like a book club where everyone gives their own interpretations?"

Anna looked pointedly at Amelia's tightly folded purse strap and grinned as she turned her attention back to the street. "You're nervous, but there's really no need. You will be as lovingly welcomed as you are at church on Sundays. As for what it's like, we simply gather in someone's living room, have a coffee, and ask questions or share anything that stood out to us from our study of the passage during the previous week."

Anna turned the final corner onto a tree-lined street and pulled to a stop in front of a sprawling, low, white brick bungalow.

"And don't worry," she continued, "no one's going to single you out for an impromptu exegesis of the epistle to the Romans! In fact, the rule is that if we haven't done our homework through the week, we're not *allowed* to talk. That's one way to avoid everyone giving their own interpretation, which usually results in a 'pooling of ignorance.' Pastor Tom always says, 'There may be many applications of a biblical passage, but only one correct interpretation.'"

They made their way past towering spruce trees along the curving sidewalk, the smell of dead leaves and wood smoke wafting through the gathering dusk.

"I've noticed a new intensity in our pastor since his wife passed away in June. Alice was a very dear friend of mine," Anna said quietly. "Tom's always been a fine preacher, but now there's just—I don't know—something more to him. A fervency, I guess you could say, that wasn't there before."

"I did read the passage you told me to," Amelia told the older woman. She'd had a lot of questions but decided to keep them to ask Anna privately later.

Dorothy Muir, silver-haired and stout, invited them into her home where a dozen others sat in a circle in the living room. It was large and traditionally furnished, obviously professionally designed in shades of robin's egg blue. There was little for Amelia to achieve playing her usual game of mental redecorating as she and Anna followed their hostess to the dining table.

Standing before the trays of assorted fruit and crackers and cheese, Amelia felt a faint flutter within her. Her hand went to her belly, while the other hand tugged at Anna's sleeve.

"I think the sight of all this food just made the peanut gallery do a tiny cartwheel!" she whispered.

"How exciting!" Anna whispered back. "You must reward him with a good helping of everything."

Giddy with excitement at the first sign of life, Amelia filled her small floral china plate. She and Anna carried their snacks and tea to the circle of chairs in the living room where Anna introduced her to everyone. From the several Sundays she'd accompanied Anna to church, she recognized a few of the faces.

In particular, she caught sight of a thirtyish man with appealing crinkles beginning at the corners of his clear blue eyes. A sky-blue polo shirt snugly hugged the expanse of his considerable shoulders; he was running a hand through a swath of blond-streaked hair when he turned toward the newcomers. His eyes locked on Amelia's in a moment of significance. She felt the heat rise from her neck as she sat beside Anna across the coffee table from him. The moment passed.

Pastor Tom cleared his throat and the chatter dribbled to a stop. He opened his Bible and in his deep, deep voice read, "'There is therefore now no condemnation for those who are in Christ Jesus.'" He closed his Bible. "That pretty much says it all, doesn't it?" He glanced around at each one in the group. "All those first chapters describing the pathetic human condition have culminated here. Let it sink in for a minute. Can you feel the relief of it? The freedom? The utter safety of it?"

Amelia was as mesmerized by the power of that truth as when Anna had first introduced it to her two months before. It meant release for her beleaguered conscience. He reopened his Bible, reviewing the preceding chapter's conflict between the human desire to do right yet the helpless inability to do so. Amelia knew that dilemma all too well, and no attempts to do good had been able to make up for the sin of ending a life—but she couldn't let herself be sucked into that downward spiral.

While the pastor went into some depth explaining the original Greek of the text, and others began to offer their insights, Amelia's thoughts returned to that dramatic opening of the eighth chapter of Romans, her personal declaration of emancipation.

Later, seeing Anna deep in what looked like a personal conversation with Pastor Tom, Amelia retrieved her jacket from the entry closet. She was putting on her boots near the front door when she felt someone standing behind her. She rose to shake his outstretched hand.

"Nelson Hogue, in case you didn't catch my name in the round of introductions," he said. "The new person always has the worst job of trying to remember them all. So, Anna tells me we have something in common. You're a teacher?"

"Clearbrook High, English."

Nelson leaned closer, gazing at her hands and whispered, "I don't think it'll fold any smaller."

Amelia followed his eyes and looked down, dropping the tightly folded purse strap to let it hang from her shoulder. "Oh, yeah. I guess not." Feeble laugh. Under his intense gaze, she suddenly felt hot around the neck and wished she hadn't already put on her jacket.

"So, aren't you going to ask me what it is we have in common?" He lifted one eyebrow neatly.

"I assumed it was—"

"Wrestling?"

Amelia laughed, shaking her head. "Where do you teach?"

Nelson eased himself onto the back of the couch. "Noble Christian School. I teach grades one to nine phys. ed, and junior high Bible and math. Oh, and I coach football and basketball. Pastor Tom's a wrestler, too, so him and me would like to get a wrestling team going, but I'm not sure when that'll happen."

Amelia nodded but inwardly winced at the grammar gaffe.

"I really love the sport," Nelson went on, "but I don't seem to be able to devote enough time to it and I'd want to do it right."

"No half-nelson for you, eh?" She smirked.

His great booming laugh drew the attention of the others in the room.

Anna made her way toward them. "You two seem to have hit it off," she said, her eyes flicking curiously from one to the other. She put on her navy trench-coat and stepped into her shoes, gathering purse and Bible.

"I'll look forward to getting to know you better," Nelson told Amelia, his face alight with interest.

Amelia picked up her Bible from the foyer table and bounced out the door behind her friend. It was a pleasure to have her ego stroked, and for a few moments she gave herself up to daydreams. Yet as they left the Muirs' home, the complexities of her present life shouted the impossibility of getting involved with another man.

"You're glowing like one of your teenaged students in a crush," Anna said, giving Amelia a brief sidelong glance

Amelia blushed. "It was a really great study. I've studied literature before, of course, but I had no idea there was so much depth and background to every sentence of the Bible. I'm definitely coming back."

"You're always welcome, Amelia." Anna gave her another searching look in the passing light of a streetlamp. "I just hope it's for the right reasons."

CHAPTER 7

And be kind to one another, tenderhearted, forgiving one another...
—Ephesians 4:32

A low slanting ray of bright sunlight burned through the curtainless living room window onto Robert's face, pulling him from sleep. He rolled over, his breathing stifled by the back of the vinyl couch. Turning outward again, he propped himself on one elbow and ran a hand through his hair. The narrow couch only accentuated his isolation. Every morning his brain needed to go through a process of waking to that reality. And every waking meant the broken pieces of his life fell back into their current state of disarray. He swung his legs over the side, sitting up, and swiped both hands over his stubbly face. He knew he'd had something planned for this Saturday—right. Yard work. It looked like the weather was conducive to it.

Ever since he'd bought this duplex, Robert had been meaning to landscape the yard. Despite the fact they had arrived in Red Deer in the midst of an oil boom, the bargain real estate prices had astonished him compared to anything in Montreal. Which is why he had so quickly begun the hunt for a rental property after the purchase of their home. That, too, his father had cautioned against, bringing up the spectre of the early 80s housing bust, a result of then Prime Minister Trudeau's National Energy Program, much despised in the West. And the stock market plunge just a few years back had Robert fearing his old man would be proved right. But the West in particular, and Canada in general, had weathered the economic storm with remarkable aplomb and the property had not lost value; it had even risen.

Yet he'd never dreamed he would live in it himself. Now that he was, the urgent need for maintenance confronted him. His duplex's backyard was the only empty one on the block where all backyards opened to one another. In the interest of building a sense of community, zoning regulations for this development eliminated a back alley and did not permit rear garages. So his barren stretch of straggly, autumn-brown grass and gangly weeds stood out among the others where homeowners had been effecting transformations from pleasantly simple to prize-winning. Each yard opened to the next for a park-like effect. With one exception. Two doors to the east, Joan Klug's waist-high board fence surrounded her yard, front and back.

Today, with the cobalt blue sky and bright sunshine setting the last golden leaves to gleaming, Robert determined to get a head start on preparations for spring planting. He hoped he wouldn't be here that long, but he couldn't quell his love of growing things and the habit of fall garden work. As he gathered his tools in the entryway, he noticed his neighbour Jesse slowly making his way to the side yard where a stack of rocks sat on the driveway beside the Fawcetts' house. At the far end of the yard, in front of a graceful planting of shrubs and trees, crouched Anna, pushing her gloved hands against a small wall of soil, twisting her head at an awkward angle to watch Jesse's progress. Her lips were set in a grim line. The young man paused uncertainly, fingering his lips and staring motionless at the rocks.

Robert had just leaned down to grab his gloves when he heard Anna through the screened window in a tone of voice he'd never expected from her.

"Just bring me the stinkin' rock, Jesse!" she barked.

Robert remained still and watched. Maybe he should have offered to help her, but this was too surprising to miss. He quietly stepped closer to the window to listen.

Jesse cringed and cowered on the sidewalk. Anna's irritable impatience, evidence of hypocrisy, added another brick in the wall of his resistance to her faith. He settled into the familiar comfort of smug self-satisfaction. He knew it would only be a matter of time before her ideas of Christian morality fell by the wayside. Nobody could be that perfect. She was just like him after all.

He continued watching as Anna gave up holding back the avalanche of earth and sat back on the grass, head hanging. Before long, she went to her son and spoke to him, too quietly for Robert to hear. Then she hugged Jesse. As she did so, her face wet with tears, she faced squarely the window where Robert watched. She gave a crooked smile and a little wave. He looked away, intensely embarrassed at being caught intruding on that tender and personal moment. What he had seen moved him. A parent's apology, a son's ready forgiveness, restoration. He had never witnessed such a thing. With Anna's repentance he felt a crumbling, a loosening, a softening of an inner wall.

Moments later she knocked at his door. Robert breathed deeply and opened it.

"You heard my nasty words, I'm afraid. I'm so sorry for my harshness," Anna began. Robert was dumbstruck. "But I wanted you to know that I've apologized to Jesse and he has forgiven me." She glanced beside her at her son, who patted her shoulder. "Whatever you do to the least of these, you do to me, Jesus taught us you know." She seemed quite at ease about the whole thing. "I'm so glad to have His forgiveness, too."

"That's... uh... good," Robert offered. He had no idea what to say, no template for such a conversation.

"Well, back to work then." She waved and returned to her own yard, Jesse trailing her.

"Wait," Robert called after her. "I'll help you with those rocks."

As his first armload tumbled onto the ground with dull thuds and clacks where they knocked together, Robert glanced sidelong at his neighbour.

"What?" she asked, catching his look.

"Stinkin', Anna?" he asked with a wry grin.

She turned with a sheepish smile back to the flowerbed border. "Never you mind, Robert. Just get to work."

Chuckling, he helped Jesse bring the rest of the rocks to the flowerbed.

CHAPTER 8

---◦---

"Who are you?" asked Shasta.
"Myself," said the Voice, very deep and low so that the earth shook:
and again "Myself," loud and clear and gay: and then the third time
"Myself," whispered so softly you could hardly hear it, and yet it
seemed to come from all round you as if the leaves rustled with it.
—C.S. Lewis, *The Horse and His Boy*[1]

Amelia burst out with a loud laugh in the empty kitchen while marking a pile of student papers. She went limp all over at the test answer in front of her. Fifteen year-old Cody Weersma's valiant foray into literary imagery made her lay her head on her arms and give herself over to a weakness of giggles.

She'd given the class an assignment to write paragraphs using metaphors and similes. Here, in his narrow slanting script, Cody had written, "the cricket made a sound like a teacher, tapping her foot right before she gives you a detention." Amelia was tempted to give him the two marks just for providing her with an endorphin surge.

Finishing her after-school grading, she checked her bank statement and flipped through the bills that had arrived that week. She groaned softly at the burden of debt. It had been far easier sliding into the pit than it was climbing back out of it.

The pleasant diversion of a stack of books borrowed from Anna that week beckoned. Amelia forced herself to write two cheques before she succumbed. She made herself some peanut butter toast, grabbed an apple and a glass of milk, and carried it all on a tray to the bedroom where she nestled in to read. Scanning the titles, she wondered where to begin. *By Searching*, by Isobel Kuhn, looked like a quick read. She paged through an overview of history and Christian thought by Schaeffer. There was *Knowing God*, by Packer, Mary Kassian's *The Feminist Gospel*, and several books by C.S. Lewis.

Though Jesus was new to her, she had recoiled instinctively at what struck her as a vague, airy-fairy tone in some of the religious literature she had found at the local chain bookstore. Worse than that was the cheesy grin of a bestselling pastor promising to make all her dreams come true.

When Amelia had complained to Anna about the dearth of good Christian books, Anna had let her take her pick from her own library.

It astounded her that there had been an entire genre beneath her radar, steeped as she'd been in literature since her teens. Amelia considered the works of poetry or fiction she'd studied in high school or university. She couldn't come up with a single tome that portrayed Christianity in a positive light. Instead, she remembered studying Browning's "My Last Duchess" no fewer than three times, while other authors seemed to have a personal vendetta against God. Where the great works of devotion and nobility by the likes of Donne and Milton had been, she was at a loss to say. And to her, T.S. Eliot's "The Wasteland" didn't count. Masterpiece though it may be, it had required constant reference checking, which for her meant she couldn't enjoy the music of its words. But perhaps it had been only her own dark age that had obscured her vision of the Light? She recalled vague references to redemption and salvation as literary themes, though it had always seemed a mere academic thing. Something cerebral to discuss in a literature course.

I had no idea it was the door to a living relationship, one that touched the deepest part of me. The transformation in her own life had been stunning. Everything was the same, yet everything was new and full of meaning. And always she was undergirded by the peace beyond understanding.

Cuddling deeper into her comforter, she picked up a simple-looking Lewis volume, *The Horse and His Boy.*

Two hours later, Amelia paused in her reading, not quite at the end. She tipped her head back against the headboard, overcome with awe at the Great Lion's retelling of the boy's life from a sovereign point of view. What had been a tale of harshness and hard luck, deprivation and danger, the great Beast had transformed into one of comfort in misery and mercy in need.

It's true for me, too, isn't it? All that alienation and loneliness, even my great sin—You were orchestrating it all, pulling me to Yourself, the real Lion.

Heart brimming and body trembling, Amelia knelt before the bed and a soul-song soared to heaven.

CHAPTER 9

The truth will set you free but first it will make you miserable.
—Title of a 1988 book by Jamie Buckingham

Wisps of wood smoke mingled through the crisp evening air as Robert lugged a couple of lawn chairs under each arm—an extra, Anna had advised, in case neighbour Joan might show up. With Anna ahead of him and Jesse trailing them both, they crunched across the fallen leaves to the neighbourhood fire pit, two houses west of his. Above the trees, the panoramic sky was bedaubed with rose and crimson and orange. It was the closest he would come in this land-locked province to the magnificence of the Atlantic sunrises he loved, but it failed to quiet his nerves tonight.

Already he was wishing he hadn't accepted Anna's invitation to this last evening gathering of the season. A pod of neighbours was huddled around the crackling blaze by the time he got there. The circle widened affably to receive them, and they settled into their lawn chairs, stretching feet to the fire.

"How's Jesse?" a few neighbours asked the young man. Robert had always hated that condescending way of asking, but Jesse spread his smile generously, unmindful of any offense.

Anna introduced Robert to the group with the smugly satisfied air of a new mother. She asked everyone to tell him their names, but Robert lost track before the circle was complete. While snacks were passed around, Robert learned that Wayne Duxbury, to his left, a dad-of-Dennis-the-Menace lookalike, and his perfectly coifed, thin-lipped wife Wendy, lived in the same duplex as Anna.

"We're so busy, I wasn't sure we could take time to come out tonight," Wendy said in a nasal voice. She explained that she and her husband ran several network marketing businesses in addition to their jobs.

"Maybe we can get together with you sometime and discuss your financial goals," Wayne said, flashing a hundred-watt smile and handing Robert his card.

Hoping he'd been vague enough in answer, Robert stuffed the card into his jacket pocket.

"Wayne and Wendy have two daughters," Anna said.

Wendy giggled. "If you think *we're* busy," Robert didn't, "Kelly and Dalia are *really* busy! They're *very* popular."

Next in the circle was Victorene Desjarlais, whom Robert had already met last summer when he'd rented to her the unit next to the one he now inhabited. She hadn't taken her heavily-lined eyes off him tonight. Her long dark hair was streaked with blond and teased in a high bump on top.

She introduced her twelve-year-old, pencil-thin daughter Brandi, who had an improbably large bust, and two sons. Ten-year-old Morrigan, apparently unhindered by the shock of thick black hair obscuring his face from forehead to chin, was intent on some game on an iPhone. Dakota, the younger boy, was slouched low in a lawn chair, gazing at the fire, his index finger diligently acquainting itself with the inside of his nostril. Nodding stiffly, Robert avoided the single mother's slow smile and dark-eyes.

"Dakota is such a dear," Anna murmured. Nose-picking and dearhood seemed mutually exclusive to Robert.

To the right of the Desjarlais family, an Asian couple introduced themselves as Preng and Yanni, originally from Kampuchea. Preng was an automotive technician at Evergreen Ford while Yanni worked at *The Needle and I* fabric shop.

From his left, Robert received a tray of veggies and dip being passed around. He grazed and then held the tray out to Anna. She chose a few cucumbers and carrots to balance the generous heap of chips on Jesse's plate before passing it on.

"Yanni is my dear friend. They're part of my church," Anna said quietly. "Their two grown sons are both in university and getting top marks. She and her husband have worked so hard to put those boys through their schooling, even collecting bottles and cans on the weekends for extra cash. Their youngest, Sareen, is in high school and also excelling."

Before the introductions had come full circle, a piercing throat-clearing turned everyone's head toward a skeletal man with patchy grey hair. His sharp cheekbones seemed about to break through the taut-stretched yellow-grey skin of his face. He leaned forward in his chair eagerly, clawlike hands gripping the arms of his chair.

"People have got to wake up to what's really happening," the man told them, his eyes burning with the urgency of his message. The attractive woman beside him rolled her eyes, her dangling silver earrings tinkling as she shook her head. Sinking further into her chair, she pulled out her phone and focused on it.

"That's Pat Siggleady and his wife Rena," Anna whispered. "And beside them, Zach Duchesne and Kaitlyn Sanderson—and Hector," Beneath the young couple's two chairs, a brindle Great Dane stretched benignly.

As Pat, the grizzled neighbour pontificated, Robert checked off the topics, noticing the others around the circle tuning out one by one. Siggleady indicted the Canadian government for pulling out of Afghanistan, the European Union for mishandling its member nations, and the WHO for being a sinister tool of the International Monetary Fund to inject third world nations with AIDS back in the 80s. As he began a condemnation of chemical trails left by passing aircraft to poison everyone, causing a multitude of diseases, neighbours around the fire pit began to break off into smaller conversations.

"Who is this guy?" Robert asked Anna behind his hand.

"They've only lived in the neighbourhood for about a year. He used to work for an oil company but took an early retirement a couple of years ago." Anna turned to offer the extra lawn chair to Joan, who had appeared on the outside of the circle.

"Everyone, make a little room for Joan," Anna said. There was some general shifting.

"I'd rather stand," Joan said, planting herself outside the circle, arms crossed tightly over her familiar camo jacket. She wore the clamp-lipped expression of one who had been personally offended by life. In front of her, Zach held his very pregnant girlfriend's hand with his left hand; his right was draped over a blue guitar.

Pat raised his reedy voice, perhaps annoyed at losing the limelight. "September 11, 2001 was like Hitler's fire of 1933 and Roosevelt's Pearl Harbour all over again. Just an excuse to go to war. 9/11 was all planned back in the 1990s to make everyone support American imperialism in the world. This whole war on terrorism is a cruel hoax pulled off by a small group of people who are sabotaging all our values of democracy and decency. They're the same elite group that brought us the faked moon landing in '69." Pat stopped for a ragged breath. "Any thinking person knows there's something horribly wrong and the whole mess has got to be exposed."

And this bozo falls into the thinking category? Robert noticed the eyes of Preng and Yanni fixed on Siggleady. Joan, too, appeared to be closely attentive. These were simple folk who needed a voice of reason to counteract all this fearmongering. He knew he had to speak up.

"What's your source?" he asked, his voice calm but loud. Suddenly there was silence.

Pat, interrupted in mid-torrent, turned toward the voice across the circle and shielded his eyes from the fire-glow.

"What's that?" he asked.

"I said, what's your source?" Robert could feel the circle of attention flicking from one side of the fire to the other.

"I've been researching this for twenty years," Pat rasped. "You wanna talk about sources! You'll never hear this in the mainstream media. They're just a puppet of the global network of forces in the background that are trying to control us. They've faked 'terrorist attacks' like the 1993 World Trade Center bombing, the Oklahoma City bombing—"

"But I asked you what your source was. All you've given me so far is a string of allegations without any substantiation." Robert's voice rose with the confidence of the more experienced debater. He blindly passed a pan of brownies along to his right.

Barely recognizing the question, Pat continued. "The research I've been doing documents all of this. We just need to open our eyes to the facts, folks. If you look at the tapes of 9/11 news reports, TV anchors were reporting that firefighters and rescue workers said explosives and bombs were going off all over the buildings."

"And that means—?" Robert's adrenaline pumped as he warmed to the topic. He'd checked into this thoroughly ten years earlier when his uncle had first raised the theory. He'd never had the chance to use his research with Uncle Stan, but the important points returned to him now.

"Remember the footage of those towers coming down at freefall speed?" Pat was saying. "Keep in mind they were over a hundred stories high. That defies the law of physics. And are we really supposed to believe that fire melted steel for the first time ever in history? Don't forget that at first the engineers said that planes and fires alone could never have caused such a deadly collapse. What it means is that this was a vile, criminal act that—"

"I've looked at the websites your 'facts' come from, Mr. Siggleady." Robert noticed Rena Siggleady look up from her phone and sit up a little in her chair. "If you check into the credentials of the writers of these sites, you won't find anything about where they got their education or what degrees they have. But you will find they have a lot of things to sell. Things like survival supplies, T-shirts, books, DVDs. There are people who will try to make money off anything. Just because it's on the Internet doesn't mean it's research."

Pat opened his mouth to respond but Robert forged ahead. "And it doesn't seem to matter how much investigation or how many facts are offered by reputable organizations, these fearmongers are never satisfied."

Zach began to strum a few desultory chords on his guitar but as Robert's professional voice carried on the night air, the young man soon gave it up.

"The National Institute of Standards and Technology, as well as *Popular Mechanics*, investigated your claims and totally rejected them," Robert continued. "Go search their websites. Civil engineers say it was definitely the impact of jets at high speed combined with fires that caused the collapse. The idea that the buildings were wired for demolition is logistically impossible. And yet these ridiculous conspiracy theories persist. Just ask yourself, what would it take to prove to you that 9/11 was truly a foreign terrorist attack? The more you preach it, the more invested in it you become, making it impossible to admit you might be mistaken. What's really at stake is truth."

"That's what I try and tell people—" Pat managed to say.

"If we're to believe your theories," Robert continued, "we have to disbelieve all other reports,"

"That's what I'm telling you!" Siggleady face darkened. "You can't trust the media! They're just puppets—"

Robert pounced. "You're being ridiculous! Why, then, should we believe your sources? They're media, too."

"They're trustworthy!"

"Sure, the media get things wrong occasionally," Robert said loudly, cutting off Pat's protest, "especially initial reports in a crisis, and sure, they exhibit bias at times, but what makes the conspiracy theorists any more believable?"

There was stirring to his left, and out of the corner of his eye he saw the Desjarlais kids disappear into the darkening night. He heard the girl whisper to her mother, "Well, that was, like, a total waste of a Saturday night." Victorene caught Robert's eye and winked. He could hardly see Pat Siggleady anymore in the dying fire glow.

"When you suspect every source of information other than your own favourite narrow website," Robert went on, "you cut off the branch you're sitting on. Throw out the media, and you ultimately cast doubt on all our ways of knowing, of getting at the truth. How are we to believe the simplest court report, or any historical document, if we throw out the most basic system of reporting we have? For that matter, how are we to believe what *you* say?"

He felt a hand firmly grip his arm and looked to his right to find Anna staring pointedly at him. Very quietly, not letting up on her hold, she said to him, "That's enough now, Robert. You've successfully made your point." She rose and, prodding Jesse, began folding their canvas lawn chairs.

Robert looked around at the others, who were quietly beginning to stir. A moonless darkness had crept over them while they sat in the well of firelight. He got up and waited for Anna, who was retrieving her empty cake pan and saying her goodnights, then followed her and Jesse up the slight rise to their homes.

"Did I say something wrong?" he asked as they walked. A shiver crinkling up his backbone told him he was being watched from behind.

Anna said nothing until they neared their houses.

"I'm sure everything you said was true, Robert," she began. "But perhaps not all of it was kind."

"I'm all too aware because of my work that it's hard to make people care about the truth. But rhetoric like his will go on and on, leading to all kinds of misconceptions for the others if we allow it—"

"I can be a stickler for truth, too, but I learned a long time ago to allow people their dignity," Anna said.

"But he was so wrong!"

"It's very important to leave an escape hatch for a person."

"Don't you think it's more important to set the record straight, not only for him but for the sake of the others listening?"

"Do you think the rest of us buy into everything Pat tells us?"

"But if, as you say, the rest of the neighbourhood doesn't believe these conspiracies, why doesn't anyone say anything?"

"Robert." Anna stopped in midstride and turned to him, her face dimly lit by the distant streetlight. "Have you ever heard the old saying, 'A man convinced against his will is of the same opinion still'? There are times when a person might be unable to express an objection, but still has a gut reaction that guides their opinion. It's called common sense. It may not be scientific but it can keep them from extremes."

"But for pity's sake! The moon landing, a hoax!"

"A person cornered is like a wolverine. They'll fight to the death, even for an idea they know is wrong. You were utterly ruthless back there."

Just when he thought he was doing the right thing! Now the old tug of war began within him: truth versus feelings.

"And there's something else you should know." Anna went on. "Pat Siggleady is not at all well,"

Go ahead, lay the guilt on a little thicker. "It was pretty obvious to me there was something wrong with his thinking," he said, unable to keep the resentment out of his tone.

"Perhaps with his thinking, but most certainly with his body. Rena tells me she's suspecting some kind of cancer, but he won't see a doctor. He's lost so much weight in the past few months, it's shocking."

What was he to do with that? Argument wrestled down pity, which in turn rose like a wounded spectre to haunt him. It really didn't seem a fair debate at all. As they reached their homes, Robert said goodnight to Anna and stomped into his duplex, letting the door slam behind him.

CHAPTER 10

Everyone says forgiveness is a lovely idea,
until they have something to forgive.
—C.S. Lewis, *Mere Christianity*[2]

Amelia checked the table one more time before answering the doorbell. She took a deep breath and let out a prayer. It had been wiser to invite Anna and Jesse to come here. There was far less chance of meeting anyone she wasn't ready to face.

She'd been looking around her house with Anna's eyes all afternoon, in the way she might have if she'd been expecting her mother to visit. Would Anna think the books with their spines turned toward the backs of the shelves was silly and impractical? Maybe it was. And the moody colour scheme was a far cry from Anna's sweet and cheerful yellows. Would the older woman read into Amelia's choices some psychological reason? Maybe there was. She had at first spread some books and magazines on the coffee table in an artless, casual way. Dishonest. Too not her. She put them away and left only a single black designer bowl in the centre.

This hospitality business was still unfamiliar, but she could learn. Too many years of indulging her and her husband's introversion, like riding a bicycle while watching the wheels, had led inevitably to a crash.

When she answered the door, there were Anna and Jesse, placidly waiting.

"I'm so glad you came, Jesse." Amelia was engulfed in his feather-light hug. She extracted herself gently.

"And thanks to you, too, Amelia," said Anna, "for being willing to let Jesse visit at such short notice. I won't be able to stay much after supper if I'm to get to the city at a reasonable hour."

Anna's vague request to keep Jesse overnight had been surprising. Amelia was eager to return her friend's many favours, but she hadn't felt free to ask what it was about.

"I'll try to be back by Sunday night, but if I'm not, my neighbour Yanni has promised to bring Jesse home and make sure he gets to all his activities next week. Jesse's left his backpack here at the door—where do you want it?"

"Oh, just leave it there for now. We'll get him settled later," Amelia said. "Jesse, you get to sleep in my new nursery."

Jesse frowned. "Not a baby."

"Of course you're not," Amelia said. "But I'll bet you'd like to try out that crib anyway."

"Unh, unh." Jesse shook his head vigorously. He wandered over to the ebony piano and poked at the keys tentatively.

"Maybe we could even wrestle him into a pair of little pink sleepers," Anna suggested. Jesse's narrow squint and lowered brow drew a chuckle out of Amelia.

"Never mind the sleepers, Jesse. But there is something in the nursery you might like."

Now he was interested. "What?" he asked, looking up from the keyboard.

"I'll show you after dinner," Amelia promised.

"What is it?" he asked again, coming toward Amelia.

"You'll see," she said. "Come and eat, it's all ready."

They followed her past the long stretches of creamy leather couches and charcoal satin walls in the living room, Anna complimenting her on her elegant taste.

"Everything is so perfectly coordinated," she said. "And so orderly. I'm a bit weak in the organizing department myself. And I can't blame the children anymore now that they're mostly gone from home."

In the kitchen, deep grey cabinets hid all things culinary, but the table was bright with scarlet carnations and square red bowls of steaming food.

Amelia was encouraged that Anna liked the red-painted chandelier hanging from the white ceiling medallion against a black ceiling.

"It started out as a great bargain, but having it painted brought the price up a bit, I'm afraid." Amelia brought the last few bowls to the table. "I thought you might like to try some of the food of my heritage."

She set a small dish of dal and a plate of naan bread in front of them.

"I've only tried Indian food once at a missions conference at church. Very spicy!" Anna laughed.

"I did try to tone it down a little," Amelia said as she sat down. "My mother didn't cook Indian, in fact, she didn't cook very often at all, not wanting to be chained to the stove. My very Canadian dad made most of the meals. But I loved everything my grandmother made the one time she visited from India."

They sat down and Amelia joined hands with them a little self-consciously. "I did a bit of a search for table grace and found this one just for you Jesse:

Some hae meat and cannot eat; Some cannot eat that want it:
But we have meat and we can eat Sae let the Lord be thankit!

"That's from Robert Burns. And this one for all of us:

Blessed are you, O Lord God, King of the Universe,
For you give us food to sustain our lives and make our hearts glad;
Through Jesus Christ our Lord. Amen.

Amelia watched as her guests nibbled tentatively at her offerings.

Jesse warmed to the meal with the exception of the cucumber raita. Though Anna seemed distracted at times, it was clear she enjoyed the chicken curry and vegetables.

"So, tell me a bit about your family, Amelia," Anna said.

Amelia paused in dipping her piece of naan. "My mother often talked about how she'd had a narrow escape from India. She was very bright, brighter than her three older brothers. When she got a scholarship to study abroad, her mother was angry. Not so much at her, but angry that her brothers hadn't received similar opportunities. My grandmother was a widow and dependent on her sons, so obviously she wanted them well-established. She was against her daughter leaving India and began proceedings to arrange a marriage for her."

"More chicken please," said Jesse, passing his plate. Amelia dished up another serving for him. When he continued holding up his plate and looking expectantly at her, she laughed and added another spoonful.

"There was a Canadian working at the university there in Delhi— I'm a little fuzzy on those details—who helped my mother apply for a scholarship. She came to Toronto and began her degree in 1966. Eventually, she got a Master's in Political Science. From then on, the women's movement took her, first on campus and then more widely." Amelia took another bite and put down her fork. She stared downward, chewing slowly as she folded and refolded the hem of the white linen tablecloth. "My earliest memories are of her getting ready for a meeting and walking out the door. My mother used to boast that when other little girls played taking their dolls shopping, I played going to a rally. Not that she really noticed. It was my dad who took care of me for the most part. Mother died of breast cancer thirteen years ago."

Anna held up her hand and turned to tell Jesse. "You may be

excused, son. Amelia, do you have any books he might enjoy?"

"Oh sure. That's what I was going to show you in the nursery, Jesse. Just help yourself," she called after him as he got up and began plodding down the hall.

"So you've been missing your mom for thirteen years. That must be especially painful now when you most need a mother. And your dad?"

Amelia sighed. "I can just imagine what my mother would think of my getting pregnant at thirty-eight. But you asked about my dad." She smiled. "Hmmm. Dad met my mother in university, and he says it took about four years for him to convince her to marry him. She had totally bought into the 'biology is not destiny' mantra of the women's movement, so when I was born in 1975, I think it must have been a major cramp in her style and beliefs. She was a fighter, though. She named me after Amelia Earhart and turned me into an opportunity to fight for women's reproductive rights. She even left my dad for a while so she could have first-hand experience championing the cause of single mothers."

"How did your dad deal with that?"

"He really loved my mother. I guess he just went along with whatever her next scheme was. I'm not sure how that separation thing ever got resolved. I was a baby at the time. But he was the original house-husband when he wasn't at work, and we either ate out or he did the cooking."

"That's very different from the way I was raised. And of course, from how we raised our children." Anna folded her hands on the table in front of her, gazing down in thought. "But a mother's heart is bound to her child. I'm sure your mother missed you terribly." She reached over and covered Amelia's hand with her own.

Amelia glanced at her guest sharply. "I highly doubt it. One of my greatest fears for this child is that I'll be the kind of mother mine was.

Now it looks as if I'll have to leave my baby in daycare just like she did. With my miserable memories of daycares and a string of babysitters, it's the last thing I wanted to pass on to my baby." Amelia could feel tears starting. "Never having a space of my own there, always afraid of the bigger kids, having to go there even when I was feeling sick—" She fought for control. Finally, she turned to Anna. "I just can't do that to my baby. But I can't think of any options."

"Why don't I help you put the food away first," said Anna, getting up and carrying a stack of plates to the sink.

Amelia was disturbed at having her deep concern take second place to clearing the table, but she rose and carried some bowls to the counter.

Anna opened a couple of drawers until she found a rubber scraper. "Now here's your best money-saving tool. The solution to so many problems is often right in front of our noses. There's a whole serving's worth of curry in that bowl." Anna swooshed the last of the curry out of the dish and snapped a lid on the plastic container. "We don't want the kitchen sink to be the best fed mouth in the house, do we?"

"I don't understand how that's a solution. Saving a penny on leftovers isn't going to help me." Amelia folded her arms and leaned against the counter.

"It's not just saving a penny on leftovers. It's the paradigm shift of going from being a consumer to being a conserver and producer. My mother used to have a German saying: *Mann muss sich nach die Decke Strecken.*"

"I must confess my German is, uh, nonexistent," Amelia said wryly.

Anna smiled. "Sorry. It means one must stretch themselves to the limits of the blanket—essentially, live within your means. There are ways to raise your child yourself if you are willing to make serious sacrifices to make that a priority," Anna said. "Could we sit in your beautiful living room?"

"I don't know what you mean by serious sacrifices," Amelia said, following her. She grabbed her phone off the kitchen counter as they left the room and showed Anna the screen. "I just got this email last night."

The older woman tilted her chin up and down, focusing with difficulty.

"I can't make it out," Anna said. "Suppose you provide an interpretation for the technically inept?"

"My husband says we have to sell this house," Amelia said, tossing the phone aside, her lips taut. "He never phones. Or texts. It's always an email. He never even writes my name. He just says to hire someone to paint so we can get an appraisal. Apparently, the research he's been doing shows that strong colours don't sell well."

"But what a shame to have to move when you've made such a lovely home and started on the nursery and all."

"It's not my idea. I have no clue what this house will bring, but I know there's still a mortgage. I may not be a financial genius, but I don't see how that will get us any further ahead—we'd still have debt. He always has a sky-is-falling attitude about money."

Amelia's eyes followed Anna's around the room, taking in the designer furniture and high-end accessories.

"And you have...?" Anna questioned Amelia from over her glasses.

"What?" Amelia asked.

"Would he say that your attitude to money falls into the grows-on-trees category?"

Amelia couldn't deny it. "How'd you guess?"

"Seems like there's one of each in most marriages. I guess that's why money troubles are a major cause of marriage breakdown."

"Yeah, well, I've already told you that's not what our separation is about. I mean, we did clash about money, but the main thing is the baby. Making me have the abortion all those years ago and having the nerve to suggest it again this time showed me I can't trust him with what's most precious to me. And his abandoning me."

"But Amelia, did you ever wonder *why* he suggested it this time?"

Amelia stared at the older woman. "I don't get it! What could possibly make even the suggestion acceptable, especially after all I've been through in the years since then?"

"I know, dear. It's a terrible thing. All I meant was that sometimes a man, wired as he is to provide and protect, is only thinking of the practical side of things, paying the bills and all that." Anna laid her hand on Amelia's arm as the younger woman started to protest. "Remember that God says the husband of a godly woman can safely trust in her. What would happen if you began to show wise management of money?"

Frowning, Amelia said, "I'm not sure I understand what you mean by 'what would happen.'" She thought of the Saturday morning lectures her husband had seemed to love to give. She could feel herself shrinking into insignificance at the memory of the many times she couldn't get what he was trying to tell her: RRSPs, mutual funds, GICs, whatever. Rubbing her temples, she closed her eyes and leaned back into the chair.

"What if the change in your life became evident to him through what he's always thought was your biggest fault?" said Anna.

"I don't know, Anna. That assumes I even care what he thinks anymore. I'm still working on forgiving the guy, and that's only because we've been discussing it in Bible study. But not one shred of forgiving feelings do I have."

"Our ability to forgive is in direct proportion to how much we see that we've been forgiven. It's something you can ask God to do through you, Amelia. Remember, I'm always praying for you." Anna rose to give Amelia a hug. "I'm afraid though, dear, that I've got to get going if I'm to make it to Calgary before it's too late. I don't much like driving in the dark, but there's no way around it."

Amelia wondered about the tension lining the older woman's mouth as she changed the subject. She could think of no way to ask its cause without prying

"I'll take good care of Jesse for you."

After Anna kissed Jesse goodbye, and he swiped the kiss away with the back of his hand, Amelia followed him to the nursery where he had books spread out in tidy piles. He picked up the unopened box of an infant gym.

"Does that look like fun?" she asked.

Jesse turned to smile at her. "It's for babies."

"Why don't you read to me in the living room, Jesse? Bring some books you like."

As they settled on the couch with a hefty stack of books, Amelia realized that Anna had again skirted around the reason for her trip to the city. It occurred to her that she knew very little about her new friend's life and background. Their relationship had been all about Amelia unloading her cares upon Anna, who seemed to have infinite capacity for caring.

Jesse starts on *The Cat in the Hat*. He knows this book pretty good. The twins, his nieces, like it when he reads it to them. Mom always reminds him to read with 'spression. So he tries to remember that.

"The sun did not shine. It was too wet to play..."

Jesse gives a sly glance up at Amelia. He can tell she likes his reading. He puts a little more 'spression into it. All the mess Thing One and Thing Two make! Jesse is glad he doesn't have to clean it up. It reminds him of when the twins come over. Sometimes he puts some of the toys on the highest shelf before they come. Then he doesn't get stuck having to clean them all up after the girls leave.

Near the end of the book, he looks up at Amelia. "Cat's the bad guy. Fish is good, right? Fish is like a conscience?"

"That's right, Jesse," Amelia says.

When he closes the book, Amelia grabs his arm. "Jesse, you're a genius! You've just given me a great idea for one of my classes."

CHAPTER 11

────────── ❧ ──────────

I'll bet with my net I can get those Things yet!
—Dr. Seuss, *The Cat in the Hat*[3]

At times Amelia had dreaded English 10-4, her most challenging class. Neither she nor any of the kids wanted to be there. And honestly, she was scared of some of them with their wild hair, metal-studded jackets, and worse, the perpetually angry expressions on their faces. A few of them towered well over her five-foot height. Connor Labchuk, with his wide shoulders and thick reddish-blonde sideburns, was the tallest kid at six foot seven—the tallest person in the entire school, in fact. By now, though, she knew him for the pussycat he was. Apparently, it was the smaller ones who had something to prove. They scoffed at each other, and sometimes even at her, with barely concealed innuendo.

Starting off at the beginning of the year with the novel *Animal Farm*, Amelia soon saw they weren't connecting. Most of them couldn't remember a book they'd ever read outside of school, nor could they remember being read to. But today she had her idea.

As usual, five minutes after the bell rang, they were still goofing off, this time playing leapfrog over the desks and into their seats. Despite her small size, Amelia had her ways of gaining the upper hand. She refused to go the route of calling in a male teacher to get order, as some of the other young women did. An almost retired teacher during

Amelia's practicum had given her a tip: "Don't smile until November." Amelia found it worked.

She slammed the heavy classroom door hard and cleared her throat. Things began to settle.

"I'm sure no one remembers what we talked about last week," she said. "It was a hard concept that some of the English 10-1 kids have really struggled to understand."

Well, maybe that was pushing it a bit. But it seemed to inspire them to think they could best the more advanced classes. Amelia wasn't above instigating a little one-upmanship if it served her purpose. Briefly, she wondered whether her new faith in the Bible precluded a trick like that. She'd check with Anna later.

"Aww, come on... Give us a hint." Logan Koss loved attention.

"Away Logan, you mouldy rogue, away!" said Jaime Willis without looking up from her phone. Evidently the Shakespearean insult fad sweeping the school had sifted down from the upper grades.

Amelia turned quickly to the chalkboard. She couldn't let them see her smile. It wasn't November yet.

She began to write on the board: P—r—o— "Anyone?" Amelia asked.

"Pro... tozoans," a boy guessed, his voice cracking.

Another guess: "Prot... estant."

At this, Amelia coughed to cover a laugh, glad her back was turned.

"Every story has a...?" She finished writing the clue and turned to face them.

"Protagonist," they chanted.

"And the protagonist is...?"

"Somebody who likes pain?" Cody Weersma said.

Amelia frowned. *What?*

"Weersma, you idiot!" Count on Kelsey Rivers to put him in his place.

"You know, *agony*. Prot*agonist*?" Cody said.

"You are a tedious fool, Weersma," Jaime said, encouraging him.

"She doesn't think so," Cody said, jabbing a thumb in Amelia's direction. "I'm the pupil of her eye!"

Amelia kept her face impassive and snapped her marker down onto the desk to cut short the escalation of insults. "Okay. Let's try it another way. Everybody come sit on the floor right up here."

Some groaned, some leaped toward the front of the room.

"Anyone remember this?" She held up the book in her best game show assistant pose.

"*The Cat in the Hat!*" someone yelled. More groans.

As Amelia began to read it to them, however, she saw a few lips moving. Before long she was stunned to see most of them, notably the toughest cases, listening raptly.

When she finished, she asked, "So who is the protagonist? Who is the story about?"

They bickered a bit over whether it was the boy, the cat, or the fish.

"Well then, who's the antagonist?" she asked next. "The bad guy."

And she had them. In the twenty minutes remaining, Amelia was able to solidify for them protagonist, antagonist, inciting incident, rising action, climax, and denouement. Spontaneously, they began making the connection to movies they'd seen, categorizing heroes and villains. Thrills of satisfaction coursed through her as she saw interest, real interest, in their eyes. It was the first time this year she'd seen it with these kids. As a teacher, she lived for that lightbulb moment. This morning, she'd nailed it. She owed Jesse an ice cream sundae.

CHAPTER 12

———————— ❧ ————————

Nature, red in tooth and claw...
—Alfred, Lord Tennyson, *In Memoriam A.H.H.*

It was Tuesday, Robert suddenly realized, turning home onto Magnolia Street, and a little thread of tension knotted once again in his gut. It was twined with relief at not having to drag out something to heat for dinner. Or as was more often the case, simply eating wieners raw from the package. His stomach caved, hungry. He'd spend the dinner hour with Anna and Jesse. By now, past Thanksgiving and well into brown October, he should be used to their pattern. But though he was grateful for the nutritional value of these dinners, he also knew they would run out of fodder for conversation quickly if it were up to him. And wariness dogged his relations with his neighbour. Her innocuous questions so often forced him to face conundrums of his own. Yet it had to be better than another futile evening of drawing a blank on his research project or fruitlessly checking his phone until he was tired enough to fall asleep on the couch.

He pulled into his own driveway and, without stopping in to check the mailbox he knew would be empty, walked over to Anna's. Before they answered his knock, the uplifting aroma of fresh baking filled his senses, bringing a smile.

"Robert! How nice to see you. And looking so happy, too." Anna drew him into the small warm home while Jesse jockeyed to take his jacket. "You have a smile that transforms your whole face."

Robert glanced in her foyer mirror. Looking happy? He had no time to ponder the remark, for she was seating him at his place at the table. Already it was *his* place.

"I could smell the buns from outside," he offered.

"Bread actually. And soup." She took his and Jesse's hands and bowed her head to pray.

His half-closed eyes fixed on a book on the sideboard, and inwardly he groaned. He'd read a review of it a few years ago. A renegade biochemist had betrayed his training with some pitiable poke at evolution. But what would an old lady be doing with it?

"Some people think soup is not a real meal," Anna said as she served him a steaming bowl. "I hope you aren't one of them. I made sure to add plenty of meat."

Thick meaty flavour, a colour carnival of vegetables, cool butter on whole wheat bread's nuttiness... Robert immersed himself in the warmth, the satisfaction of it. Though he was repelled by Jesse's open-mouthed chewing, he could feel himself gobbling.

Anna gazed from one to the other of them as they ate, smiling as if they were both her sons. "An old question of mine came to mind the other day when I was watching you come home from work and the wind sent a few of the papers from your briefcase flying."

Robert gave a rueful smile.

"The courses you teach on evolution remind me of something I've puzzled over since I first heard about it," Anna said. "Years ago, Robert, I heard a story from a photographer that you might be able to explain to me."

"A photographer? What did you want explained?" he offered, pleased to be able to help.

"While this man was in Africa, he'd been at a river waiting for hours to catch some good shots of elephants. Well, no elephants showed up, but he did witness something he found amazing—and he managed to capture it on film, too. He showed us the photos. This young gazelle came to the river and was just bending its head for a drink when, quicker than quick, a crocodile lunged up, grabbed its leg, and began to drag it under the water."

A gasp diverted Robert's attention and he saw Jesse's eyes had widened as he listened to his mother's story. Anna laid a hand on her son's arm.

"By this time, you can imagine my photographer friend was busy snapping pictures. But what was so surprising was that a large hippo he hadn't noticed earlier came close to the struggle and somehow managed to wrestle the gazelle away from the crocodile. The gazelle escaped and bounded off, and of course the hippo had no worries from the crocodile, which, I suppose, went off pouting." She turned to Jesse. "No lunch for the croc!" Her eyes twinkled at him. His relieved sigh was audible.

"Now, Robert, why do you think the hippo did that? It couldn't have been competing for a meal, could it, since the gazelle got away?"

"Well no, hippos are herbivores," Robert said.

"That means they eat plants," Jesse put in. Robert was surprised he knew this.

"Right you are, Jesse. What happened there," he began, shifting to his professorial tone, "must have been a territorial dispute. The crocodile encroached on the hippo's marked territory and the hippo—"

"Huh, huh, huh," murmured Jesse, who rose to leave the table. Robert found these unpredictable distractions unnerving.

"But what I don't understand is this: why would it help the gazelle to get free? Why not just oust the lot of them from its territory?" Anna asked, unfazed by the interruption.

Jesse brought a large book to the table.

"It's 'H' for hippo. Very good, Jesse. Yes, let's look it up." Anna stacked their empty bowls and put on her reading glasses to look at the encyclopaedia. Finding the entry on hippos, she showed Jesse the pictures and had him read the first three sentences in his slow and singular way of smoothing off the hard edges of the words.

Robert questioned the value of her efforts, yet marvelled at Anna's patience. And he noted the pleased look on Jesse's face.

Taking the book from his mother, the young man sat down, clicking his tongue as he earnestly scanned the pictures.

"My real confusion, Robert, has to do with what I've read about these cases of animal altruism," Anna said. "And there have been lots of them."

"You probably mean something like the meerkat that has one of its clan stand guard for the others, or the honeybee that does its complicated dance to let the other bees know where the nectar is," Robert instructed. "But these are all systems the group has evolved for the survival of the species. So even though a meerkat might 'waste' energy caring for young that aren't its own, or spend time standing guard, they are doing it for the survival of their own kind."

"I see," said Anna, thoughtfully staring at the salt and pepper shakers as she stroked smooth a wrinkle in the tablecloth. He was about to make his excuses and get up from the table when she asked, "What about the many other cases where animals have sacrificed themselves but there doesn't seem to be anything in it for them or their kind?"

"Like a dog defending its master? That's just conditioning—"

"Actually, what I have in mind is more like dolphins and whales who have supported sick animals of a completely different species. There was one story where a man was swimming when a shark attacked him and bit into his arm and ribs."

Jesse looked up from his book, suddenly motionless, listening.

"When he screamed for help, three dolphins came and formed a circle around him. They kept flapping their tails and fins to frighten away the shark until the man's friends came up in a boat and rescued him."

"That sounds a little fanciful to me," Robert said.

"I've been reading about accounts like these for years, always wondering about that first story I heard." Anna reached for a notebook from the sideboard and rummaged through a fluttering of loose notepaper. "Here's something I found that Charles Darwin said." She adjusted her glasses. "'We may feel sure that any variation in the least degree injurious'—I assume he means injurious to an animal—'would be rigidly destroyed. This preservation of favourable individual differences and variations and the destruction of those which are injurious I have called Natural Selection, or the Survival of the Fittest.'"

"Yes, of course," Robert said. "But I fail to see your point."

"So, it seems to me that it might be 'injurious' to an animal like that hippo if it takes the time—and the risk, I might add—to rescue another creature."

"Not at all. Hippos have few predators," he said. "How could it be injurious?"

"Well, the hippo wouldn't be feeding during the time it took to do the rescue," she said thoughtfully. "And it would be taking the risk of getting slashed by the crocodile. Plus, there doesn't seem to be any benefit to the hippo itself."

"It was probably just an anomaly," Robert snapped.

He saw her chin pull back as she glanced away. He felt he was being watched and looked across the table to see Jesse frowning at him over the top of his book.

Conciliatory now, he said, "Maybe the animal that was helped would be able to reciprocate at a later time."

"Oh, you mean like Androcles and the Lion? But I thought that was a fable?" Anna asked, round-eyed.

"I like that story," Jesse said.

His hypothesis reduced to the mythological, Robert searched his memory for anything he'd read that would put this matter to rest. While he did so, Anna began clearing the dishes of leftover food.

"You must understand," Robert began, "that animals do whatever promotes survival, and they do these acts that appear altruistic to promote survival. We just don't know why yet. Probably it'll be found that animal groups that have altruists among them survive better than groups with only selfish animals."

Anna laughed. "Now you're pulling my leg!"

Robert found this disconcerting.

Anna sobered. "I'm sorry, it just sounded a little like circular reasoning."

He stiffened and rose from the table. "I've got to get back." Robert turned to the door, mumbling something about papers to mark.

"Please don't be upset," Anna said.

"Not at all," he said. "Thank you for supper tonight. And the, er, conversation. Until next time."

Jesse is still reading about hippos. They sure have big teeth. He goes to the foyer mirror to practice yawning that wide.

"Well, Jesse, I'm not at all sure that went well," Mom says, still looking out the window after their neighbour. "But at least he said he'll be back."

Jesse glances back at the place where Mr. Fielding ate. "Didn't clear his dishes," Jesse says, knowing he'll be the one to have to do it. "Hmph."

CHAPTER 13

---~~---

A proud man is always looking down on things and people:
and of course, as long you are looking down,
you cannot see something that is above you.
—C.S. Lewis, *Mere Christianity*[4]

Sitting in his sticky black vinyl office chair later, war broke out within Robert. A rush of accusation came at him. He had snubbed an old lady. One who had shown him nothing but kindness and generosity.

Yet another voice, too, spoke quietly.

Why did you feel that way, cut her off that way?

There are rational, scientific answers to these questions. I can check with—

But why does it matter so much? She may be well-read, but she's not an educated woman.

These are questions everyone asks themselves at some time or another. Regular people need to know that science, not superstition or religion, can answer their questions. Robert tapped the mouse to awaken the computer for a little light in the darkened room.

Could it be that you have something to prove?

Issues with tenure at the college are entirely beside the point.

What if Anna is right? What if these occurrences in nature contradict the tenets of natural selection?

He snorted. Abandon any hope of tenure, all you who enter here and let something like that slip at the college

What about the truth?

That's what I was trying to give her.

You very much like to look important. That's why you were so irritated that she had questions for which you weren't prepared.

And round and round it went. Self-justification and that other voice, each in turn. In disgust, he finally shut down the computer and shoved away from the desk. Flopping full-length on the saggy couch, he punched his flat pillow, pulled up the ancient, too-short sleeping bag, and hoped he'd fall asleep quickly.

The sides of Robert's mouth were stiff with frustration and his forehead tightly-knit when he woke in the early morning darkness from a disquieting dream. Details surrounding his interrogation by a panel of lawyers were nebulous, but the feelings of inadequacy and worthlessness were bitingly clear. He had been called for jury duty. When it was his turn with the lawyers, they asked him question after question, their frowns lengthening with each answer he gave. His feeling of desperation grew.

Finally, after conferring in whispers, they turned to him and said, "We're sorry, Mr. Fielding. This is very disappointing. Your level of intelligence is not sufficient for the position and you have been rejected as a juror for this case."

Fully awake now, Robert became aware of how tenaciously he was clinging to the sense of certainty in what he believed. Yet he knew a desperate grip like that could blind him to clear thinking. His old motto, "follow the evidence wherever it leads," had never yet failed him. But the stakes had never been so high. He'd based his life on truths he now saw challenged. Letting out a long and slow breath, he resolved to be true to his motto.

He groped the floor for his phone to check the time. An hour before the alarm would ring. He could mark a few more lab reports before leaving for work.

CHAPTER 14

——

Through love serve one another.
—Galatians 5:13

Joan answered the door after four rings and stared blankly. There stood Anna, her old friend. The two of them went back a long way, though they'd only been getting reacquainted for the past four years. Joan had been about fourteen when she'd been asked to help Anna's mother with her brood for a couple of weeks one summer. On later reflection, Joan now realized the do-good family had been offering mere charity, couched in a job opportunity. She remembered all too vividly young Anna and her little sisters staring at her, whispering unintelligibly in German and giggling incessantly as they watched her go about the cleaning chores in their home.

"You said come early, so here I am," Anna explained.

"Oh yes, I suppose I did. Well, come in. I haven't had my breakfast yet, but you can get started while I have my coffee." Joan led Anna into the kitchen and sat on her favourite stool. "You didn't bring Jesse?"

"No, I'm just a few doors down and he'll be all right for a little while. He knows where I am if he needs anything."

Joan rummaged through a pile on the table. "I was hoping he could do a few jobs for me, too. I had a list somewhere here." With Anna taking in the scene, Joan began to see her home through her neighbour's eyes. There was cat hair in mounds on every seat, piles of stuff and more stuff on every surface, cat toys and cat food dishes in quantity. Well, Anna was the one who'd offered to do this, after all. *If she so much as breathes a word of criticism...*

Peeved, Joan gave a sigh. "It was here last night, but I don't know. I'll have to make another one, if I can just find a pen—"

"Why don't we start with this table? I've learned from my daughter that if I get started with one thing and make a dent in it, it gives me courage for the next stronghold of confusion."

Joan shrugged. "Be my guest."

"This, for instance," Anna began. "An article clipped from, it looks like a 1998 issue of *The Advocate*. Do you have a filing cabinet?"

"Well now, I finally found that article and was going to send it to my oldest daughter. She has a weight problem, you know, and this article had some research on nutrition that I thought might help." Joan feared the health problems that would arise if Louise didn't get serious about her diet. And health problems could lead to early death. "I don't know why people can't lose weight. It's so unhealthy and it must *feel* horrible with all those extra folds of flab. When I started to put on weight about fifteen years ago, my doctor said I should diet and I just did. It only takes a little—"

"But Joan, I was just wondering what you wanted done with newspaper clippings. I'll tell you what. Why don't I use the method Beth uses with me? I know how nervous I get when she starts pitching things in the garbage. So I won't throw anything out—I'll just sort it all and then we can decide where to put things. Fair enough?"

"I suppose." Remembering her manners, Joan added, "Are you sure you don't want some coffee first?"

"I've already had breakfast, but you go ahead and I'll just start sorting."

While Joan puttered about in and out of the kitchen, toasting and eating a leftover pancake with saskatoon jam and flossing her teeth, she thought how pleasant it was to have someone around the house to talk to.

"I had more luck at garage sales this summer than ever before," Joan said. "That new subdivision to the west, mostly young families. They get rid of perfectly good stuff, and not just kids' clothes. Young people these days take so much for granted. But it meant I got more clothes for my little project."

"You can handle all that walking? And carrying home the heavy bags, too?"

"It's nothing. The exercise does me good. There's a lot of people who should be doing more walking, that's for sure. Anyway, I've got my winter's work cut out for me: mending, treating stains and spots, replacing zippers. I can turn the worn collars on some of those plaid shirts and they'll be good as new."

"Such a lot of work! It's quite a project," Anna said.

Was she being sarcastic? Joan frowned. "And on each garment I make sure I remove every speck of lint from the pockets and seams. It's such a shame to see all this perfectly good clothing go to waste when there are people around the world with nothing to wear." *Anna's not the only do-gooder in town.*

"Have you had any luck yet, finding an organization that'll ship it overseas?" Anna asked.

"Not yet. After all the work I've put into this over the years, I don't know if I can trust anyone to get it there safely. And besides, I'm not much for making phone calls. Though I did have a few calls this week that got my goat." She described in detail the misunderstanding about her dental appointment. How unfair it had been; she had been dreading it so long but had finally prepared herself for the inevitable, only to have them reschedule and dredge up the dread again. What if the anaesthetic didn't take and she felt everything?

Then, catching sight of the state of her yard out the window, she shared with Anna her dilemma about who to get to rake leaves.

Keeping busy, Anna murmured her sympathies and suggested Joan hire one of the Desjarlais boys.

"Those kids? Don't you know they're involved in a gang?"

Anna's wide-eyed surprise showed clearly. "How do you know that?"

"It's obvious, Anna. You just have your head in the sand." Joan disliked having to prove everything to Anna.

"I've always found them pleasant boys," Anna said.

Forty-five minutes later, there was no change in the quantity of miscellany on the table, but the teetering mounds and haphazard heaps were now neat stacks and piles with the surface of the table showing between. Joan was glad to find her favourite grey sweater draped on the back of a chair. She'd been missing that one. It had been causing instability at the bottom of the whole towering structure. There were stacks of clipped newspaper and magazine articles, unused paper and stationery. An empty tin can now held pens, pencils, and erasers. Packages of cat food sat with three cat leashes, an animal brush, and pet vaccination records.

"I'm amazed how easy this is at someone else's house," Anna told Joan when she was finished. She pointed to each orderly stack in turn as she explained. "Now, sunglasses and lip balm are here, and I've bookmarked all the books where you had them open and they're stacked here. Anything that looked like mail, opened or unopened, I put here. These are photos and camera supplies, food and grocery items, empty packages, bags and containers in these stacks, clothes here, this jar for money and coins. Four wooden clothespins. Three tubes of lotion, two pillowcases, and a printer cartridge in a pear tree!" Anna sang triumphantly.

Joan had no idea what the singing was about. Anna was always trying to be cute or something. Joan reached out a hand. "Let me see the mail. Maybe that's where that credit card statement is. I've been after them three or four times on the phone for hours trying to get them to take off this charge from a spa for $79.95. I'd never go to a spa. What would I want from them? I can't afford all that fancy stuff."

When life squeezed Joan, she couldn't help it. She dripped contempt.

"It is hard to remember, sometimes, what each item on a credit card statement was for, isn't it?" Anna said.

Now that—that right there was the kind of thing that irritated Joan. Anna was always trying to put her happy spin on everything. She'd had to put up with this for years, always being corrected into finding the bright side. Well, a lot of life didn't have a bright side. In fact, it was downright miserable out there and some people should wake up to the fact. But then, Anna had always had it easy with her doting husband, adoring children, and picture-perfect farm.

"Well now, why don't I get these piles put in their proper places? Then I'll be getting home to get lunch for Jesse," Anna said as she started for the door.

Joan looked up from her bills, disappointed that Anna was leaving already. No one ever came to stay and visit.

"Can't he make himself a sandwich or something?" said Joan. "I was hoping you'd be able to do something with my living room today, too."

Anna glanced through to the front room. Joan watched her eyes scan it and felt sure there was disappointment and disapproval in that look. To her, it was home. She surrounded herself with things that held meaning, precious and purposeful things. And those stacks of boxes along the wall were her reason for living in recent years. Oh, why had she ever suggested to Anna that she come help her get organized?

"I've got to leave now," Anna said, "but I can come over for another hour in the afternoon if you like." Joan heard no eagerness in her neighbour's tone.

"Never mind," she told Anna. "I can do it myself."

CHAPTER 15

As far as the east is from the west, so far has
He removed our transgressions from us.
—Psalm 103:12

Amelia had already sat like this, legs dangling over the side of the bed, for a long time. Pleating the hem of her nightgown, she shivered as guilt wrung out all she thought she'd known of God's love. On impulse she grabbed her phone off the nightstand.

Only after she'd punched in Anna's number and heard the phone ring twice did she note the time. While she'd been awake for hours, it was only 6:22 a.m.

Oh no, it's far too early to—

"Hello?" came a croak.

"Anna?"

Throat clearing. "Yes..."

"I haven't slept at all. I'm so cold and I'm just shaking—"

"Amelia, dear, what's wrong?"

"I'm so afraid. I've been thinking about something I read last night in—I think it was—" Amelia turned the crisp new pages of her Bible. "Yeah, right here: Hebrews. 'Vengeance is Mine, I will repay.' That's me, isn't it? He's going to pay me back for what I did!" She thought she had expended all the hard, rasping sobs her body contained, but there were more.

"Now, Amelia—"

"I took a life and now He's going to take one. I can see that would be justice but, oh, I can't stand the thought! I look at these prenatal development pictures and I love what I see because that's my baby. And then I hate what I see because that, too, was my baby. And I killed her. I *killed* her! I didn't want to but I did it anyway. I just know—"

"Amelia! Now stop this. You *must* listen to me." Amelia had never heard the sharp tone in Anna's voice before. "You are doubting the goodness of God and His promise to forgive. You're thinking that God is out to get you. You aren't considering the context of that passage."

Amelia's sobs subsided.

"Do you have any bleeding or cramping?" Anna asked.

"No..."

"But you're cold and shaking?"

"Yes, but I suppose it's mostly the stress from what I was reading and thinking about."

"And other stresses, too, I expect," Anna added.

"Well, yeah. But what do you mean, the context? It keeps on going and says, 'The Lord will judge His people' and 'It is a fearful thing to fall into the hands,'" her voice began to rise, "'of the living God.'"

"Context, context, context, my dear," Anna said.

Amelia heard pages flipping.

"You must know that from your own training in literature."

"You mean the context of the whole dictates the meaning of its parts?"

"Exactly. That whole section is a warning against apostasy," Anna began. "It's about what would happen if those folks were to follow through with what they were considering. Because of persecution, some of those early Christians were thinking about going back to Judaism. They hadn't expected that following the Messiah would be hard. Do you see?"

"So far," Amelia answered, still unsure.

"This is a warning that once you know Jesus and have forgiveness of sins, if you reject Him after all He's done to forgive you, you're insulting Him supremely. The whole point is that there is forgiveness only in Jesus. Were you thinking of rejecting Him, dear?"

"No, no, of course not. I see what you're saying... It's about forgiveness." Wonder filled Amelia.

"Now listen, Amelia. Here's something else in the same book: 'He is also able to save to the uttermost'—that means *completely* and *forever*—'those who come to God through Him.' That means no matter what they've done."

"But what if there are still physical consequences in this life for what I've done?"

"I can't promise you there won't be. Sometimes there are."

"That's what I'm afraid of."

"But I can promise you what God promises, Amelia. He only allows into your life what He knows is for your good. The history of God's people shows that even when they were being disciplined for rebellion, God loved them and was with them. 'In all their affliction He was afflicted,' it says. He feels our pain, dear. He's with us in the hard things. I'm preaching to myself here, too, dear," Anna told her, her voice cracking. "And here's something I often turned to when I was pregnant, love. Let me just find it here... Ah yes. 'He will feed His flock like a shepherd; He will gather the lambs with His arm, and carry them in His bosom, and gently lead those who are with young.' That's you, Amelia. You are 'with young.'"

"Mmm. I love that," Amelia murmured. "Sounds like that means a lot to you, too."

"Yes, it's still true for me. Jesse may be twenty-five, but he's still young. And even though my others are grown, they'll always be my 'young.' We never stop being mothers. He gently leads us," Anna whispered hoarsely.

Amelia pondered that for a few moments. "There's something else that haunts me, Anna. I keep wondering what has become of that first child of mine. I know from what Pastor Tom has been teaching us that sin is pretty much embedded in our DNA. And sin requires judgment. So I wonder—"

"Let me reassure you on that score, dear." Pages crackled. "Only an understanding of grace allows us to know that God takes those little ones to be with Him. Or even adults who don't have the capacity to understand sin and salvation. You know that *we* make no contribution to our right standing with God, right?"

"Mmhmm."

"And we have to rely on God choosing us and bringing us to repentance, right? So it's all His doing. That's how I know He shows grace to little ones. We don't have any ability to remedy the sin we've inherited and neither do they—unless God intervenes."

"How do you do that, Anna? How do you just pick up and run with these questions I throw at you first thing in the morning?"

"You're not the first to wrestle with these questions, dear. You see, years ago, I lost a little one at five and a half months gestation." Anna paused, then began again with a tremor in her voice. "I held him in my hand. A boy, perfectly formed in every way, but oh so very, very tiny. And blue. Later, when I went to the hospital, they told me I wouldn't have been able to tell what it was. But I knew he was a boy. I remember the doctor saying, 'Don't cry. You'll have other children.' What a thing to say to a grieving mother. But I had big questions. I wondered if my sin had caused this tiny one's death. Or if God had just made a mistake and decided to start over with the next one? And later, I realized I never would have had my precious daughter if that other baby had lived." She cleared her throat. "These thoughts puzzled me for years. Women face these enormous matters of life and death in the conception and carrying of children. I finally took the time to study it.

You know that old saying, 'God helps those who help themselves'? Well, it's not in the Bible. What I learned is that God delights in helping those who *can't* help themselves. He can be trusted because He has infinite mercy and loving-kindness for us. He gently leads those who are with young, remember? There are references all through the Bible about God's special care for the helpless. I can give you the list when I see you at church if you like."

"I'd like that." Amelia checked the time and gasped. "I have a staff meeting at school in less than half an hour and I haven't even showered and dressed yet. I have to go, Anna! Thanks so much. See you Sunday."

Amelia ended the call and reached for her robe.

"Gently leads those that are with young," she mused. She paused as she walked through her large walk-in closet to the bathroom, tears starting as she hugged her arms.

CHAPTER 16

———— ∿ ————

If we had no faults, we should not take
so much pleasure in noting those of others.
—Francois de La Rochefoucauld, *Reflections; or Sentences*
and Moral Maxims, Maxim 31

Walking along the wide hallways with Jesse and Anna in tow, Robert wondered if they walked in awe as he'd done the first time he went to a college open house. He'd have been about sixteen then, with a hunger for academia that mystified his business-minded father. That aura carried by busy students of being in the know—he'd wanted that.

Today, a Saturday, young people were scarce, and he was surprised to notice a few of the female students smiling past him at Jesse.

"Just a minute, Robert," he heard Anna say.

Turning, he saw Jesse lagging, and waited. Beyond Robert's neighbours, he was annoyed to see Jamie McCoy coming toward them at a brisk clip. All three caught up with Robert simultaneously. Reluctantly, he made the introductions, aware of this quiet clash of worldviews. His breath caught in apprehension as he anticipated what might come out of the exchange professor's opinionated mouth.

But McCoy warmly shook hands with Anna and Jesse and within minutes had the young man laughing. Robert stood amazed as his fellow prof took a few moments to chitchat amiably with both guests. Before long, McCoy clapped Jesse on the shoulder, made his apologies, and continued on his way.

The meeting took less than five minutes, but it soured Robert's entire morning. He did his best to follow Mr. Congeniality's act, leading them past classrooms and lecture theatres to the Science Department's central office. Noticing the name plaque on Robert's office door, Anna asked what the Q and M stood for.

"Q is for Quentin, my mother's maiden name. M for Marlowe, after my father." Smiling sheepishly, he said, "When I was in elementary school, there were two popular TV series I told kids my initials stood for—Quincy, the medical examiner, and Matlock, the lawyer."

Anna laughed. "I like to hear a secret tidbit like that about you. Brings you down to my level."

Opening the door of the laboratory launched a mix of pungent smells—cedar shavings, formaldehyde, plants. As Robert began to describe the lab's current research projects, he observed Jesse's eyes wandering followed by a wide, uninhibited yawn. *Wait till he sees the newborn rats. He's going to love them.* But before they reached the cage of squirming pink rodents, McCoy breezed in.

"Have you seen these, mate?" he said to Jesse, drawing Anna and Jesse's attention to the litter of young at the far end of the row. Jesse was fascinated as he and McCoy huddled together, pointing and exclaiming over the small, hairless bodies. Anna watched from the side, but Robert, miffed, retreated to the opposite end of the lab until McCoy waltzed out again. He rejoined his guests and tried to resume the tour but couldn't disguise his annoyance.

Before long, he sensed Anna glancing his way.

"Is something wrong?" she asked, her eyes searching his face.

He paused in front of the row of rustling rat cages and looked down at her, the lines on her concerned face bracketing her gentle smile.

"That guy is a big fake," he blurted, instantly aware of his petulant tone.

"You mean Dr. McCoy?" She lifted one eyebrow, accentuating the wry skepticism in her eyes. "Oh, that was quite obvious."

"It was? What made you think so?"

"Robert, you should know by now that I have a pretty well-honed baloney detector. Aside from your friend's charming accent, I saw a man utterly full of himself who adapts to fit whatever circumstances he finds himself in. Just so long as he shines."

Spot on. Her insightful analysis made Robert curious. "How could you possibly know that after a single meeting?"

Anna's eyes crinkled further. "Some men's sins are clearly evident, preceding them to judgment." She patted his arm. "But I wonder why he gets under your skin so much. Hmmm? Sometimes we are most irked by the flaws in others that we share with them."

She gave him a searching look that Robert evaded by straightening one of the rodent water bottles. He heard the door to the lab open.

"But I've said too much already." Anna lowered her voice. She extended her index finger toward him. "I used to tell my children, 'When you point a finger at someone, there are three fingers pointing back at you!' Dr. McCoy is still a person, made in the image of God."

The arrival of Dr. Baldwyn spared Robert a confrontation on that doctrine. He introduced the dean to Anna and explained Jesse's interest in the lab animals.

"Oh, but we already know each other, Robert. Cliff and I have both been part of the community churches' singing Christmas tree choir for several years now," Anna explained.

Cliff? Most of the faculty didn't even venture that level of familiarity with the dignified department head.

"Most notably, Handel's *Messiah* last year. And it's good to see you again, young man," Dr. Baldwyn added, pumping Jesse's hand and laying his other hand on the young man's shoulder. He turned to Robert. "How is it that you know my friend Anna?"

Robert looked at his boss with a wry smile. "I thought I was introducing my friend to you. Actually, Anna is my next-door neighbour. It was the food that first lured me."

"Oh? Next-door neighbour?" Baldwyn's furrowed brow made Robert shrink a little at the implied question. His superior was known for his traditional views and while other members of the faculty spoke freely of their personal lives, Robert was sensitive to even a mild dose of Baldwyn disapproval. At work he had scrupulously avoided any mention of his marital breakdown. And now his surprise that these two were acquainted had made him drop his guard.

"Well, the lure of food is no wonder. The cherry pies she baked for the party after our last performance were—" Baldwyn put his fingertips together and kissed them "—a taste experience!" Baldwyn started to leave the lab, but turned back and pointed at Jesse, a twinkle in his eyes. "Be sure you show this young man my boys before you go!"

When the door clanged shut, Anna looked quizzically at Robert. "His boys?"

"Dr. Baldwyn is uber-proud of his collection of piranhas in the staff lounge aquarium. Come on, I'll introduce you." He ushered them out the door and down the hall toward the lounge. He looked down at Jesse, walking beside him. "And be sure you don't put your hand in the tank, Jesse. Those fish have mighty sharp teeth."

CHAPTER 17

———— ❧ ————

Christ, who said to the disciples, "Ye have not chosen me,
but I have chosen you," can truly say to every group of
Christian friends, "You have not chosen one another but I
have chosen you for one another."
—C.S. Lewis, *The Four Loves*[5]

Anna had promised she'd teach Amelia to sew and they'd decided on a maternity top as a first project. They were to meet Anna's daughter Beth on Saturday to shop, a suggestion Amelia had no reason to refuse. She chided herself for her irrational desire to have Anna to herself. Entering the fabric store together, Amelia heard Anna's blissful sigh as her friend slipped her hands out of her gloves to finger the cloth. Amelia looked around at the prismatic array on the shelves, marvelling at the way the older woman experienced everything.

"It might be best to find a pattern first. Then we'll know what kind of fabric to choose," Anna said.

Amelia followed her to the pattern desks, already glad for a chance to sit down.

Anna eyed her. "At the rate you're puffing, we're not going to get around to too many stores."

They both turned as Beth arrived, breathless, her rosy, round nine-month-old boy in a stroller.

"Whew!" Beth said, greeting her mother with a hug and shifting her oversized aqua bag further up her shoulder. "Steve said to enjoy myself with you two today and I intend to. He's taking the girls to the rec centre for the day. The twins were frantic to see Jesse. Anything exciting happen yet?"

Typical 'life is so busy' Mom-boasting. But with sudden pleasure, Amelia realized her days of being on the outside of such talk would soon end.

"Amelia, this is my daughter Beth and my youngest grandson Dusty." Anna turned to Beth. "You mean have we found any bargains? Just waiting for you."

"With the move coming up, I'm not looking to acquire any more stuff," Beth said. "But I'll help spend your money."

Anna was already crouching to make much of the little one, his face alight with anticipation. She whipped off his small leather slipper first thing and nuzzled the chubby foot, then held it out to Amelia; it was almost as thick and wide as it was long. A throaty chortle burst out of the baby when Anna's fingers crept up his pudgy arm. "Round and round the garden, goes the little bear; one step, two step, tickle you under there!"

Beth smiled, all motherly pride, at her mother's delight in the child, then turned to Amelia. "I've heard wonderful things about you, Amelia, most notably your home decorating capabilities."

When Beth also greeted Amelia with a hug, it was so spontaneous, so natural, that Amelia was ashamed of her earlier inner pique of jealousy. She felt embraced by a sense of family, belonging in a way she never had.

"Back to work," Anna said, beckoning to Amelia and turning to the oversized pattern books. The older woman vetoed one, then another, and yet a third designer pattern that had drawn Amelia's attention involving a notched collar or bound buttonholes or some such mumbo jumbo.

"You do gravitate toward the complicated styles, don't you, dear?"

Finally, they agreed on a design Anna said was simple enough for a beginner.

There were a few false leads choosing fabric, but at last they settled on a fun, bold orange print Amelia liked.

"What serendipity, finding it sixty percent off regular price." Anna helped her find matching thread and buttons and sent her to the checkout. "I'll just go say hello to my dear friend Yanni."

Anna hurried to the rear of the store where a tiny Asian woman carried a tottering stack of fabric bolts that nearly obscured her vision. Amelia couldn't make out the words, but there were enthusiastic squeals and heartfelt hugs.

"I guess they haven't seen each other in a while," Amelia said.

Beth laughed at the idea as she pulled Dusty up out of his chariot. "Yanni's her neighbour! She's always like that with Mom. Absolutely fawns over her. Mom makes friends with every stray kitten she finds."

"Thanks!" Amelia grimaced.

"Oh no! I didn't mean—" Beth buried her head in the drowsy baby's blanket on her shoulder as she rocked him slowly. "What I meant is that it's like she has a sensor for people who are hurting. Or they sense something about her that draws them to her. It's the only way I've ever known her. We kids all used to take turns after school, in order of age, telling her all the school bus or recess drama. In high school I even brought my friends home for her to solve their problems."

"Didn't you resent sharing her with all those others?"

Beth paused and tilted her head, her blond curls bobbing. "You know, I don't think I ever did. She may have packrat tendencies that drive me crazy, but the best thing about Mom is her way of making me feel like I'm the only one that matters. My brothers and I have compared notes and we all feel that way." There was a pensive pause. "Well, maybe not David."

A dart of envy pinned Amelia to her place in the queue of fabric-fondling women at the checkout. Beth cleared her throat, thrusting her chin at the gap in the line-up ahead of Amelia.

"It sounds like you have wonderful memories," Amelia managed to say as she moved forward.

Beth's blue eyes peered back in time and she giggled. "I do. It's not every mom who lets her kids use the sofa cushions as rafts, or load real wheat into our toy trucks and combines on the living room rug."

When Anna rejoined them, Beth asked, "Is it all right with you two if we stop in at the mall across the street?"

Anna gave Amelia a questioning look. Amelia laughed. "Be still, my beating heart. Yes, I think I can resist temptation."

"Am I missing something here?" Beth looked from one to another, but neither Amelia nor Anna offered anything but a smile. The young woman shrugged, causing the baby to snuffle and shift. "I was really hoping to help you find something new, Mom. It's been a long time since you got something for yourself."

Anna demurred, insisting she didn't need anything. But when they arrived at the mall, Beth marched her into a quietly lit shop, scanning the racks for age-appropriate clothes. She and Amelia held out a series of possibilities which Anna declined on one pretext or another.

Finally, Beth pulled a periwinkle blue jacket and skirt off the rack, holding her hand over the tag. "You're forbidden to look at the price, Mom. Please try this on."

Anna sighed but gave in. Taking the outfit, she disappeared into a cubicle.

Dusty had wakened and Beth made her way to the chairs near the fitting room. Amelia took mental notes as she watched the young mother cover her shoulder and the baby's head with a blanket and, judging by the sucking, smacking sounds, nursed him.

"I knew it was only a matter of the price," Beth began after a few minutes. "Mom's never been much good at buying things for herself. I'm sure if we didn't ask, we'd never find out anything about her finances, but it's not like she doesn't have the money." The baby's dimpled fist clutched at his mother's finger in a way that set Amelia yearning. It was a photo-worthy vignette that could have been captioned *Trust*. "My brothers and I laugh sometimes about how secretive Mom is. Not sure why. Maybe she's reacting to some of our relatives at family reunions who went on and on about every detail of their health. Organ recitals, Mom called them."

Amelia considered this aspect of Anna, the discretion she'd perceived about her almost instantly from their first meeting. "One thing about a secretive person is that you can be sure anything you tell them isn't going to go any further," Amelia said.

"There is that, I suppose." Beth looked down to play peekaboo with the baby, straightening her clothes as she pulled the damp-curled blonde boy to a sitting position on her lap.

"How did you learn to do that?" Amelia had to ask.

"What? Oh, you mean nurse a baby?"

Amelia nodded, fascinated by the little white dribble at the corner of Dusty's dewy red lip.

"To some degree it comes naturally, I suppose. They put the baby to your breast as soon as he's born. And of course, there are lactation consultants who can help if you have any trouble. Where are you planning to birth?"

The salesclerk sang a dramatic intro just then as Anna made her entrance. Beth whistled, poorly. Amelia clapped.

"You look like an aristocrat!" Amelia said.

Anna rolled her eyes but pirouetted anyway. The skirt flared obligingly.

Surrounded all day at work by young people, it was new to Amelia to get to know a senior. Early on, she'd begun to reconstruct in her mind Anna's face as a younger woman.

There's beauty in her face, aged as it is. Could there be some point of beauty in every woman, no matter her age or size or shape?

"You're gorgeous! It really brings out the blue in your eyes," Beth told her mother. "You'll wow them at church this Sunday."

"'It would be mortifying to the feelings of many ladies, could they be made to understand how little the heart of man is affected by what is costly or new in their attire,'" Anna quoted.

Amelia laughed. "That's got to be from something by Jane Austen!"

"*Northanger Abbey!*" Anna told her, a pleased smile on her lips.

"You have quite the memory." Amelia said.

"You don't know the half of it," Beth said to Amelia. "Poems, Shakespeare, hymns, scripture, old television ads... just don't get her started." She turned to her mother, who was still shifting this way and that before the three-way mirror. "You are going to take it, right, Mom?"

"Yes, she is," Amelia said. "And matching shoes? No? Then maybe lunch."

Over an Italian lunch, Amelia finally had the chance to ask the two women about giving birth. They shared their experiences, Anna in reserved terms, Beth enthusiastically sharing the details of her home birth.

"Have you been to a prenatal class?" Beth asked.

"Yes, but it was so awkward and uncomfortable going alone that I quit after the first session. I probably take up way too much time at my doctor's appointments asking questions. She never seems to have much time for me. So I watch birth videos on YouTube a lot." She grinned.

"That could scare you more than anything." Anna handed over the rest of her garlic toast to Amelia. "I saw you eyeing it."

Amelia laughed and took a large bite of the toast.

"You're what?" Beth asked. "Maybe fourteen or fifteen weeks

along? It's probably not too late to find a midwife. They give you a full hour at each appointment—more if you need it. I'll give you my midwife Sherry's number." Beth popped tiny bits of tomato and cucumber into Dusty's mouth whenever he started his droning, wrist-twirling hungry signal. "Hasn't your mother ever talked to you about what her experience was like?"

"I learned two things from her on that topic. I remember her once mentioning an elite group of feminists whose membership was restricted to those who had given birth alone."

"Preferably in the woods, in a hut they'd built themselves?" Beth's eyes sparkled mischievously.

"Something like that. My mother talked about it with admiration, I remember that much."

"And the other thing you learned?" Anna asked.

Amelia looked down and began meticulously picking up the crumbs resting on the small but growing built-in shelf where her waist used to be. "That there was no way it was worth it."

Almost in unison, the two women protested. In the dimly lit restaurant, heads turned toward their table.

"Forgive me for disagreeing with your mother, Amelia, but that is absolutely not true."

"Not true!" Beth said. "There's nothing that brings more fulfillment than pushing out a living human being." Dusty squirmed as Beth squeezed him tightly.

"Well, maybe one thing rivals it," Anna said. "Seeing a person come to new life in the spiritual sense." She looked with love at Amelia.

"That brings me to something I've been meaning to ask you, Anna," Amelia said, tipping her head to one side. "It would mean a lot if you would be willing to be my labour coach when the time comes."

"Oh dear. It would be an honour. But I'm not sure I'd know what to do."

"Just what you've done for me, Mom," Beth said. "Be there. Sympathize. Encourage. All the stuff you're good at."

Amelia nodded. "You know, Beth, your mother threw me a lifeline once before when I didn't know where to turn."

"Oh?"

"It was a particularly bad time for me. I... I was overwhelmed with guilt and need and emptiness. Anna introduced me to Jesus." Amelia's throat tightened, threatening tears. She took a deep breath. "It's changed my life entirely."

"I've always wondered how it came about that you bared your soul to me that day, Amelia. Being the private person you are, I mean."

"Isn't it what you'd call Providence? Actually, I somehow knew that you'd tell me the truth. I knew you wouldn't say what I'd done was okay. That it was the 'responsible' thing to do. That it was only a blob of tissue and I had a right to do what I wanted with my own body. I'd already heard and told myself those answers for years." Amelia breathed deeply, aware of Beth's eyes growing rounder at her revelation. She kept her own eyes wide to keep tears from spilling out. "They were never enough to quell the guilt."

Anna took her hand, compelling Amelia's trust with her earnest gaze. "You will not be alone when your time comes."

CHAPTER 18

Teachers affect eternity; no one can tell where their influence stops.
—Henry Brooks Adams, *The Education of Henry Adams*, 1907

In the milling and clatter of kids leaving the classroom as the buzzer faded, Amelia was aware of a large shadow passing in front of her desk. Where previously she would have demanded a student's attention, her growing interest in her students as individuals alerted her to their sensitivities.

"Connor, can I see you for a minute?" Amelia spoke quietly, not wanting to stigmatize him for being singled out.

"You're in for it now, Labchuk, thou lump of foul deformity," Cody Weersma said. He took a leap and slapped Connor's shoulder with his backpack, then raced out of the room. The blow had as much effect on Connor as a squirrel colliding with an oak tree.

The rest of the students filed out with snickers or looks of sympathy at the class giant.

Amelia looked up at him when all was quiet. A sandy lock dropping onto his forehead was all that was out of order on the clean-cut kid in his blue Henley shirt, size extra-large. The sleeves were still a little too short, she noticed.

"Have a seat, Connor," she said.

He hung his backpack on the ear of the chair and sat, his knees lifting the front of the desk.

"I've been noticing something that has made me wonder why you're in this class." Amelia came around to the front of her desk and eased herself up onto its edge. "Your marks in English and Social Studies—"

"I know, they're pitiful. But Ms. Ashton, I've been trying." Connor leaned his chin on his fist, smushing his lips.

"What do you think the problem is?"

"Haven't a clue. I know the stuff, but then I get a test back and I've just bombed."

"Can I see your notes?"

He rummaged through the paper muddle in his pack, pulling out a purple ring-bound notebook.

Amelia thumbed through the many pages of scrawl. The only things she could decipher were occasional numbers. She closed it softly and handed it back to him.

"Are you able to read that?" she asked.

"Yeah. Well, most of the time. Not really." He stared down at the desk, his thick blonde eyebrows shading his eyes from her view.

"What I've been noticing, Connor," Amelia tilted her head to catch his eye, "is that you do well on essays and homework where you can use a computer, but tests where there are essay questions are your downfall."

"I know," he mumbled.

"So I have a plan."

"Yeah?" He glanced up at her from under the brows.

"I have a friend who homeschooled one of her sons during junior high and high school. She told me one of the reasons she did it was that he had this infantile handwriting all the way into his teens even though he was a bright kid. Teachers couldn't understand his work, so they kept giving him zeroes. It was really demoralizing for him."

"Tell me about it." Connor's shoulders slumped lower than ever.

"Not so great knowing the material and not being able to prove it to teachers, is it?"

"So how'd she fix it?"

"The magic wand."

"Uh-huh."

"Right here." Amelia pulled a thin workbook out of her briefcase. "My friend said that before she started work on any of his courses, they spent a while working through this italic handwriting course. It's kind of halfway between printing and cursive. His writing went from looking like a preschooler's to looking like an adult's in just a few weeks."

Connor took the book, flipped its pages. "Looks simple enough."

"It is. But it's going to take discipline."

"Ms. Ashton, I have a job, I play football, and it may not show, but I do study. I know about discipline."

"I believe you, Connor." Amelia smiled into his blue eyes. "So, you should have no trouble adding this to your homework routine. It's broken into daily lessons, see? And when it says to do a page or two, or three of extra practice, promise me you'll do it, okay?" She clasped her hands, her index fingers in front of her lips.

"Okay. Promise." Connor stuffed the workbook into his pack. "You think it'll make a difference?"

"If you don't skimp on the practice, it definitely will. Just like in football. But you'll be learning a new habit and that always takes some time."

The boy got up to go, towering over Amelia. She began filling her briefcase and putting on her sweater around her baby bump.

Halfway to the door, he turned and took a few steps back toward her. "You're different."

She looked up at him, way up.

"All through last year, it was like, to you, we weren't even here," he said. "Now you're seeing us."

A lump began to grow in Amelia's throat.

"Must be the baby." He gave a crooked smile. "You're going to be a great mom."

CHAPTER 19

A man who isolates himself seeks his own desire;
he rages against all wise judgment.
—Proverbs 18:1

She used to put her knees up, making the sheets a little tent of cool air. Maybe she hadn't been trying to annoy him. It had turned out to be an irritation he now missed. Robert was awash in memories. It was early on, probably while he was still in grad school. Those lazy Sunday mornings had been the only time he really relaxed. Not quite awake, he had grumbled something about her, on the other side of the bed, doing all that flapping. She'd begun stroking his back.

"Poor, poor Bobby," she'd said, snuggling closer behind him. "He's just jealous. He wishes he had my flapping ability. But no, he's never been to flapping school. Jealous, jealous, jealous. Only those with special flapping talents are admitted. The competition is tough. And poor Bobby is jealous. That's why he lashes out at flappers who flap... flap... flap... so beautifully—"

Not wanting to think about what had followed, he got up abruptly from the tangle of sleeping bag that had slid off the couch during the night. When had the playing stopped? When had he stopped being able to laugh at himself?

Halfway through his ritual bowl of Saturday morning Froot Loops, he remembered something. His neighbour Joan had asked him to come over that morning and see what needed to be done to look after her cats. She was going away for three days and nothing less than a biologist would do to care for her babies.

When she opened her door, he was confused by her first words.

"Will you marry me?" Joan asked, standing at the door but staring back toward her kitchen.

Robert stood before her, uncertain and tongue-tied, distracted by a flash of fur darting past him and down the basement stairs.

"I need a handyman around here all the time," she continued.

From the kitchen, a muffled voice answered. "That should just about take care of it now."

Joan addressed the wide, florid-faced man in the red plaid jacket emerging from beneath the kitchen sink. "So how much do I owe you?" she asked the plumber as he wiped his hands and gathered his tools.

Well, that was awkward. Robert was relieved he wasn't the object of her proposal. He could see that living in the duplex next to Joan could mean further social discomfort.

She paid the plumber, who passed Robert with a nod on his way out. Joan motioned Robert in. "I've trained all my cats to go on the toilet, but what with me being away and all, I've set up the litterboxes just in case. You'll need to clean them every morning. Here's the whatchamacallit." Joan held up a slotted scoop.

Despite seven cats living here, Robert was surprised there was no detectable odour or obvious damage to the place. Just a lot of cat hair on everything. He followed her to the kitchen and eating area, carefully navigating his way through the gridlock of furniture and towers of boxes.

"Here's the food in the pantry. This special food is for Snuggly. Eighty dollars a bag for that stuff. But she won't eat anything else. Be sure you leave the pantry door open a little bit so she can get at it, but not so much that the others can get into it."

How that feat was to be accomplished remained unclear to Robert.

"You'll need my key, and I've written down everything that needs to be done. I'm glad there's finally someone whose experience with animals I can trust to care for my feline family."

Joan handed Robert a detailed list of instructions, the house key on a fob clattering with plasticized photos of the cats. There'd be no way to remember the animals' daily schedule, personal habits, and likes and dislikes. No fewer than thirteen dishes sat on the kitchen floor, offering a plethora of sampling from the pet food aisle. Now she was calling out the door for the cats.

"Snuggly! Miss Cuddles! Tenderfoot!" Joan cleared her throat. "Darn those cats. They know I'm leaving, and they don't want to be locked in the house. They're just trying to make life difficult for me."

"I think I can handle it," Robert said, sidling around her. "I've got your list here. I'm sure they'll be fine."

He hurried out the door, leaving Joan hollering for her pets.

Half an hour later, he glanced out the front window and watched an altercation between a taxi driver and Joan. She gesticulated jerkily, while the driver froze in the act of hoisting her suitcase into the trunk. Finally, she got into the rear seat, slamming the door. The driver dropped the trunk lid, got in behind the wheel with a scowl Robert could see even at his distance, and they were off.

Robert worked on marking and evaluations clear through dinner time. He was browsing the freezer, hoping something would tempt his appetite, when he remembered the cats. He hesitated, his hand on a box of frozen food. He thought of the one fleeting glimpse of fleshy feline he'd seen skittering past his legs when he'd been at Joan's this morning and decided starvation was not imminent. The animals could wait while he finished his Hungry Man dinner.

Opening the door at Joan's, he managed to squeeze through without letting out any of the cats. In fact, the moment they saw him, the two nearest started a scrabbling stampede across the kitchen floor, presumably to hide in their favourite recesses.

That crawly, watched feeling of being alone in someone else's home made him hurry, wanting to get out as soon as he could. Sweeping the cat food bag out of the pantry and toward the cat dishes, he inadvertently brushed a sheaf of papers from the counter onto the floor. His curse seemed overloud in the silent house. He crouched to gather the stack and replace it on the counter. Among the mix of newspaper clippings, envelopes, and advertising flyers, an almost-blank page with a single handwritten notation caught his eye.

I seem to have driven away everyone I love,
and I don't know what to do about it.

Robert recognized the same hand as the instruction list Joan had written out for him. The raw vulnerability of that simple sentence gave Robert pause. The paper in his hand trembled. He was a voyeur at the window to Joan's soul and it seemed an accurate assessment, a summary of a life weighed in the balance and found wanting. He thought of interchanges he'd observed in the short time he'd known Joan: the embarrassing flirtation with the handyman this morning, the altercation with the waiting taxi driver, his own first meeting with her—a confrontation over a stray dog. The image of her standing outside the circle of lawn chairs at the neighbourhood fire circle months earlier returned, a portrait of alienation. Now the pathos of this stark admission frightened him. It gave him a tender understanding of her, the kind one has toward one's own flaws and failings. He wondered what his epitaph would be.

We are flock animals and every species is drawn to its own kind. Unexpectedly, he began to feel an affinity for this abrasive neighbour. *Why do some of us, wanting community and family, still put out the prickles? Is it so that when relationships inevitably fail, we can be vindicated, telling ourselves we tried but the failure lies with others? Is it easier being lonely?*

CHAPTER 20

The course of true love never did run smooth.
—William Shakespeare, *A Midsummer Night's Dream*, Act I, Scene 1

Robert gingerly opened the door at the Fawcetts' and called, "Anyone home?" It was usually Jesse's proud duty to open the door, take his jacket ceremoniously, and welcome him in.

"C'mon in! I've just got my head in the oven," came Anna's muffled voice from the kitchen.

While she was busy there, he enjoyed another browse through the titles on the bookshelf. She was certainly a woman of eclectic interests. Martial arts mingled with philosophy, needlework with theology, organic gardening with fiction classics, and prominently, at least it seemed so to him, several titles on intelligent design versus evolution.

He turned when Anna bustled in with a plate of steaming baked ham in one hand, and a small dish of something creamy in the other.

"Could you get that bowl of broccoli from the kitchen counter for me?" she asked.

Robert found the faded china dish among the detritus of meal preparation and followed her to the table in the wake of the oniony aroma.

"Where's Jesse?" he asked.

"At rehearsal. Another cast member picked him up. Rehearsals are ramping up, what with the production date coming up in a couple of weeks."

"He's part of a theatre backstage crew?"

"Oh no, he acts. And loves it, I might add. Hasn't missed being involved in a community theatre production for about five years now. This one's a pantomime— a spoof on Goldilocks and the Three Bears. Jesse's a villager and for the first time has a couple of spoken lines. We've been practicing them here at home every day, so they'll be perfectly clear. Maybe you could come see it?"

"I think I'd like that," Robert said, surprised that he meant it. Anna motioned to his chair and they both sat down.

Reaching for his hand, she said, "That son of mine. I've got to tell you a story Jesse's supervisor at the senior's centre told me today. But let's pray first."

Raising her head after her oblation, she continued. "He was—" she leaned in close to him and put her hand on his arm. A little laugh erupted before she could go on. "He was helping Alison shelve returned books in the little library they have there and she said she kept hearing these sighs. They were getting heavier and heavier and finally he just busts out and says, 'If I have to look at one more of these books, I'm leaving!' So she looks over at him and asks, 'What books?' and he says, 'These ones. They're all about *kissing*!' Alison says, 'You don't like kissing?' and he says, 'Well... I'm *immature*.'"

Robert grinned, picturing it. Jesse was a master of the unexpected.

"It seems empty without him sitting across from me trying to avoid a large helping of salad," he said.

A delighted smile warmed Anna's glance. "It does, doesn't it?" Her smile disappeared. "With the loss of my husband, I feel a vacuum every day. And when our children moved out, they left a huge gap, too. In fact, the vacancy seems disproportionately large to the person. The most recent one to leave was David, my son just older than Jesse. He was so very quiet, and there was strain between us, but the gap has been huge nonetheless."

Her voice wobbled and she looked toward the wall of family photos, clearing her throat. She inhaled deeply and, turning to him again, began slicing pink slabs of succulent meat.

"I'll bet you like pineapple with your ham, don't you?" she asked.

"Mmmm. I do. But it's all right if you don't—"

She dropped the serving spoon and scurried into the kitchen. He heard the cranking of a can opener. Minutes later she was back with a bowl of the golden rings.

"Perfect," he said, forking two onto the meat.

"I have a question for you." Anna settled herself back in her chair.

Robert lifted an eyebrow and flared his lips, shaking his head. "Oh no," he said, tossing a hand in the air.

"It's nothing you're unqualified for." She smiled at him. "As a biologist, I understand that you rely on an evolutionary model as the basis for all your understanding of the world around us. Am I right so far?"

"You are."

"So is there a fair bit of lending and borrowing of scientific data and theory between the various disciplines?"

"Yes, I suppose so. Why reinvent the wheel, as they say. After all, with the high degree of specialization these days, few of us can be an expert on everything. But what, exactly, are you getting at?"

"Just one more question?" Anna gave him her sweetest smile.

"Hit me with your best."

"Has it ever happened that in such lending and borrowing, a scientist has drawn a wrong conclusion because his work was based on a faulty premise?"

Robert leaned in and set his elbows on the table. "That's the beauty of the scientific method. It's specifically meant to eliminate wrong conclusions in a couple of ways. The hypothesis sets out what the scientist expects to discover—his premise—and the method of carefully controlled testing with changing variables either confirms or disproves his theory. It's also subject to peer review by being repeatable."

"It *is* a wonderful method, I'm sure. But one thing puzzles me."

Robert's love for imparting knowledge drew him in. "And what's that?"

"When I read or listen to information on non-scientific topics, I often hear social scientists use evolution as their foundation for making certain deductions. They treat it as a given rather than a theory, but if the theory isn't true, their findings would crumble, wouldn't they?"

"We should establish one thing first," Robert began. "Evolutionary psychology is significantly different from biology or other areas of hard science. Their area of study is quite subjective, making it difficult to put it to the rigorous testing required by the scientific method."

"What I'm thinking is, if everything we do is just a result of biological urges for the survival of the species, we can't be blamed for even our worst behaviour. It used to be that psychologists would blame a cold mother for problems in the child. Now everything gets blamed on genes. So murderers and rapists aren't culpable because they're just victims of their DNA." Anna stopped for a breath, looking to Robert.

He raised his eyebrows. "I think everyone can safely agree that those are antisocial behaviours." The doubt in Anna's eyes prompted him to add, "You must be thinking of a specific example."

"Well, let's take some phenomenon that's been observed, such as parenting or love. These sociologists will always reason backward to its evolutionary roots. For example, I once heard a program on why we associate the colour pink with girls and blue with boys. You know what they said? Prehistoric men looked for good hunting weather—clear blue skies, while women were the gatherers of fruit and therefore interested in the colours of ripe fruit—shades of pink. But if that's true, how would they account for Victorian Britain where blue was associated with girls because of the Virgin Mary, while pink was for boys, because it was seen as a diluted version of the fierce colour red?"

Robert could only chuckle.

Anna held up a hand. "What brought this up for me today was hearing about a study where a group of women were to sniff the sweaty T-shirts of men, proving the idea that women choose men they perceive will be good providers as a throwback to our primitive days."

"What puzzles you about that?" Robert asked. "It seems obvious to me that that would be a sensible conclusion."

"I'm not sure I can express it... Hmmm, let me try a simple analogy." Anna pulled out a scratch pad. "What if I say that 1+1=3 and, making that assumption, I try to build a birdhouse." She sketched a lopsided house on a leaning pole. "It might not matter much on that small scale if it's a bit screw-gee, but I'll run into trouble trying to build a real house. It seems to me it's the same with science. If I'm wrong on one theory, won't I be mistaken if I apply that theory to other disciplines?"

"I suppose that does cast it in a different light," Robert said. "You're objecting to the building of one theory using premises from another theory. But remember, evolution is a robust model of how things came to be, so it stands to reason that other disciplines would use it as a guiding principle. Your example of women choosing men who are the best providers has direct correlation to the survival of a species."

"Perhaps it does," she said, looking unconvinced. "Yet I find it strange that sociologists speak of courtship in those terms. It seems to fly in the face of modern life and the women's movement."

"They don't mean it prescriptively—that women today have to follow that pattern in choosing a man. It's simply descriptive of the way our early ancestors went about mating. Obviously with the human race well-established on the planet, there's no further need for reproducing at the same rate we did millions of years ago."

"Are you saying that survival of the fittest no longer applies? That mankind has evolved beyond natural selection?" Anna peered over the top of her glasses with mischief in her eyes. "Someone should tell men that. It's far too easy to come to the conclusion that men want to spread their genes far and wide, taking no responsibility for their offspring or—"

"It's not always men who are irresponsible about spreading their genes around," Robert said in a low tone. His mouth tightened as he sat staring at the open weave of the green tablecloth.

Anna tried to tilt her head into his line of vision. Her smile had faded. "We seem to have ventured somewhere beyond the scope of our initial discussion. Do I detect a note of bitterness, Robert?"

Now how was he to answer that? The silence between them opened a chasm where all the confusion of his heart lay. Long moments passed before he could squeeze a response past the swelling in his throat.

Anna laid her hand on his arm gently. "I've thought since I met you, there was a sadness about you. Would it help to tell me about it?"

Robert cleared his throat and looked at her for a long moment. Then he looked away, focusing on her wall of family photos. "My wife has been unfaithful to me."

Her gentle touch became a firm grip. "I'm so sorry, Robert." They sat in dreary mutual silence for some minutes.

"Tell me," Anna said at last, "do you want to reconcile with her?"

He met her steady gaze. "More than anything," he murmured.

She had wrenched the truth out of him by its roots, something he had not yet been able to admit to himself, leaving him raw and hollow inside.

"You know, Robert, a woman wants to be fought for," she said

117

finally. "Not literally, of course, but she wants to feel cherished. To feel she is worth some effort on your part. Have you tried winning her back?"

Robert's mind resisted the medieval images Anna's old-fashioned advice evoked. He said nothing. After all, of the two of them, she was the one with a lifelong experience of marriage.

But she pressed on. "Wouldn't she be surprised if you reversed your reaction to some bone of contention between you? Maybe investing something of yourself in her somehow? You could do something uncharacteristic, unpredictable to show her you care."

"Such as?"

"I'm sure you can come up with something. Just make it memorable."

When he got home, Robert went straight to his computer to transfer funds into his wife's account before he could change his mind. It went against everything he had previously thought about the need for her to earn his trust with money. He doubted this would work.

It wasn't so much the cash outlay; it was the inevitability that she would blithely spend beyond reason again. And deeper still, the fear that this uncharacteristic generosity left him open to having his motives maligned or misunderstood in some way.

According to Anna, to love was to be vulnerable. If that were true, he was a squirming nematode on a gull-encircled promontory.

CHAPTER 21

And say to mothers what a holy charge Is theirs—with what a kingly power their love Might rule the fountain of the new-born mind.
—Lydia Huntley Sigourney, *The Mother of Washington*

Amelia watched Anna smooth the orange fabric across the kitchen table, mesmerized by her thin, worn hands. The older woman's narrow gold wedding band, also worn thin, looked like it would never come off her large-knuckled finger.

"I've been meaning to ask you, Anna," Amelia began. "You were married many years..."

"Yes, thirty-six to be exact."

"Well, I was wondering whether you ever had major disagreements?"

Anna laughed.

"Oh about once a week."

Amelia couldn't smile.

"I'm sorry, dear. You must be meaning something specific."

"I was. I mean, I know you have children." Amelia faltered.

"Yes. Five to be exact, all girls except four."

Amelia's brows bunched, then smoothed as she did the math. "So, how did you decide to have children in the first place? And then, how did you decide to have five?"

"You make it sound like it's a corporate plan," the older woman mused. She winced at Jesse squeaking his fork across his plate as he sat at the counter, finishing the last of the chocolate cake Amelia had served him. "Can we get Jesse occupied in another room?"

Amelia tucked her long sweater around her and began to lead Jesse to the bookshelves in the nursery, but he took his own bag of books and trotted ahead of her to the living room. She offered him a chair, but again he had his own ideas. He arranged himself cross-legged on the rug, pulling out his books to lay them in three neat stacks in front to him. Finally, he chose an illustrated chapter book and Amelia left him, reading.

Anna looked up when she returned to the kitchen. "You know, I've been thinking about your question. It's something I've searched the scriptures about since my daughter and daughters-in-law asked questions. But here, let's just get this pattern cut out first."

Amelia tried to take in Anna's explanation of the finer points of selvages, straight-of-grain, and cutting on the fold.

Anna looked at her sympathetically. "You'll catch on with experience," she said.

Together they pinned the pattern pieces to the fabric and Anna handed her the scissors.

"Just cut along the innermost dotted line for the smallest size." Anna sat down on a kitchen stool, watching as Amelia bent over the table and began cutting rapidly. "There's no rush, Amelia. Take it slowly and you'll be more accurate."

Anna tapped her finger to her lips for a moment.

"Now where were we, again? Oh yes, of course, family planning. All this about planning your family was big in the women's magazines back in the seventies when I was a young wife. The pill was in common usage by that time. But in real life, you know, babies just come." Anna waved a hand. "Usually when we're least ready for them."

"Do you mean yours were all accidents?" Amelia said without looking up from the sleeve she was cutting out.

"Don't forget to reposition that sleeve pattern and cut a second one, dear. See here? It says 'Cut four' because the sleeve is to be lined." Anna grew serious. "No, our children certainly weren't accidents. Not at all. They just weren't planned by us."

"Oh, you mean God." Amelia straightened up and thought for a moment. "So you didn't have a good reason for having children?"

Anna giggled. "A reason? We were married! Babies are just a precious gift from a God who likes to see his children loving each other. I think if having a good reason were the prerequisite for having children, the human race would have gone extinct a long time ago. But what makes you think you have to have a reason for having children?"

Amelia set down the scissors and leaned back against the counter, looking out the kitchen window. "It's something my husband used to say," she said, twisting and folding the hem of her sweater.

"And did you come up with an answer?"

"Not one that he thought was valid." Bitterness tinged Amelia's reply. "Apparently simply wanting one was not a good enough reason."

"It's all mixed up in our world, you know," Anna said, shaking her head. "Babies are a natural result of the act of marriage, under normal circumstances. Since the advent of the pill and other means of prevention, people have gotten the mindset that *they* are in control. But God is the giver of life. Just ask anyone struggling with infertility. They know they're not in control. So since bearing children is natural, the onus is on those who *prevent* children from being conceived to have the good reason for doing it."

"I've never thought of it that way."

"And those reasons are often very selfish," Anna continued. "'A baby will ruin my education, or my career plans, or my financial goals, or my home, or—heaven help us—my figure.' She rose to help Amelia stack up the cut pieces of the maternity top and lay them aside.

Together they set up Anna's sewing machine. "It's significant, I think, that the reasons for abortion are so often the same as the reasons for contraception."

Amelia bent toward Anna. "Are you saying using birth control is wrong? Where do you get that in the Bible?"

Anna smiled. "You learn quickly. You're right to check with God's Word for direction on these things. No, I'm not saying the use of birth control is always wrong. What's very clear in the Bible is that God is the Author of life, that he is completely in charge. We call that his sovereignty. What's also clear is that he wants us to trust him with every aspect of our lives."

"I didn't give any thought to my motivations for using contraceptives." Amelia teared up. "The biggest issue for me was being so consumed with guilt about... k–killing my first baby—oh, that's hard to say—"

She gulped. Anna came around to her side of the table to embrace her.

"Just remember," Anna whispered into Amelia's ear. "There are these wonderful things called grace and mercy. Mercy is not getting what we deserve. Grace is getting what we don't deserve. Like forgiveness. And a new life."

Anna patted the younger woman's back. When Amelia had composed herself, the older woman went back to the table and threaded the sewing machine.

"Here's where you start," she said, pointing to the pattern instruction sheet. "They make the steps so clear these days, I don't think you'll even need me on this. Come and sit, it's all yours."

"Would you mind if I asked you another personal question?" Amelia asked, taking her seat and studying the diagram. She began pinning the front and back pieces together. "Did you know about Jesse before he was born—that he had Down syndrome, I mean?"

"No." Anna grew pensive. "No, we didn't. They weren't doing routine ultrasounds back then and my doctor didn't request one. I had an exceptionally easy pregnancy that time. When he was born, I recognized the short fingers and slanted eyes immediately, of course, and blood tests confirmed it. But you know, I'm so glad we didn't know in advance. As I read up on Down syndrome in those early days, I used to get overwhelmed by the potential for future problems. Then I would scoop him up from his cradle and just hold him. Because of his low muscle tone, he was wonderfully comforting to hold—like a bag of warm Jell-O, my husband used to say. If we had known about his condition in advance, I would have had all the worry and none of the comfort." Anna covered Amelia's hand with her own. "But you must have some reason for asking that."

Amelia stared down at the bright fabric under the presser foot of the sewing machine. "I'm thirty-eight, having my first baby. Because of that, my husband insisted I have amniocentesis. 'We can decide what to do once we get the results,' he said. Can you believe that? After everything I suffered all those years, how could he talk about deciding what to do?" She exhaled hard, looking up into her friend's denim-blue eyes. "This time I refused. I even refused to have an ultrasound. I mean, what was the point? I knew I would never go through an abortion again and, like you said, there'd be months of worry..."

"And yet, you still wonder, is that it?"

"I do. And I've got to admit, I'm scared. The midwife says everything is perfect with the baby and my health, but... I hope you won't take this the wrong way. I know Jesse is really high functioning and brings everyone lots of joy, but I'm not like you. I don't think I have what it takes to meet the challenges of raising a special needs kid. This may be my only chance and I really want a normal child."

Anna took a seat at the corner of the table adjacent to Amelia and shook her head with a sigh. "It's perfectly normal, and I would say even right, to have that desire. Two things come to mind, though. First, human life has intrinsic value, period. We don't have value because of the contribution we make. We have it because of the Creator who endowed us with that value. Without even knowing that, you've already affirmed it by spending years grieving over the loss of one life, invisible and not apparently contributing, but precious nonetheless."

Amelia listened, nodding.

"Secondly," Anna continued, "people who do well at parenting a special needs child weren't born that way. The whole idea that God looks down to find someone special he can entrust with this kind of child is sentimental nonsense. I believe the degree to which a parent rises to the challenge has everything to do with how God grows them up to meet it. Some do and some don't. And thirdly—"

"I thought you said there were two things that came to mind." Amelia looked at her slyly.

Anna threw back her head and giggled. "Nothing gets by you! What I thought we could do is pray about it."

She took Amelia's hand and together they laid the future of her baby before the One who knows the end from the beginning.

Raising her head, Anna peered at Amelia. "Can I have a turn asking personal questions?"

"What?"

"Nelson?"

Amelia could feel the flush rising into her cheeks under Anna's probing look. "What about him?"

"I've noticed his interest in you, Amelia. But I've been wondering if he knows your, uh, marital status?"

"Well, it's not exactly something I announce the minute I meet a person." Amelia instantly regretted her waspish tone. "I'm sorry, Anna."

"I understand, dear. I know how pleasant getting some male attention can be. It's just that knowing Nelson, he wouldn't want to come between you and your husband or any possibility of reconciliation. It would only be fair to him for you to let him know."

After an uncomfortable pause, Amelia sighed. "I know."

CHAPTER 22

She herself had the gift, than which there is none more enviable,
of finding great pleasure in little things.
—L.M. Montgomery, *Mistress Pat*, 1935

Southern gospel tunes greeted Robert as he stepped into Anna's inviting home out of the unseasonably mild autumn night.

"Come on in. I'll just get Jesse to turn that off and then we can sit down to eat," Anna told him. But catching sight of something beyond Robert, she grasped his arm. "Ah look, a harvest moon!"

Robert turned and beheld the heavy golden orb like some shimmering giant peach rising in the eastern sky.

"'Never lose an opportunity of seeing anything beautiful, for beauty is God's handwriting,'" Anna quoted. "Ralph Waldo Emerson." She gazed transfixed for several moments more and then turned to look up at him. "I had an old-fashioned teacher in Grade Three who used poetry as handwriting practice."

She ushered him in and motioned to Jesse to come and take Robert's jacket. But Jesse's hoedown ended only when the song was done, despite Anna's repeated commands to turn it off.

"He can't stand cutting off a song before it's finished," Anna explained as Jesse slowly and deliberately hung Robert's jacket on the hook.

"I'm a little the same way." Robert couldn't help smiling as he followed her to the table set with steaming dishes. Jesse asked the blessing in his unique, detailed way and with a grin, carefully offered Robert the salad first.

"Have lots," Jesse told him. The thinly disguised attempt to avoid greens made Robert laugh.

"You know, Robert," Anna said as she laid two enchiladas on his plate, "you have a wonderful smile. It'd be good to see it more often."

"Yes, well..." He occupied himself with his salad. They ate in silence for a time.

Anna anticipated his cleaning off his plate by bringing a jar of raspberries and a frosty tub out of the kitchen. "Can I interest you in dessert?"

"You could indeed," Robert said.

"Me too!" Jesse said.

"You'll have to finish your supper first, though, Sonny Jim," Anna told Jesse, scooping a generous mound of vanilla ice cream into two of the bowls. "I wasn't sure, Robert, if you were one of those people who insist on gilding the lily, adding ice cream to perfectly lovely fruit."

Robert nodded, taking over the scoop when he saw her struggling with the frozen confection.

As Anna began spooning the preserved raspberries over top, she said, "These are the berries Jesse picked at the farm on August 5. And do you remember whose birthday that is, Jesse?"

"Twins'. They're two. We watched 'Winnie the Pooh' with them," Jesse said, a smile spreading across his face.

"My daughter's girls. They live about an hour east of here, near Broad Valley. There you go, a little taste of summer." Anna set a bowl of the ruby-tumbled cream before Robert and took the berries without ice cream for herself. She motioned to Jesse to finish the last of his salad before starting on dessert.

His eyes shone at the sight and he hummed to himself as the lettuce began to disappear rapidly.

The sweet-tart treat melted on Robert's tongue with a pleasant contrast. "You like country music, Jesse?" he asked.

"Southern gospel," Jesse corrected. "I like Johnny Cash an' the Stewart kids and the Josts and the Fehr family."

Anna smiled. "Those last three are local Alberta families who tour and have done some recording."

"And I like Johnny Cash." Jesse opened one side of his mouth to sing, "Far from folks on poison, Thass where I wan' to be..."

Robert choked slightly and flashed a look toward Anna at this misquote of the famous country song. She seemed oblivious and was dipping her head back and forth with the tuneless singing. Jesse dropped his chin as he followed the tune south. And he was off. He ran to put on another CD. Johnny Cash walked the line through the rest of their dessert. Faster than Robert had ever before seen him move, Jesse cleared his plate and a few other items off the table. Soon he was back pulling at Anna's arm, then Robert's.

"Come dance," he ordered.

Anna looked at Robert and laughed.

"Dance," he insisted, tugging on both of their arms. "Y'know y'want to."

"Oh, I don't think so, Jesse. Not this time," she said, but Jesse kept asking.

"C'mon, get on with it! Dance," he insisted, drawing them upward.

"Well, why not?" Robert said.

Anna glanced at him quickly in wonder, but she too rose and pushed the coffee table to one side. Jesse put on a gospel CD and the toe-tapping rhythms soon had them swinging their partner. Jesse joined in, arm in arm with both of them in turn. Round and round and clapping hands, they whirled through song after song. The set ended and the three of them flopped on the couches puffing and laughing. Jesse's face was red and glistening. Only then did they hear the loud rapping at the door. Anna jumped up to answer it.

It was Joan. "I hope this isn't going to go on all night," she said, taking in the red faces and the room in disarray.

"Oh no, not at all, Joan," Anna said. "You could hear us all the way over at your place?"

"Yes. I actually missed the news because of all this racket."

"I'm so sorry we disturbed you," Anna offered.

"Well, just don't let it happen again," Joan said. An unaccustomed smile stretched her face.

As soon as the door shut, Jesse quietly began to sing, "Every party needs a pooper..."

"Jesse," Anna warned. "No more of that."

But a look at Robert's half-suppressed smile brought her hand to her mouth.

As he walked home, there was a new feeling in his chest. A simple joy, an inexplicable contentment. It had been a long time since he'd felt it. If he ever had.

CHAPTER 23

How can I live without thee, how forgo
Thy sweet converse and love so dearly joined,
To live again in these wild woods forlorn?
—John Milton, *Paradise Lost, Book IX*

No clean underwear. Robert grabbed the cleanest ones he could find in the array on the bathroom floor, knowing it might bother him all day. No matter. He had slept late, but there was just enough time to make his first class.

By the time his first two classes were behind him, he was desperate for a coffee. Stepping into the green and blue staff room, a faint smell of burnt popcorn assailed him. Dr. Baldwyn's piranhas cast peevish eyes on him from the eight-foot aquarium on the wall opposite the windows. The room was empty except for Phil Thiessen, slouched low on the blue couch, his laptop propped on top of his short muscular thighs. He nodded at Robert.

"How 'bout them Oilers, eh?" He sported a smug grin.

"Don't rub it in," Robert said, heading straight for the coffee station. "It's early days yet." The Canadiens, for whom he kept a moderate affinity, had just lost to Edmonton last night and generally were performing abjectly so far this season. "Cramming before class?" Robert asked him.

"Ha. Naw. Just checking some probability numbers."

"Oh yeah? Probability of snow this winter? Of getting a raise? Of McCoy leaving before the year is up?"

Phil looked up at him, eyebrows cocked. "Probability of snow this winter might depend on your view of climate change. A raise? Nil, due to government deficit. McCoy leaving early? Outside the realm of mathematics. Sorry."

Robert smirked. "I thought math was the absolute science. So what are your figures?"

"Actually, they kind of overlap your field. Probability of life arising on earth."

Not you, too! No more questioning of basic science.

Robert fumbled the coffee mug, splashing scalding liquid on his wrist. It slipped from his grasp and he cursed the cup, the coffee, his hand, the college and life on earth.

"Whoa, whoa, whoa! Baldwyn's piranhas are covering their ears!" Phil laughed. "What's your deal?"

The tender skin of his wrist felt as though it were afire. Robert held it under the faucet while trying to soak up coffee with a wad of paper towels in his left hand. Tossing shards of ceramic into the garbage can, he gave up on making the coffee and came to sit opposite Phil.

"What've you come up with?" Robert asked, grudgingly.

"Seriously? You're not going to like it."

"Yeah, well, break it to me gently."

"So what I've been looking at is the ratio of functional arrangements of amino acids—"

"Your basic building blocks for life," Robert said.

Phil looked up from his laptop. "—among possible combinations for a protein 150 amino acids in length. The fewest amino acids needed for viable life would be 278." Phil grinned and returned to his screen. "I figured I'd stay on the conservative side *and* use a round number. So," he typed rapidly, "the probability is... just a sec here...

one-in-ten to the seventy-fourth power."

"Yeah, so?"

"That's seventy-four zeroes. Apparently, that's larger than the number of atoms in the entire Milky Way galaxy." Phil gazed at Robert steadily, raising his eyebrows. "About the same likelihood as a blind man finding a certain grain of sand out of all the deserts of the world."

Robert squeezed his scalded wrist, considering. "Nothing new here. We've discarded the idea that chance had anything to do with the origin of proteins decades ago. Hence the theory of life transported on crystals from elsewhere in the universe."

"But are you teaching your students that? Popularly, Joe Public still thinks science proves life developed spontaneously in the primordial soup."

The door of the staff room burst open before Robert could reply and he was surprised to see Sarah-Mae and Jamie McCoy come in together, laughing. McCoy scanned the room as the secretary homed in on the coffee urn.

"What's all this then?" McCoy said, flopping down on one of the green chairs that formed the square conversation grouping. Phil and Robert exchanged glances.

"We were just discussing the impossible mathematical odds of life having spontaneously arisen on earth," Phil said.

Not "we," Phil. Thanks for dragging me into it. "Actually, I was busy spilling coffee." Robert got up to run cold water over his hand again.

McCoy put his feet up on the glass coffee table and crossed his arms, staring Phil down. "Oh, come on Teeza. I s'pose you're going to preach us a sermon, too, then?"

The math professor slouched a little further into the couch and performed his trademark quirk. He lifted a hand behind his head and scratched the top of it without disturbing his wavy, dark hair.

Imitating it had become a sort of salute among math students at the college.

"Not sure what you're thinking of, Dr. McCoy," Phil said, "but figures don't lie."

"We all know that figures can be made to say anything anyone wants them to." McCoy's snappish tone intrigued Robert.

"Would you like to see the odds? Basically, the chances of—"

"No, I would not like to see the odds," McCoy sneered. The bubbling of the aquarium filter seemed suddenly loud.

"No problem, you don't have to," Phil said with a smile.

Sarah-Mae, bringing a mug of steaming coffee to McCoy, failed to distract him.

"Dressing up ignorance and religion in technological terms gets you nowhere," McCoy said. "This is not science, but it does sound suspiciously like the kind of rhetoric spouted off by a creationist." He spat the word. Jabbing a finger at Phil, he added, "Just watch yourself, mate. I'm onto you. It's pernicious ideas like this that can ruin your career." He pulled his phone out of his pocket and checked the time. "I don't know about you, but I've got class." He sprang up and swept out of the room.

"I guess that makes at least one of us with class." Phil shrugged, closed his laptop, and grabbed his briefcase. "Talk to you later, Robert."

Sarah-Mae, lagging behind McCoy, frowned at Robert. "He *had* been in a good mood..."

Robert was confused about the camaraderie he'd observed between them in light of her vitriolic outburst earlier in the school year. He opened his mouth to ask her about it when she averted her eyes and hurried out the door.

On the way home, Robert's mind examined the interchange between Phil and McCoy in the staff room. It was embarrassing to witness a polemic like that when McCoy had represented the responsible view. Why the reactionary anger? In proper debate, ideas could be presented, impartially compared, and accepted or discarded based purely on their merits.

An uncomfortable memory surfaced. He distinctly remembered lambasting his neighbour Siggleady, several months earlier for a similar lapse in logic. *The more you preach it, the more invested in it you become, making it impossible to admit you might be mistaken.* Robert fidgeted in the driver's seat.

Knowing he'd meant to pick something up on his way home, he pulled into the Walmart parking lot. He'd have to wander the aisles for a while until it came to him.

The incongruity of the argument in the staff room wore at him and he was barely aware of his surroundings. *Oh right. Underwear.* The vague discomfort he'd been aware of all day should have been an urgent enough reminder. He couldn't find the brand his wife had always bought for him but chose some that looked adequate.

At home, the shower wheezed and spit at first, but gradually its heat melted some of the tension in his overwrought body and mind. After towelling himself dry, he ripped open the new package of underwear and pulled up a pair... and up... and up.

What the—?

Who were these made for? He peered into the foggy mirror and saw the navy-blue briefs skimming his rib cage. They would definitely show through a light-coloured shirt. He'd have to return them. But no, the package was torn open. Perhaps if he rolled the waistband down. They were about right when he rolled it down three times. Except it would look like there was a hula hoop under his trousers. This was really too much.

He sat down on the closed toilet seat, frustrated. A sudden image of her impish face if he were to share this ridiculous episode made him laugh aloud. It almost startled him, echoing as it did against the porcelain and metal of the small room.

As he stuffed the appalling garment into the garbage, along with the package, he guffawed. And while he began gathering scattered clothing to start some laundry, Robert positively roared. But the laughter morphed into a strangled howl. He slammed his hand down on the countertop.

How could she do this to me? To us?

The emptiness of the house was his only answer.

"So when I put them on, they nearly came up to my armpits." Robert enjoyed the telling at his next dinner with Anna, even if it was at his own expense. Tears were rolling down Anna's cheeks as she laughed.

"Mom can fix 'em for you," Jesse suggested, nodding earnestly.

Robert started to protest but Anna quickly told him he shouldn't worry, she didn't need to subject him to a fitting.

"Just measure where they should fit and I think I can solve your problem." And she let out more giggles.

CHAPTER 24

Hadst thou been firm and fixed in thy dissent,
Neither had I transgressed, nor thou with me.
—John Milton, *Paradise Lost, Book IX*

As she left the school for the day, Amelia chuckled at the email reminder on her phone from the school secretary regarding pension plan changes. Apparently, they were to return the "singed" copy of the document to school administration by Friday. She pulled the document out of her briefcase and signed her name, briefly toying with the idea of taking a lighter to its edges. Her husband would have loved that malapropism. She recalled some of the howlers he'd shared with her—"a virile strain" instead of virulent. Amelia sighed. Well, Anna would appreciate this one. She'd have to save it for her.

She snapped shut her phone and tossed it into her purse on the passenger seat. The parking lot was icy and she was too tired now to run back into the school to turn in the form. Grunting, she reached under her seat for the ice scraper. There was no one to clear her windshield for her anymore. She was finding independence highly overrated.

As she pulled out of the school lot, she thought she heard a clunking somewhere in the back end of the car.

Oh no! Not a car problem. They're always so expensive! Was it wishful thinking, or had it gone away as she kept driving?

Stopping in at Walmart for a few grocery items, Amelia was conscious of a decided swagger to her walk, and a swagger was just one step above an outright waddle. If she hadn't quit shopping-as-therapy for budgetary reasons, she'd have had to quit for the sake of her hip joints. And this was only the fifth month. How much worse would it get? Everyone at work told her she didn't look pregnant from the back, or that she was so small that she hardly showed at all. *Tell that to the pelvis, Elvis.*

And now, there, coming toward her was that other walk she knew so well—loose-jointed, raw-boned: her husband. It was inevitable that they should meet sometime, somehow in this small city of ninety-some thousand. She'd done her best to avoid him but he would see her now, all hundred and twenty-four pounds of her.

Instinctively, Amelia placed a protective hand across her belly and pulled her jacket as nearly closed as she could. He didn't see her. He'd disappeared into an aisle of men's wear. Just a brief glimpse of his face told her he was preoccupied with some deep thought. His hair had gotten shaggy. She smiled sadly to see his green shirt didn't match the navy pants.

Hurrying back to the grocery department, Amelia gathered and paid for the yogurt and bananas she needed and left.

She realized her initial reaction to seeing him, her hand to her belly, revealed that she still saw him as a threat to her baby. But really, what would have taken place if they'd met?

He might have said in his uniquely formal way, "How are you doing? Are you well?"

She would have nodded, said, "Doing really well. You?"

And that's true. I am doing better, in one sense, than I ever have. But not in a dimension he would understand. He would take that to mean she was better off without him entirely.

Would he have stared at her round middle? Or looked past her, pretending it didn't exist? Would he have been repelled or, as she was, fascinated? Would he have warned and scolded about the foolhardiness and risk of having a child at her age? She felt a bitter frown distort her face and the heat of her inner turmoil rise along her neck.

And what would she ask him? How's work? Are you eating healthy? Do you want to come with me to a midwife appointment and hear your child's heartbeat?

Right.

Again, Anna's suggestion returned: her husband, while misguided, had his own fears in not wanting her to have this child. And with it came a truth that haunted her; he had no more forced her to abort their first child than he had this time.

No matter that she had been only twenty-four at the time. She could have stood, even then, for what she knew was right. Yes, she'd been filled with fear at his dire predictions that the prescription medicine she'd been on would result in a handicap. She still could have done some research and discovered then, as she did years later, that the defect might have been as minor as discoloured teeth. No excuse held water about just following his lead and trusting the doctor's credentials and experience. If the political rhetoric were to be believed, it was entirely a woman's right to choose. Amelia was left shouldering the full load of guilt, something she'd been shifting for fourteen years. The familiar ache of it was almost physical.

That hidden child, the one who'd never seen the light of day, the one her husband had never acknowledged, Amelia had kept alive in memory all these years. She'd been a mother! The only one who'd known the child. It —*she*—Amelia always thought of the child as a girl—was significant. Her years of commemorating the day of the baby's death, as well as her due date, made her so. Yet there had been no commiseration from co-workers as had other women who had miscarried or had stillbirths, no sympathy cards or casseroles brought. The culturally enforced silence around abortion meant she'd had no right to speak of her loss. Because it was self-inflicted—a right and a freedom.

The load was crushing. Always had been. Blaming her husband had only increased and spread the pain, not eased it. Yet now, from under the burden of condemnation, she remembered the assurance that no sin was too great to be expiated. Someone had paid her impossible debt and she was freed. Walking out to her car, she literally felt lighter.

She knew, too, what her response should be. One who'd been forgiven much, loved much. And forgave much.

But in full mother grizzly bear mode, she fought the softening she'd felt toward her husband. His first response to the news of his own precious child had been to kill it. Again! Forgive that? She wasn't there yet.

CHAPTER 25

———————— ✐ ————————

The pleasure we derive from doing favours is partly
in the feeling it gives us that we are not altogether
worthless. It is a pleasant surprise to ourselves.
—Eric Hoffer,
The Passionate State of Mind: And Other Aphorisms[6]

It was Wednesday, so Robert wasn't expected at Anna's. But she waved at him from her front window as he pulled into their shared driveway.

He gathered his laptop and stuffed several files into his shoulder bag before he saw her come out the door. Pulling a shapeless sweater around her shoulders, she hurried over to his car.

"Robert, I have a very big favour to ask of you."

"Oh?" It was a reflex for him to begin thinking of excuses to bypass this kind of disconcerting familiarity. But he reminded himself of Anna's weekly hospitality. Here was an opportunity to show he wasn't entirely thankless.

"Yes," she said. "I'll be needing to go help my daughter Beth when they move. Normally I'd take Jesse with me, but he has a few commitments of his own coming up. So I asked Joan and Yanni to check on him a couple of times a day. His aide will pick him up for the afternoons as usual. And I was wondering if you would mind taking him to floor hockey on Saturday?"

"I could do that," said Robert, relieved he wouldn't be babysitting the entire weekend.

She gave him the location of the school where they played and a little background on the Special Olympics Jesse had been a part of for the past eight years.

So on Saturday afternoon he drove, towering above Jesse in the passenger seat, who looked as awkward as Robert felt.

As they parked in the school lot, Jesse turned toward him, working his jaw intently. Finally he said, "If you go shopping, you gonna pick me off right after?"

What? Pick him off? Robert stifled a laugh and banished the sudden image of himself in sniper gear, aiming amongst the players. Anna must sometimes go shopping during these games and pick up her son when he was finished.

"Uh, no. I don't need to do any shopping. I'll just stay and watch you play."

A slow smile spread across Jesse's face as they left the car and made their way to the school, the wind fluttering their hair and flapping their pant legs.

Robert perched on the lowest level of bleachers under the inverted bowl-shaped lights of the gym, the kind that turned everyone's face a purplish grey. The ridged metal of the seating alone had him hoping the game wouldn't last long.

Jesse went to put on his red pinny and grab a stick. One of the young assistants, short, neckless, heavy-shouldered, and small-headed, nodded at Robert as though he should know him. Must be from the college. Sizing him up, Robert pegged him, perhaps unfairly, as a C student.

Robert watched as two short men with Down syndrome and their aide, a taller black man came down the hall toward the gym. The coach spotted them and called, "Nathan, Otto, hurry up and get your sticks. We gotta get going!"

"Yes, coach. I will, coach. Be right there, coach," they said, nodding happily.

But their pace did not vary as they slowly set down their backpacks. Coach patted their shoulders anyway. With much deliberation, they opened the zippers and began to put on their gym shoes and shin pads. Painstakingly they patted down each Velcro strip, straightening them if they closed unevenly. The coach glanced at Robert as Nathan and Otto finally went to get their sticks.

"I call these two my turtles," the coach said, grinning, and ushered them out to the centre of the gym where the other athletes were doing warmup exercises.

"I want chicken nuggets!" one tiny, wiry man called out, punctuating each jumping jack. "From McDonald's! And a shake! And large fries!"

As Coach tapped heads to divide up the team, Robert counted at least twelve with Down syndrome. Roughly a third of the team. But it was odd. They all seemed quite a bit older than Jesse. Hard to tell. With that expression of innocence on each face, they were perennially young. There *was* the grey and thinning hair, though.

It was soon clear that this game would be no nail-biter. Everyone got a chance on the floor and there didn't seem to be any scorekeeping. Jesse, notwithstanding his earlier promises of scoring twenty goals, seemed more concerned with waving at Robert as the herd lumbered by than with shooting on goal. And Robert couldn't help grinning and waving back. Every time. Whenever anyone scored, there were high-fives and calls of encouragement regardless of whose team they were on.

At one point, just after faceoff, the ref blew his whistle. "Tim!" he said, pointing at a tall skinny lad with giant feet. "Penalty! High sticking!"

"Aww, ref," Tim said. Looking around for a likely candidate, he settled on Jesse. "*He* can take it for me."

Jesse cheerfully turned to go sit on the penalty chair.

"Oh no you don't," said the coach, steering him back onto the floor. "C'mon Tim. You get a chance to rest."

Tim dutifully loped over to the chair and plopped down.

It was quiet on the way home, driving through the now-darkened streets.

"That guy who was helping you practice shooting, what's his name?" Robert asked.

"Miles," Jesse said. And after a pause, he added mildly, "Looks like a pug."

A huge bubble of a laugh burst out of Robert when he thought of the bulging eyes, thick neck, and heavy shoulders of the body builder. An apt description.

As they drove along the Strip, a truck stop's EAT GAS sign flashing its offensive welcome, he began to hear murmurs from Jesse every block or so.

"Wendy's. They have fros'ies," Robert heard Jesse say. Then a little louder, "McDonald's. They have cones."

Robert was starting to catch on.

"Dairy Queen. Banana spli's and peanu' busser parfaits!" Jesse burst out.

"You want ice cream?"

Immediately Jesse turned his head away. "Not s'posed to beg."

Robert turned left and doubled back on the access road. "So what'll it be, Jesse? Banana split or peanut buster parfait?" The face that turned up to his was pure joy.

CHAPTER 26

---_⁓_---

It is very iniquitous to make me pay my debts;
You have no idea of the pain it gives one.
`—Lord Byron, *Letter to Douglas Kinnaird*, 1818

Late Friday afternoon the low autumn sun, far to the north at this time of year, streamed into the corner window of Amelia's bedroom, dappling the grey wall with the chevron pattern of the sheer curtains. The white rectangle of wall where her husband's dresser had been, however, spoiled the effect. It was testament to her impatience with "doing things the proper way," as he'd always said. She really should paint over that someday soon.

In her soft fuchsia chenille robe, balancing her laptop on her knees, Amelia sat in bed propped up by a plethora of pillows. On the computer, Schubert's Trout Quintet bathed her in bliss as the strings frolicked nimbly after the piano. She took a sip of her mildly bitter raspberry leaf tea, intended to tone the uterus. Then into her mouth she popped a piece of red wood—also known as an out-of-season strawberry—followed by a glossy dark chocolate-covered almond. The chocolate was the justifiable compensation for enduring the tea. Absently, she continued alternating, tea, fruit, heaven, as she browsed her favourite home design blogs.

Thinking about these reminded her that she hadn't gotten a call from a realtor since her husband's unilateral decision six weeks ago to sell their home. Amelia wasn't sure what that meant, since there had been no further communication from him. Although she had already bought primer and a neutral paint for the living room, she was in no hurry to proceed down the path of selling the house.

Which brought her to the topic of finances. As much as she dreaded it, she would have to tackle balancing her chequing account again. And pay some bills. And worry about her future. Without looking, she groped for another chocolate to go with the last strawberry and came up empty.

I hate it when things don't come out even. Heavy sigh.

She swung her legs over the side of the bed and, gathering the dishes, padded to the darkened kitchen. It was time for a real meal. She began heating the beef vegetable soup she'd made the weekend before. Anna had advised apportioning the huge recipe into single-serving containers for just such a night as this. Amelia searched the memo app on her phone for the web address of the online financial advisor her friend had recommended. Dave Somebody-or-other. There it was. She took a tray with the soup, some cheese, a few slices of cucumber, a pumpernickel roll, and a glass of milk back to the bedroom and settled in to face the financial facts.

Reading through the money guru's advice, she began to recognize some of the principles of sound financial practice as points her husband had advocated: a written budget, an emergency fund of three to six months' worth of expenses, the imperative of getting out of debt, eliminating the use of credit cards.

Amelia shoved the computer off her lap, thinking hard. Anna's money-saving tips of staying out of stores and restaurants, reusing anything and everything, and cooking from scratch had been a start. Now she pulled her journal off the nightstand and began making notes.

Two hours later, Amelia stretched and sighed. She had a plan. And a hope for freedom. She had a budget with envelopes marked by category— food, gasoline, and so on, even a tiny bit for entertainment—ready to be filled with cash come payday. She had performed plastic surgery by snipping her credit cards into tiny shards. That was an act of sheer courage. Her fridge would soon sport a poster of the debts to be paid. And she'd even written a cheque for $59.87 to Canadian Tire, which eliminated the smallest of her debts.

As she was using a marker to colour a segment of the poster's debt thermometer, her phone rang.

Hoping it was Nelson, she shook her hair smooth, then gave an embarrassed laugh at the reflex. They'd only seen each other at Bible study or talked on the phone. She had to admit to finding him attractive, yet there were small things that loomed large. She knew the irritants were insignificant in light of his genuine love for God and his students, but it had been a mighty act of the will for her to suppress the reflex to correct solecisms like "supposebly" or "irregardless". And such faux pas were even more glaring by contrast: her husband had never trespassed in that manner.

She dug her phone from among the pillows and answered.

Ironically, it was an offer to increase her MasterCard credit limit. When she told the telemarketer, with triumph in her voice, that she'd just cut up her card, there was a moment of silence. Then, "Good for you, ma'am. I wish I could do that."

Amelia laughed aloud after ending the call and gave a snap and a clap.

CHAPTER 27

Suspicion always haunts the guilty mind.
—William Shakespeare,
Henry VI, Part III, Act V, Scene 6

A powerful gust of wind tore the screen door out of Jesse's grasp as he held it open for his guest. Robert caught it and, making sure the latch was fastened securely, turned around to see the young man standing before him. Jesse gave a slight bow, one hand on his middle. *He bows to me now?*

"Welcome-may-I-ta'-your-coat?" Jesse said with a self-conscious smile.

Robert looked over Jesse's head and caught Anna's wink. He handed his jacket to the doorman. Grinning and bending down to stare closer into Jesse's eyes, Robert said, "I hope you'll be able to remember which coat is mine."

Jesse giggled his high-pitched trill.

"Come and sit, you two. Everything's ready." Anna put the last bowl of food on the table. "Tell me, what was the highlight of your day, Robert?"

"I saw something Jesse would have liked," he said, taking his seat.

"What is it?" Jesse sat down, looking up at Robert expectantly.

"I was on Gaetz Avenue coming down the hill where the forest valley is on the right side of the road and Tim Horton's is on the left."

"I like Tim Horton's! Breakfast sandwiches!" Jesse burst out. "Apple fritters!"

"Let Robert finish," Anna told Jesse, patting his arm.

Robert folded his arms on the table in front of his plate and leaned in toward Jesse. "It was almost dark and getting hard to see, but I thought I saw some shadowy figures," he put a tremor in his voice, "walking down the road out of the Tim Horton's drive-through."

Jesse's blue eyes widened, his dark eyebrows rising.

"One was quite tall, the others shorter. Some of them wore tall headdresses. The smallest wore a fur coat with just a couple of faded spots on it. So I slowed down because it looked like they were going to cross the street right in front of me. I actually had to stop. It's a good thing I did. One after another, five of them walked right across the street and into the woods on the other side of the road. Who do you think they were?"

Jesse looked at him intently, then to his mother. "Who?"

"Were they carrying coffee cups and brown bags of doughnuts?" Anna's eyes twinkled.

Jesse turned to Robert and again asked. "Who was it?"

"Five mule deer. A buck, three does, and a fawn."

Jesse clapped his hands and giggled. Robert found himself pleased with Jesse's obvious admiration and joy in the recounting of the simple event.

"You'd be a wonderful father, Robert," Anna told him. She bowed to ask the blessing, oblivious to the smile vanishing from his face.

When she released his hand, he cleared his throat and picked up his fork. He put her comment firmly behind him as he made his way through the hearty meal. It was a wonder to him that meatloaf and mashed potatoes could be such a savoury feast.

Jesse was still only halfway through his meal, the slice of peach pie beside his plate beckoning a golden promise, when Robert saw the opportunity to catch Anna alone. He took up his own plate and one of the half-empty serving dishes and followed Anna to the kitchen.

"I've meant to ask you something, Anna." He fumbled to put his knife and fork into the dishwasher.

"Yes?" she asked, glancing up at him as she put away potatoes, carrots, and meat in single-portion containers.

"When I took Jesse to his floor hockey game, I noticed he seemed to be the youngest person there with Down syndrome. There were other young players, but they seemed to have other handicaps."

Anna's hands stopped moving and she turned to face him. "I've noticed the same thing myself. At first, I thought it might be a result of the younger Down syndrome kids being involved in school sports instead, but..."

Robert followed her gaze out the kitchen window at the strong wind breaking small twigs off the box elder in her backyard.

"But what?" he finally asked, leaning against the fridge.

She turned and looked up into his eyes, sadness shadowing the droop of her eyelids. "We found out that Jesse had Down syndrome after he was born. There were no routine prenatal ultrasounds at the time and I had no reason to seek one. But that was twenty-five years ago. Since then, the Supreme Court has struck down Canada's abortion law and we are without any law whatever."

"Yes, I'm aware of that, but I fail to see what that has to do with what we were discussing." Robert's tone came out sharper than he'd intended, suspecting the direction she was taking the conversation. He looked away from her intense gaze.

Anna pulled back from him. "Let me try to explain from a different angle. I expect you're familiar with Dr. Jerome Lejeune—"

"The biologist who identified Down syndrome as a trisomy of the twenty-first chromosome. Yes."

Anna gave a slight smile. "So you've done a little research on us, eh? Did you also happen to research aging Christian farmwives?" Her eyes held some of their old twinkle again.

Robert shook his head and smiled. "About Lejeune, you had started to say...?"

"If you've read up on him, you're probably aware that he had hoped his work would lead to a cure."

"I didn't read that specifically, but it seems obvious."

"Yes, it does, doesn't it?" She gave him another searching look. "But did you do any reading about Lejeune's later life?"

"No, but I suspect you're going to tell me."

"He was horrified and heartbroken when he began to see that his findings were only being used to eliminate babies with Down syndrome by screening for them. He called it 'chromosomal racism.' He devoted much of his remaining years to fighting for the rights of these helpless little ones."

"You're saying that people with Down syndrome are a dying breed?" Robert's mind raced. Every pro-choice argument he could think of was defeated by the presence of Jesse in the next room. Jesse, whose quality of life, if sheer *joie de vivre* counted, was superior to most people Robert knew, especially himself. Jesse, whose contribution to society, measured in hugs and smiles and easy contentment, was beyond price. Jesse, who created a "burden" for those who cared for him by generating love and patience and joy. Robert's palms began to sweat, thinking and rethinking his position on the issue. His silent angst was so deep that Anna's answer startled him.

"When they speak of preventing it, that's what they mean. That's where the idea of natural selection leads. Survival of the fittest." She leaned towards him. "Think of it, Robert. Over ninety percent of babies found to have Down syndrome are aborted. That's how they're preventing it."

Her eyes were swimming; Anna sniffed hard and cleared her throat. Tipping her head to the side, she looked more carefully at him.

"Sit down before you fall down, Robert. You look a little pale. Supper not agreeing with you?"

Robert sat down hard on a kitchen stool.

She filled a glass with water. "Straight from the Fawcett," she said, pointing her thumb at herself and laughing feebly. "As I was saying—"

"You've made your point, Anna. But I would have to verify those statistics."

He accepted the glass and took a long draught. Standing jerkily, he made his way to the door, passing Jesse who, with bliss on his face, was savouring his last morsel of pie. Anna stayed behind in the kitchen for several moments, then caught up with Robert at the door where he retrieved his jacket.

"Just a minute, Robert. I have a piece of pie with your name on it. You can take it with you for tomorrow's lunch."

CHAPTER 28

⸺ ⁓ ⸺

Thus they in mutual accusation spent
The fruitless hours, but neither self-condemning;
And of their vain contèst appeared no end.
—John Milton, *Paradise Lost, Book IX*

On a star-pierced November night, Robert found his solitary seat in the almost-filled Memorial Centre for the opening of Goldilocks and the Three Bears. Feeling conspicuously alone in the milieu of couples and families, he scanned the program for Jesse's name. There it was, listed under *Forest Bears* and also *Villagers*. Anna would be kept hopping backstage, he knew, changing her son's costume for the various scenes. And as the lights dimmed and the curtain rose, there was Jesse in his brown fur suit, smiling into the audience in a decidedly un-ursine manner. Robert settled into his chair preparing to be entertained.

Despite predictable puns and the repetitious shtick of the family-oriented comedy, he was still smiling as he followed others ascending the steps of the theatre, remembering Jesse's enthusiasm and studiously enunciated lines. He was just stepping out into the crowded foyer when, on the opposite side of the room, he was arrested by a familiar sight. A burst of sudden elation filled his chest.

What was it about the human form that, of the billions of people on earth—well, at least these hundreds here—one could stand out so singularly? The tilt of the head, the set of the shoulders, the sweep and sway of hair and hips—all were as unique as a fingerprint. Yet he knew her indubitably. He caught only one glimpse of her back in an orange top, but he knew her.

She seemed unchanged except for longer hair. Such dusky, lustrous hair. Beautiful. A crazed yearning tore through him and he began to wade through the crowded foyer toward the coat check where he'd seen her.

It was time to set aside his anger. Time to terminate the feud and resume life together, whatever their differences. He knew now that he was ready to overlook her indiscretion and face the inevitable changes.

But when he arrived at the coat check counter, his frantic eyes searched the milling crowd futilely. She was gone.

He stood rooted in an inertia of disappointment, the flame of hope ebbing. Gradually, the crush of people eased, and with it the wild impetus to make amends. He plodded toward the doors. Pricked by the frosty air, Robert felt again the bewildering sense that control over his own life had evaporated.

CHAPTER 29

---·~·---

A sure sign of a good book is that you like it more the older you get.
—Georg Christoph Lichtenberg, *Vermischte Schriften*, 1789–1793

"I see you bought low-VOC paint," Anna said, setting down the can on the swath of old newspapers she'd lined up against the wall.

"That's what my daughter-in-law Cassie has switched to. She's always up on whatever is healthiest, and apparently this type is kindest to the environment."

Anna was wearing what she'd called her Rembrandt shirt, spattered with the memories of other makeovers, while she taped the generous white baseboards in preparation for priming Amelia's living room walls.

Amelia had been banned from lifting so much as a paintbrush, relegated instead to the role of reading aloud an old favourite of hers, *Pride and Prejudice*. Anna's own reading of it had been so long ago that the plot was all novelty now.

The previous Saturday, Amelia and Anna had spent the day exploring the world of thrift stores and second-hand shops with Beth. Amelia had overcome the initial ewww factor to become an aficionado of the previously owned and gently used. Though she'd had no luck finding maternity clothes to fit her petite frame, she was now completely ready for the baby, and at minimal cost. Selling some of her high-end furniture had provided the funds and even allowed her some savings for maternity leave. The loss she felt most sorely was the baby grand piano. She was no concert pianist, but it soothed her soul at the end of a stressful day to tinkle away. And she'd had more reason to keep it with the hope that the baby would grow up musical. To let it go had meant saying goodbye to all the rent she'd paid toward owning it, but it freed up another chunk of her monthly budget. Maybe someday...

Shopping with Anna had changed her own taste almost imperceptibly. At first Amelia had thought she'd have liked to edit some of Anna's things out of the older woman's small duplex. It had all been too busy, too dated, and without any cohesive design. But the few visits she'd made to Anna's home on her days off had taught her to appreciate the story behind everything. Amelia had borrowed books, heard the history of the quilts, seen the grandchild-ready toy cupboard, and snuggled in the shapeless couch sipping tea from heirloom china. And she had come to cherish it all.

This Saturday, however, they were following Elizabeth Bennett's foibles of the heart. Amelia was curled around her growing pumpkin belly, Anna at the wall, covering Amelia's beloved charcoal satin with the last strokes of a second coat of primer.

"Stop for a minute, Amelia," Anna laughed. "That line you just read? It's so true! Can you read it again?"

"'The power of doing anything with quickness is always much prized by the possessor, and often without any attention to the imperfection of the performance,'" Amelia read, grinning.

"Oh, ha ha! That's particularly noticeable in some people's sewing. But home renovations, too. I know I may be slow, but it's worth it to do a job well."

Anna laid down her paint roller and began opening one of the cans of safe and realtor-friendly neutral paint that Amelia called "greige."

"There is no colour so repulsive that a clever name can't make it fashionable," Anna said, staring into the can. "I'm waiting for the day they call this what it really looks like, Stale Oatmeal." She poured some into the paint tray, switched rollers, and began rolling it onto the walls in a W motion.

Amelia looked up from the book. "But really, my dear Mrs. Fawcett," she said, "I'm afraid I am deeply offended. That shade was specially selected to show off my handsome figure." She rose and stood against the wall, chin up, tightening her sweater for the full benefit of her bump.

"You are so cute!" Anna threw her head back, giggling. "Forgive me, but from the back no one could know you're pregnant. And from the front it's a volleyball." Weakened by laughter, Anna sat down, then jumped up looking at the spot where she'd sat. "Whew! I was afraid I'd left some paint smears on your new couch."

"My 'new' couch, that I paid exactly forty-five dollars for," Amelia said.

"Okay." Anna rose and took up the roller again. "One more wall and I'll have to get home before Jesse gets there."

"Where was he again? Oh right, you said he was going to the zoo with your neighbour."

"Isn't it strange to have zoo-going weather in December?" Anna said above the rhythmic squeak of the roller. "But I'm not complaining. It's so nice not to have to put on boots or drive in icy conditions."

"So shall I carry on with the adventures of Elizabeth and Mr. Darcy?"

"Carry on, my dear," said Anna, covering the last of the primer with the first coat of dreaded neutral paint. "I'm feeling a special fondness for Mrs. Bennett in particular."

CHAPTER 30

And the King will answer and say to them, "Assuredly,
I say to you, inasmuch as you did it to one of the least of these
My brethren, you did it to Me."
—Matthew 25:40

Jesse can't keep from twirling his wrists with the bubbles of excitement inside him as he waits for Mr. Fielding.

"Now Jesse, remember to speak clearly and loud enough for Mr. Fielding to hear you," Mom is saying. She kisses his cheek. He wipes the spot, as he always does. She laughs.

"I know, Mom. I be fine. I'm not a baby."

"Of course you're not. Have you fed Hanky and the fish?"

"I always do, Mom." This morning he has done all his chores before Mom came out of her room. He knows Hanky, the gerbil, has rolled himself into a little ball under the shavings at the back corner of the cage.

"I know you do, son." Mom smiles at him. "Don't forget to say please and thank you for everything. Do you have your money?"

"Yup. In my pocket, see? Where we going for supper?"

"I don't know, Jesse, but I'm sure it'll be good. Make sure you eat—"

"...my veg'ables." Jesse knows she'll say that. She always does. He doesn't like vegetables. If they are in a hamburger, okay. But not broccoli. Like eating little trees. Or carrots. Too much chewing.

Mom looks out the window then. When Jesse looks out, his

neighbour is coming to their door. Jesse zips his orange and grey jacket, puts on the red and yellow Calgary Flames toque he got last Christmas from his brother Burk, grabs his purple mitts, and leaves the house. "Hi, Misser Fie'ding," he says. "Ready for the zoo."

"We'll be home by eight or nine," Mr. Fielding tells Mom.

He opens the door to his car. It's a lot lower than Mom's car. Jesse strokes the cool, black leather along the full-length of the inside of the door. He finds the seatbelt way back there and pulls and pulls. The clicky part wiggles a little so he grabs it with his other hand, aims the flat buckle into it, and pushes until it clicks. He's all ready now and so excited. This is just like it used to be when Dad would take him places. Jesse takes a sharp breath inward. It's like it was when his brothers Burk and Don were still at home.

Turning to look at Mr. Fielding, he says with a grin, "You're like another brother."

Mr. Fielding opens his mouth, then closes it. Then he smiles and says, "Do you want to hear some music?"

Jesse turns to him. "Johnny Cash!" He wears a big grin.

"One and the same," says Mr. Fielding, and he hits the button to start the music.

Jesse knows every song. He sings along while he flattens the folds along his pant legs. He likes things to be smooth. He likes it, too, when Mr. Fielding starts to sing along.

When they get to the zoo, Jesse can't keep still. He bends and bobs as they wait in line, wrists flapping. Mr. Fielding buys tickets and they start looking for animals.

"What do you want to see first, Jesse?"

"Monkeys!"

Walking together to the monkey house, Jesse takes Mr. Fielding's hand. It's kind of stiff so he swings it a little. After a bit of swinging it feels looser.

Jesse loves monkeys. Mr. Fielding reads all the signs by the cages. "*Cercopithecus neglectus*," he reads, and points to a monkey with a long white beard.

"Looks like he's wearing glasses," Jesse says.

"*Colobus badius.*"

These have very long tails and fluffy white hair all around their little dark faces. Two of them are hanging upside down by their tails. Jesse points to the one who is sitting on a high ledge with a large lettuce leaf hanging from his mouth. Mom would sure say something to him if Jesse ate like that.

They walk along to the next window.

"*Pongidae troglodytes.*"

Jesse sees Mr. Fielding grin and then laugh when a dad chimpanzee, with both hands, pounds two young wrestling chimps on the tops of their heads. Jesse laughs, too.

"How about the large animal house next, okay?" Mr. Fielding asks him.

A mom and dad ahead of them are trying to pull apart two scuffling little boys. Jesse looks up when Mr. Fielding murmurs, "*Braticus badius.*"

"The dad should pound 'em on their heads," Jesse says.

Mr. Fielding laughs loud then. Jesse doesn't know why. He thinks the dad really should do it.

Up ahead there are hippos. "*Hippopotamus amphibius*," Mr. Fielding says. Next there are giraffes—"*giraffa camelopardalis*"—and gorillas. There are two fuzzy baby gorillas playing and wrestling. The way they tumble over and over tickles Jesse's insides and he giggles.

A man beside him slurps the last of a milkshake and Jesse looks around to see where he might have gotten it. He spies a counter where they're selling chips and drinks. He tries not to look. Mom always tells him he's not supposed to have too much of that kind of thing. But as he and Mr. Fielding walk past it, Jesse's steps lag. Licking his lips slowly, he looks for a long time past Mr. Fielding on his left, to the concession.

"Want a snack, Jesse?" Mr. Fielding asks.

How did he know? "Yes please!" He feels good that he remembers the please.

At the concession, he carefully unzips the inside pocket of his jacket. The girl behind the counter looks at him and he asks for chips. Salt 'n vinegar chips. He takes out a blue bill with a five on it. That should be enough. She gives him his change and he puts it back into his pocket.

He should share some chips with Mr. Fielding. But Jesse has seen him eat when he comes over for supper to their house. And this bag is not a *very* big one. His mom would tell him to share. He crunches down on two more of the large chips.

Finally, he says, "I guess I have to—" and offers the bag to his friend.

Next comes the elephant pen. "*Elephas maximus,*" Mr. Fielding says. He and Jesse sit on the bleachers finishing the chips while they wait for the elephant show to begin. Jesse sees Mr. Fielding pull out his phone. The door opens to the pen where the elephants will perform.

Jesse nudges Mr. Fielding. "They're comin', Misser Fie'ding."

Mr. Fielding, still staring down at his phone, doesn't look up. Lots of people do that. They sit with their heads down. They don't look at each other. They don't do anything together. Mom sometimes used to pop the phone out of David's fingers so he'd pay attention.

Jesse snatches the phone out of Mr. Fielding's hand and drops it into the pocket of his neighbour's brown leather jacket. Jesse keeps his eyes on the zoo-men bringing the elephants into the pen, but he can feel Mr. Fielding staring at him.

A slow grin creeps across Jesse's face. He puts his hand up to shield the side of his face.

The elephants are very smart. They can do a lot of things people don't think animals can do. Watching them get their peanut treats for moving logs and carrying a bucket with their trunks, Jesse starts to feel a rumble in his belly.

"It's supper time, Misser Fie'ding," he says, tugging on the jacket sleeve beside him.

"Well, Jesse, if I can't look at my phone, how can I check to see if you're right?"

"You can look now," Jesse says with a smile.

Mr. Fielding is surprised when he checks the time. "It's only four, but I'm kind of hungry myself. What do you want for dinner?" he says, getting up to head out to the parking lot.

Jesse knows he'll ask that and he has his answer ready. "Spaghetti 'n meatballs."

"I know just the place," Mr. Fielding says.

As they were leaving, an episode in the zoo parking lot had Robert rattled. A gaggle of junior high kids hanging out at the underpass tunnel were twirling their wrists, tongues out, jaws waggling. Some were pulling their eyes into slants, swinging each other's hands, all unmistakable imitations of Jesse. It occurred to him that he'd become accustomed to the quirky mannerisms and barely noticed them anymore. But when Jesse stood stock still and began breathing heavily, emotion pulling down the corners of his mouth, anger surged through Robert.

Brats! When he stopped directly in front of them, their laughter evaporated. He fished his car keys out of his pocket and handed them to Jesse.

In a tone loud enough for the kids to hear, he said, "Why don't you drive today, Jesse?"

He'd guessed right. All of them were too young to drive and as they gawped, Jesse and Robert walked on toward the parking lot. He recalled the repugnance he'd harboured toward this handicapped young man when they'd first met. Now here he was, ready to defend Jesse with his car.

Robert hadn't thought he'd actually put Jesse behind the wheel, but evidently Jesse had other plans. And of course, he still had the keys.

"Hunhhh, hunhhhh." The young man quivered with excitement as he belted himself into the driver's seat. From the other seat, Robert swung his legs over the console, then guided Jesse's hand to Reverse. Robert could scarcely believe he was doing this as he slowly let out the clutch and gave his precious BMW a little gas. With minimal help, he let Jesse steer as they took a turn around the parking lot.

"Time to go eat now, Jesse." That wide, small-toothed grin stayed in place all the way to the restaurant.

After they were seated in The Old Spaghetti Factory and had ordered, Robert googled Down syndrome for a refresher. He was soon lost in the science of genetics. Pasta arrived and disappeared and he was still engrossed until a muted squawk disturbed him.

Glancing up from his phone and across at Jesse's face, he saw it altered grotesquely. The young man's eyes were crinkled crescents and his teeth were bared. He emitted a fiendish, guttural laugh. Robert stared, then glanced around the mostly empty restaurant. At this early dinner hour, they were alone. But looking around he caught sight of Jesse's reflection in the fireplace glass. A shaft of mischief assailed him. He shifted his chair a bit and smiled his own best fiend-face into the glass. Jesse rewarded him with a long giggling fit. So there they sat, contorting and distorting until a familiar voice behind them startled him into propriety.

"Dr. Fielding?" It was Sarah-Mae, her voice on the verge of a giggle. "I wasn't sure that was you."

He swivelled to find her and Jamie McCoy standing behind him in sweatpants and turtlenecks, puzzled, amused looks on their faces. Of all the times, of all the company, of all the activities—that he should be caught this way.

"What are you two doing here?" A poor opening remark, Robert realized the minute it came out of his mouth.

"G'day mate." McCoy nodded at Jesse. "How ya doin', Big Guy?" The Aussie's smile was set in place but his eyes were scanning the booths in the restaurant. "We're just coming back from Fernie. It was fantastic! Love the skiing here."

"Jesse and I have just enjoyed a day at the zoo." Robert glanced at the couple's locked fingers. He lifted his eyebrows at Sarah-Mae, who simply shrugged and looked away.

"Well, carry on." McCoy guided his date to a table in a dim corner, far from the one the hostess offered.

CHAPTER 31

Mother of science! now I feel thy power
Within me clear, not only to discern
Things in their causes, but to trace the ways
Of highest agents, deemed however wise.
—John Milton, *Paradise Lost, Book IX*

At one-thirty on the last Friday of classes in December, Phil Thiessen poked his head in Robert's office door.

"You coming to the staff lounge for coffee today?"

Robert tipped his chair upright, raking a hand through his hair. "I've got one more class at three." He glanced at his watch. "Yeah, sure, why not."

As they ambled down the busy hallway, Phil glanced up at Robert, eyeing him from behind his thick, black-framed glasses.

"You look about done in. I figured the Habs' first win of the season would have pumped you up. Of course, they weren't up against the Oilers."

The jab failed to elicit a response. Phil tried again. "Been a long semester?"

"I guess you could say that."

"I just did."

"Funny."

"Got a joke for you," Phil said.

"Better than the last one?"

"Baldwyn thought so."

They entered the lounge, empty except for two women in a pair of chairs beneath the piranha tank. Their murmured conversation mingled with the hum and gurgle of the aquarium pump.

Phil poured two cups of coffee and they crossed over to the couches. Partway into the story, Robert vaguely recognized it from a PhD humour website. but he enjoyed Phil's dry retelling of it.

"Night after night a philosopher had a recurring dream. He would meet one of the ancient philosophers who promised to give him the foolproof, universal, irrefutable final answer to every argument. But just as the ancient was about to impart it, he'd vanish and the guy would wake up. Finally one night, he insisted Socrates tell him the answer before he disappeared."

Phil paused to slouch a little further in his seat, the bare hint of a smile moving the corner of his mouth. He scratched the top of his head in his peculiar gesture.

Robert was already grinning, anticipating the punch line.

"When the guy got his answer, he willed himself to wake up, rush over to his desk and write it down. The next morning, he went to see what he'd written. There it was, the foolproof, universal, irrefutable final answer to every argument. It was 'That's what *you* say.'"

Chuckling, Robert said, "Takes you right back to elementary school, doesn't it?"

Phil took a long draught of his coffee and sighed. "Two more classes this afternoon and then exam week." He looked up at Robert. "You coming to the faculty Christmas party tonight?"

"I guess so."

Phil raised an eyebrow at him.

Robert shrugged one shoulder. "It's a free meal, usually a good one. I don't plan to stay to the bitter end."

"Maybe my wife and I will see you there then." Phil got up, stretched, and took his cup to the sink to wash it.

"I've been doing a little checking on the whole matter of creationists and their complaints about evolution," Robert blurted.

Phil turned from the counter toward Robert, his cup halfway home to the shelf. "Yeah?"

Robert considered how to proceed. He genuinely liked Phil and had no desire to demolish him or any of his pet theories. But as an educator, as *fellow* educators, they had a responsibility to the truth.

Phil sauntered back to the couch and sank down, putting his feet up. He aimed an expectant look at Robert.

"I suppose what I'd have to say is that we do a disservice to scientific endeavour if, when we come up against something we don't understand fully, we simply sit back, throw our hands in the air, and say, 'It must be God.'" Robert looked away from Phil's intense gaze and continued. "That approach seems to undermine science in the worst way and, I think, threatens its future. Once we appeal to an omnipotent deity, it means that at any moment the regularities of nature can be disrupted. From there on, science as we know it can't proceed. Intellectually, it's just giving up and letting superstition take over." He paused, waiting for his colleague to respond.

Phil nodded but said nothing.

Finally Robert said, "So, what have you got to say to that?"

"Do you consider me superstitious?"

The spurious question took Robert by surprise. "Only with regard to the Oilers."

"Ha ha!" Phil threw back his head. "How about Blaise Pascal? Was he superstitious?"

"I don't associate him with superstition, no."

"Isaac Newton?"

"Not where scientific matters were concerned."

"Louis Pasteur? Lord Kelvin? Werner von Braun, father of space science—"

"Okay, okay. What's your point?"

"Just this: those are only a few of the scientists who've made their contributions to our body of knowledge *because* of their belief in the God of the Bible. Obviously, their belief in a deity didn't hinder their scientific pursuits. It was their very reliance on a God who established the regularities of an orderly universe that guided their discoveries of the laws of science. Science may be restricted to examining physical effects, but it doesn't have to fudge the facts when an intelligent cause might be inferred by the data." Phil pushed himself up from his slump and leaned toward Robert over the coffee table. "Look. You, as a biologist of all people, should know what theory held sway for over a thousand years before it was debunked."

Phil waited for Robert, who crossed his arms and shrugged, letting Phil take his course.

"Remember spontaneous generation?" Phil asked. "The idea that life could come from non-life? It was a given in the scientific world for centuries. Pasteur's careful experiments finally demolished that old idea. But the opposition from the biological establishment of his day was intense." He glanced at his watch. "What I'm getting at is, every radical idea seems to have to go through four stages in challenging the status quo. First, it's *preposterous*—doesn't even merit consideration. Second, it's *pernicious*—dangerous in some way. Third, it's *possible*. And fourth, it's *plausible*, and a status quo emerges. That's the point where we wonder how people in times past could have believed anything else."

"So where do you figure evolution is in that continuum?" Robert asked.

"It's the status quo, man," Phil said. "The radical idea is that all the complexity we observe in the world around us and the universe beyond has been unbelievably fine-tuned by a super-intelligence. And the way I figure it, intelligent design is at a stage somewhere between *pernicious* and *possible*." He stood. "I've got to get going, Robert, but I'll send you a list of titles by current thinkers in the field to get you started. Anybody in your position needs to know what's going on in the intelligent design movement. It's asking biology and a lot of the other scientific disciplines some tough questions."

CHAPTER 32

---~~---

[H]e, who will not reason, is a bigot; he, who cannot, is a fool;
and he, who dares not, is a slave.
—Sir William Drummond of Logiealmond, *Academical Questions*, 1805

Getting dressed that evening, Robert pondered Phil's words. He resented Phil's implication that he didn't know what was going on. Or, for that matter, the assumption that he wanted to "get started" looking into renegade scientists' claims. And from what he'd seen on the Internet, it could hardly be called a movement. Yet the tough questions were clearly filtering down to the layperson. Some of his conversations with Anna were evidence of that.

In the bathroom mirror, he surveyed the crooked knot of his tie. Frustrated, he pulled it out and started over. It had always been something his wife fixed for him. The memory reminded him that he'd be on his own at this year's Christmas party. Dinner, conversation, dancing—it all filled him with apprehension. He paused to consider simply staying home. But he'd paid for his ticket weeks ago.

At the country club, cocktail hour was just drawing to a close and he hoped to find the Thiessens or Baldwyn before he was the only one standing, drawing all eyes as he hunted for a place to sit. He checked his coat and scanned the large foyer for a familiar face. There was Dr. Baldwyn's craggy silhouette, bobbing above the crowd toward the dining room doors. A strong mingling of perfumes and aftershave rose as Robert threaded his way through the milieu to safe territory.

Baldwyn nodded at him and Robert noticed Phil, spiffed up in tie and jacket, with his pregnant wife Carol. Or Carla?

"Robert, you remember my wife, Kallie?" Phil asked.

Saved from one embarrassment, anyway. Thanks, buddy.

"Of course. Good to see you again." There was no room to shake hands in the crush, so he simply nodded at the attractive red-haired woman whose green eyes shone from among her many freckles.

They found a round table not far from the long buffet, an important consideration, Baldwyn had maintained. As Robert pulled out the grey upholstered chair, trying to avoid pulling the entire tablecloth with it as he'd done two years back, he was dismayed to see McCoy making his way to their table. He had a barely clad Sarah-Mae in tow. Robert was conscious of her long, satin thighs in the short black dress. Their knees bumped when she sat down.

When their table was called and he and his colleagues lined up for the buffet, Robert's innards began their inevitable complaint at the late dinner hour.

Phil glanced back at him, lifting one eyebrow at the yowling. "Pretty famished are you?"

Robert clamped an arm against his midsection and smiled weakly as he grabbed a plate. Phil paused in front of a festively colourful Greek salad, helplessly scanning the salad bar for a spoon with which to scoop it. Kallie finally tapped a passing caterer on the shoulder. The woman, was stout, no more than five feet tall, with jet-black hair beyond the one-inch white roots. Her pouchy eyes searched the table for a spoon.

"If they haven't gone and done it again!" she said in her singsong Newfoundland accent. "Them serving spoons grow legs and walk off at a tremenjous rate!"

She scuttled toward the kitchen and returned with several utensils.

"There y' be, luv," she said to Phil, who thanked her, smirked at his wife, and delved into his favourite salad.

They returned to their table with plates piled high, followed by Baldwyn, McCoy, and Sarah-Mae. Sarah-Mae's plate held only green salad.

Robert stared at her until she turned to look at him. He shifted his gaze to her plate, then raised his eyebrows. She turned away, lips compressed in a thin line.

"Apparently, I've been gaining weight," she muttered in a tight voice.

Robert huffed and rolled his eyes at the ridiculous idea.

"Really!" McCoy burst out from his place on the other side of his girlfriend. "I find this unacceptable!"

"What seems to be the trouble?" Baldwyn rumbled, raising his head ponderously toward McCoy.

"Am I the only one without silverware?" Half-rising, McCoy took in each place setting and then his own lonely plate.

Sarah-Mae shoved her chair back and strode over to the empty table behind them. She brought back a white napkin-wrapped package of cutlery and set it at her boyfriend's place.

With a twinkle in his eye, Phil looked across the table at McCoy. "Must be another case of spoons growing a set of legs and walking off."

"And the dish ran away with the spoon," Kallie quipped.

McCoy paused with his first forkful of prime rib midway to his mouth. His eyes narrowed as he cocked his head and laid down the fork. "I assume you meant 'growing a set of legs' to be some kind of jab at evolutionary science. So what is it you're getting at, Thiessen?" He folded his arms across his chest and stared at Phil.

"Nothing but a bit of a joke, Jamie," Phil said with a flip of his hand.

"Because I sincerely hope you're not one of these flat-earthers who believe in creationism."

Despite the thrum of conversation and dish clatter in the hotel's large dining room, the silence at their table was palpable. Robert noted that Phil was the only one who seemed at ease; everyone else was either fidgeting or frozen in place.

"Do you consider dissent from the status quo a dangerous thing, Dr. McCoy?" Phil asked, placidly buttering a dinner roll.

McCoy's chin jutted. "I do if it represents stubborn anti-intellectualism and threatens the progress of science."

"Isn't exploring ideas the very nature of science?" Kallie asked with a gentle smile.

"All this intelligent design hocus pocus spells the end of science," McCoy huffed.

Sarah-Mae shrugged and began munching on her greens. The others, too, relaxed enough to resume eating.

"I don't see it as the end of science at all," said Kallie softly. "You know, at Christmas, Phil and I always plan a hunt for our kids to find their gifts. As they get older, it's getting harder to make it a challenge and we have a real job making the clues clear enough without giving the hiding place away. I think of the Designer doing the same thing. It takes true genius to put enough clues in place to allow us to discover Him but without revealing Himself fully and spoiling science—the fun of the hunt."

McCoy gave a brief smile that didn't reach his eyes. "All a nice bit of hubris, I'm sure, but religion has no place in the realm of science." He went on cutting his prime rib with firm strokes of the knife. Robert caught Sarah-Mae eyeing her boyfriend's plate.

"So would you quash all controversy in the interest of a scientific consensus?" Phil asked.

The Aussie hesitated a moment. "Yes, for the sake of the public who needs reliable answers and a united front, I'd say so."

"Ah, Plato's philosopher kings deciding on behalf of the masses what they can and cannot think," Phil said. "But don't you think a scientific consensus is precisely the opposite of the spirit of free inquiry?"

"There's a difference between free inquiry and ignorant meddling on the part of the religious."

"We don't need to bring religion into the discussion at all. There's enough evidence coming to light about big bang cosmology, the Cambrian explosion, DNA, and cell biology to turn Darwinism upside down. Of course, it always takes time for new ideas to be accepted in the scientific community, and even longer for them to filter down to a layman's level."

McCoy stiffened, appearing to resent being categorized as an academic dinosaur. But before he could swallow his bite of baked potato, Phil continued.

"Even in my short lifetime, I've discovered some inconsistencies. In high school, we were taught the ancient Greek idea that the universe had always been, but that idea was already being debunked decades earlier. Starting in the 1920s with Einstein's realization that his theory of relativity didn't allow for a static universe and Hubble's discoveries that the universe is expanding, it's been proved that the universe had a beginning." Phil glanced around the table at his listeners. "Whatever begins to exist has a cause. Since the universe had a beginning, it must have a cause."

Robert pondered this pithy syllogism. There was an inherent satisfaction in its neat cogency, but he was uneasy with its implications.

McCoy half-rose in his chair to pop the cork on the Cabernet in the centre of the table. Pouring some for himself and Sarah-Mae, he passed the bottle to Dr. Baldwyn.

After an extended wine savouring, McCoy sighed and shook his head wearily. "Teeza, Teeza, Teeza. Thanks so much for the astronomy lesson, but what's your point?"

The math prof finished chewing and wiped one corner of his mouth with his napkin. "The point is that it takes too long for scientific discoveries to make their way into popular use. If you're concerned about what really threatens the progress of science, that's one of your culprits."

Phil took in a breath as if to go on when Robert noticed Kallie cover his hand with her own.

McCoy contemplated his goblet as he swirled the liquid ruby in it. "It's immaterial to us in the biological sciences how things began; we can leave that to the cosmologists. What we deal with are the facts, and evolution is the proven mechanism that has resulted in all the lifeforms we see today." He finished the wine and poured himself another glass.

Phil pulled his hand out from under his wife's and set his elbows on the table. "It might be premature to use the word 'proven'. What's the current estimate on the age of the universe?"

McCoy sighed deeply. "About ten to twenty billion years."

"And dates for life appearing would be—"

"Around six hundred million."

"What I've been reading indicates that given the rate of the incidence of mutations, even twenty billion years is not enough time for the evolution of a single protein molecule, let alone a living cell."

McCoy snorted. "Then isn't it astounding how evolution accomplished it? Whether by punctuated equilibrium or some other means, we *know* the facts. What we don't know is how to satisfy the impossible demands for proof that ignorant religious nuts keep yammering about."

The Aussie's grating, sulky tone soured Robert's enjoyment of both the excellent dinner and conversation. He decided to plunge in with a question of his own. "What's your take on this, Dr. Baldwyn?"

The dean laid his fork down and laced his hands on the table. He looked from one to another of the professors at the table and cleared his throat. "Armed with all the data available to us now, and knowing the many conditions required for the origin of life, it would be only honest to concede that in some sense it had to have been almost a miracle." Baldwyn held up one hand at their surprised murmurs. "I personally favour a theistic beginning, and subsequently an evolutionary mechanism as an explanation for all that exists."

Setting down his empty wine goblet deliberately, McCoy reached for the bottle. "If evolution is the means by which a god created everything, he or she couldn't have been much of a god. With all the death and destruction over the millennia, it has to have been the most inefficient of all possible means to produce the world around us."

"It doesn't seem logically possible," Robert added. "By definition, evolution is an undirected natural process. It doesn't make sense to me to talk about a purposeful process that is, nevertheless, purposeless."

He leaned back. *That came out remarkably well.* Then he noticed Phil nodding and realized the math prof thought Robert was coming down on his side.

"That's exactly right," McCoy said, co-opting the argument. He avoided Baldwyn's craggy frown and focussed his gaze on Phil. "Natural selection works via random genetic mutations. We're the result of a purposeless process that never had us in mind, in a universe of pitiless indifference."

"If we're simply pond scum, all grown up, what place is there for morals?" Phil leaned forward slightly. "What difference does it make how we behave toward one another? Teaching a course like your Bioethics seems a bit irrational then, doesn't it?"

"It's only science that's rational." McCoy's voice began to rise. "Only science can arrive at the truth."

Phil wore a crooked smile. "Seems like if we say science is the only source of truth, we'd be contradicting ourselves. The statement itself can't be tested by the scientific method."

Angry red blotches mottled McCoy's handsome face as he leaned forward with both hands flat on the table. "That's what *you* say," he hissed. There was a moment of stunned silence as Dr. Baldwyn, Phil, and Robert exchanged significant glances. Then they erupted in laughter.

McCoy stood and reached for Sarah-Mae's hand. "That's it. We're done. Let's go to the bar."

She yanked her hand back, but in his hurry, he scarcely gave her a backward glance.

There was a last call from the emcee for buffet seconds before the band began to play, its volume ending any hope of conversation.

Robert took the opportunity to ask Sarah-Mae for a dance. Before they hit the floor, however, he steered her over to the buffet and urged her to fill her plate. Back at their table, he watched with approval her enthusiastic devouring of the beef dinner.

When she was finished and smiled her thanks at him, they found a spot on the dance floor in the darkened room. He kept his eyes on her throughout the fast-paced popular song as Sarah-Mae lip-synced the lyrics.

You think I'm keepin' you back but it's all about your pride. You can't give me what I lack—something in me has died! Fitful sleep, fit for nothing, since I found out you lied, Having fits. Nothing fits. I'm just fit to be tied!
Survival! Survival!
Survival of the fittest!

She was a luscious and intelligent woman, and Robert wondered why she stayed with McCoy, who at the moment was immersed in animated conversation with a pink-haired pixie at the bar.

During the next slow dance, she whispered in his ear, "Jamie's father is an Anglican minister."

Robert had been enjoying her body next to his, trying to forget how long it had been since he'd held his wife this way.

Sarah-Mae pulled back to look intently at him. "Well, don't you think that's kind of significant?"

"You're saying his belief in science is mere reaction to his upbringing?"

"Something like that." She rolled her eyes. "Maybe all that bluster kind of extinguishes the little flames of conscience."

"Why do you stay with such an insensitive, arrogant man? You deserve better."

Sarah-Mae turned to look across the half-full dance floor. She shrugged. "What other kind is there? Isn't that just the nature of the beast?"

"Thanks," Robert said wryly.

A slow smile spread across Sarah-Mae's perfectly made-up face and she pulled close again. "So how come you're here alone this year? Things not so good at home?"

He stiffened, wondering how much she knew. "I'd rather not talk about it."

She pulled back again, looking at him skeptically. "Robert, you are way too easy to read. You've lost weight, you're preoccupied, and you have no interest in the hockey pool this season. You're obviously floundering without her. Why don't you go find your cute little wife and kiss and make up?"

CHAPTER 33

---~~---

Long lay the world in sin and error pining
Till He appeared and the soul felt its worth
A thrill of hope, the weary world rejoices
For yonder breaks a new and glorious morn.
—Placide Cappeau de Roquemaur, "O Holy Night"

An inner swell of excitement brought a smile to Amelia's face as she wished her students and the other staff Merry Christmas. In years past, the holiday season had been a particular source of pain, focused as it was on Santa and children. This year the simple greeting held such wondrous meaning for her, a significance beyond even her own growing child. *Pregnant with meaning.* She'd always wanted to use that phrase. The thought of its current triple meaning made her giggle in wonder: her own spiritual rebirth now gave her a genuine appreciation of the marvel of Jesus' birth—Almighty God invading His own creation. And third, the impending birth of her own baby.

Amelia buttoned the top button of her tightly straining coat against the dry cold and made her way to her car. She reminded herself to fill up with gas before she left it at the airport car park, proud of herself for thinking of a detail her husband had always looked after. The trip to Toronto for Christmas was an unexpected surprise provided by an anonymous donor. At first, she thought the red envelope of cash she'd found in her front door mailbox had come from Anna, but a look into those surprised innocent eyes when she'd asked told Amelia it must be someone else. The idea of such a large gift from Nelson was flattering but troubling. And unlikely, as she gave it more thought. His interest in her had seemed to shrink in recent weeks as her midsection had expanded. But she couldn't imagine who else would have given the money.

Whatever the source, she was thrilled to spend Christmas with her dad.

"The skunk!" was all her mild-mannered father had said when she'd informed him months ago about her separation. Since then he'd respected her silence on the matter. She was grateful that she wouldn't be spending Christmas at home alone with all her memories. As the months had gone on, Amelia was surprised by how many memories of home and her husband were happy ones. Was that because of Anna's frequent admonitions to "keep a thankful heart"?

A disturbing thought made her frown. She knew what the Bible said about forgiveness. God would forgive her in the same way she forgave others. It meant she was compelled to forgive her husband. But letting go of fourteen years' worth of resentment and bitterness was no easy task. She knew Anna expected her to let him know it, too. As much as she told herself there was no need to try to meet Anna's expectations, questions about the nature of forgiveness continued to arise.

Can you forgive a person who hasn't asked for it? Won't you just anger them if you say they're forgiven while they're convinced they've done nothing wrong? Is forgiveness, after all, simply an inner mental release? Or does it require both parties?

The city limits were already in sight. Amelia rummaged in her purse for her flight itinerary and anticipated Christmas with Dad, the first in at least five years. And the first where she had something special to show him.

He's going to be thrilled.

And he was. From his first hug at the airport to the day she left, her dad had done it all: carried her bag, held an umbrella over her, pampered her, worried over her. Amelia easily gave up her self-sufficiency of the past four months, surrendering to the bliss of being cared for.

How lovely it was to share tidbits about baby development and prenatal pictures with someone who anticipated the child's birth as eagerly as she did. How lovely to bask in his solicitude, to be made to rest with her feet up while he cooked a perfect turkey dinner. For three.

The third was Janet, a chunky, smiling widow in sensible shoes whom her dad had met in a digital photography class. Amelia had wondered about the new boxwood wreath on the door that had replaced the tattered paper one she'd made in Grade Four art class. There were other small improvements, too. She'd immediately noticed his new clean-shaven look and the classy sweater that matched his sky-blue eyes. Now they began to make sense to her. With her father's resistance to social media and his awkwardness on the phone, there had been no previous clues. It was completely unexpected to Amelia that he would find someone new to love. And love her he very evidently did.

A full forty-five minutes after leaving his condo to see Janet to her car, he returned, whistling. Amelia was still sitting on the couch with her feet on the coffee table, waiting for him.

"Well?" she asked, giving him half a smile.

"Well what?" He glanced around the room, picking at his thumb cuticle.

"Janet?" She drew out the name slowly, enjoying his shy embarrassment.

"Look, Amelia," he said, sitting beside her and taking her hand in both of his. "I'm sorry I didn't tell you sooner. You know how bad I am with the phone—"

"That's the way you end every phone call." Amelia elbowed him in the ribs.

Her father jumped a little and a smile flickered across his time-creased face. "When we first met, we found we had a lot in common, living alone and all. And it got more and more natural to do things together. It seemed like something to tell you in person."

"It's all right, Dad, really."

He gazed into her eyes. "I know she's not beautiful and charismatic like your mother." He squeezed her hand, searching her face for approval. "But she's steady and intelligent and just... so... comfortable."

"I can see how comfortable. She knows her way around your kitchen pretty well." Amelia shook her head quickly at his effort to explain. "It's totally fine. I'm glad for you. I didn't like the thought of you so far away from me and all alone. And it's been over thirteen years."

They sat gazing into the fireplace in silence a while, still holding hands.

"Were you ever sorry you married Mom?" she asked.

He was quiet so long that Amelia wondered if her dad had forgotten the question.

"In the early years, sometimes. But I never let myself think that way after you were born. I knew she'd take you from me. Men don't fare well in custody disputes. I feared I'd never see you again and I couldn't have borne that. Ever."

Amelia shifted to face him, trying not to worry him by any little grunts. "She'd have been that spiteful?" Even as she asked it, Amelia knew it was all too possible.

"It was all about her version of the world, little girl."

"You mean 'Men oppress women, men have always oppressed women, men will always oppress women'?"

"You learned it well." Her father paused and gave a sad smile. "When that woman got an idea in her head, dynamite couldn't dislodge it. And woe to anyone who tried. I made that mistake a couple of times early on. So I learned to go along with things to keep the peace. But mostly to keep you." He turned to look at her. "I did do some fancy footwork to get you into McGill University, you know." He smiled when Amelia raised her eyebrows at him. "Your mother wanted you to go to the University of Toronto where she could get you involved in her women's focus group and have you mentored by the venerable Betty Oysskin."

At the memory of the women's rights activist, Amelia choked, laughing and grasping her dad's arm.

"You remember her?" he asked, chuckling.

"When the meetings were at our place, you and I used to snicker about her crazy outfits."

"Elephant pants, I believe they were called."

Tears streamed from Amelia's eyes when her dad brought back that old memory.

"Most of her 'cool' wardrobe was at least a decade out of date. What I remember is being fascinated by her... 'stringy' saliva!" Amelia snorted with laughter.

When the joke was spent, her dad reached over and stroked her cheek. "As hard as it was to see you leave, little girl, I feel my efforts were well-rewarded. You are nothing like your mother."

On the flight home, Amelia smiled as she relived the memories of her two weeks with Dad. If she were honest, she felt displaced by the competent Janet—in his kitchen, in choosing new clothes for him, even in tying his tie. Though it was entirely incorrect in a modern world, she missed tending a man. But those feelings were eclipsed by her joy in seeing her father genuinely happy. She was especially thrilled that he and Janet had been quite agreeable about attending a

Christmas Eve service at a nearby church. The minister had emphasized the name of Jesus, Emmanuel—God with us.

When somebody's grandmother, a heavy, greying woman in a frumpy green print dress, had risen to sing, Amelia had braced herself, knowing her dad's impeccable ear for music. But the contralto's obviously professional, mellifluous voice put all doubts to rest. Her offering of an excerpt from Handel's Messiah was lodged in Amelia's heart. Even now she hummed it to herself: "He shall feed His flock like a shepherd; and He shall gather the lambs with His arm... and gently lead those that are with young." It was the same passage, she now recognized, Anna had offered several months ago when Amelia had been distraught with the guilt of her past.

The flight attendant offered her juice and Amelia shifted her seat back the full two inches of its capability. It made little difference to her cramped legs. Only three more hours to Calgary and the realities of her own life. She would be a single mother. Maternity leave would end before June of the following school year. And after that? Amelia closed her eyes and gave her future to God, as Anna had taught her to do.

He shall feed His flock...

Recalling the conversations Amelia and her dad had had during the holidays about relationships, she now considered another perspective on her own marriage. It pained her to think of Dad throughout the years, doing his wife's bidding, held hostage by her moods, holding his peace. Yet again she pondered her father's statement that she was nothing like her mother. Amelia thought of the years of her marriage, and in a flash of lucidity she saw her husband going along with her plans for the house or for their schedule, held hostage by her moods of grief or depression, holding his peace. Had she, like her mother, been guilty of revisionist history? Of thinking all of the past could be funnelled into a single paradigm—or in her case, a single panicked action?

This point of view was so unfamiliar and so unpleasant that she tried to slam the door on the images. But like the contents of her overfull suitcase, the truth kept popping out. Being forgiven, she would have to forgive her husband. Yet to reconcile with him seemed an act of betrayal of the child she carried. The child *he* had wanted to get rid of. And after all, she had not been the one to leave.

Amelia sat up straighter and breathed deeply. *Perhaps if he contacts me. Maybe then.*

CHAPTER 34

——————⟋ℰ⟍——————

Peace on earth, and mercy mild; God and sinners reconciled.
—Charles Wesley,
"Hark! The Harold Angels Sing"

Sleet slammed against the windshield as Robert left Calgary behind him. At least his flight's noon arrival left plenty of daylight for the hour's drive to Red Deer. Sunset was at about four-thirty this time of year.

He was glad he'd only promised to be in Halifax over the Christmas long weekend. He'd been unable to get any time alone with his father for anything other than the usual question of Robert's earnings and a hint that maybe he should talk to his brother Randall about stocks. His stepsister Trudy's outstanding debt to him rankled all the more now that she was married to an NHL hockey player and freely divulged the plum financial details of his recent contract. Robert enjoyed a good game of hockey as much as anyone, but the dollar value placed on a thug in skates was obscene compared with someone who had sacrificed so much to get an education that would benefit society. Yes, four days with his family was entirely enough.

With Randall spending the holidays in the Bahamas with his wife's family this year, Robert was more than ever an outsider in his father's home. He was old enough now to see that his stepmom and stepsisters and their families didn't mean to shut him out. They were simply absorbed in their own lives. His wife had always been a buffer for him, interpreting him to his family, providing a diversion for him. She had always made him someone by her presence.

Hunched over the steering wheel, he felt his grip tightening. Visibility diminished the farther north he went. Now, big sloppy wet flakes drove mesmerizingly toward him.

Robert was aware that he was only exchanging one scene of loneliness for another. What awaited him at home was miserable in its own way. He wondered what he'd do with himself until classes started on January 4. The thing to do would be to drink himself into oblivion. If only alcohol didn't give him migraines.

Looks like they've had a white Christmas here. He recalled Jesse's eagerness for the white stuff. But before he got to the Red Deer city limits, he suddenly drove out of the snow into bright sunshine. Like coming out from behind a curtain, his glance at the rear-view mirror showed a thick grey-white cloud behind. Around him now, everything was winter brown. *Poor Jesse.* But he could feel his body relax, not having to fight the weather anymore.

He stopped for a few groceries to replace what he knew would be furry and lumpy in his fridge at home. Experiments like these must have given rise to the theory of spontaneous generation.

A white SUV with Louisiana plates and a Ford Taurus rental filled Anna's driveway. Two hockey nets occupied his. Robert parked on the street and was just getting out when a fortyish man in dark-rimmed glasses and a Calgary Flames jersey hurried over from Anna's door to move the sports gear.

"Sorry about these," he said. "You can park up here now."

While Robert moved his Beamer forward, the Flames fan waited to shake hands with him.

"I'm Burk Fawcett. Anna's my mom."

"Robert Fielding."

"Ah, you're the one she's been singing the praises of. I've got to thank you for all you do to help her. She's been telling us some wonderful neighbour has been doing yardwork, chopping firewood. Even taking Jesse to his games. We all appreciate it."

"I'm in her debt. She feeds me twice a week."

"If I know Mom, she'll be wanting you to join us for supper tonight."

"But I really shouldn't intrude."

"No intrusion. Unless you've had enough turkey dinner to last you till next year and would prefer," Burk peered through the thin white plastic of Robert's grocery bag, and looked up grinning. "Hot dogs? No contest!" Robert went indoors and put the groceries into his fridge, then followed his nose through Anna's door that Burk held for him. Turkey and sage and pumpkin scents filled the mild winter air.

"C'mon in and I'll introduce you to everyone," Burk said. He guided Robert through the bright confusion. Bowls of mandarin oranges, nuts, and candy vied with Lego on the coffee table. Errant bits of ribbon, wrapping paper, and toys were strewn around the living room. Faint strains of orchestral music could be heard between the peaks of conversation.

"My brother and lifelong rival, Don." Burk introduced a muscular, pink-faced man with a shaved head.

Don shook Robert's hand in a powerful grip. "Great to meet ya."

"Don is the family dispenser of law, while I," Burk jabbed his thumb into his chest, "am the dispenser of grace."

"I'm the cop, he's the preacher," Don explained, lunging down to intercept a tiny, curly-haired girl crawling speedily toward the glittering Christmas tree. "Not so fast, baby girl." He picked her up and set her atop his shoulders where she hugged his shiny smooth head with both chubby hands and laid her cheek against it.

"He works on the outside of man, I work on the inside," said Burk.

"I chase 'em, you face 'em."

Burk shook his head at that. "I make 'em believe, you make 'em behave."

"Not too shabby," Don said as he pulled the baby girl down from his neck and into his arms. "You thump the Bible, I thump the skulls."

Burk groaned.

"All right, y'all, that's enough." A tall, fine-boned brunette came in from the kitchen.

"My wife, Katie," Burk said, slipping his arm around her waist while she shook Robert's hand.

"Try to ignore these guys. They're always cuttin' up," she said in a soft drawl, her black eyes sparkling.

"What's this? Are these two at it again?" An athletically built blonde with clear blue eyes came in, followed by three little girls in sparkly pink.

"I'm Cassie, by the way. I'm with Don." She put her arm up around him in an attempted headlock. Don eluded her and lay down on the floor where a flurry of pink immediately piled onto him. The big man was completely under the control of his four small daughters. "These are ChelseaAnyaGraceOlivia," Cassie said. "Which is how we always seem to refer to them. And if you think I said that fast, well, that's the way they came."

Anna came in carrying a couple of aprons, scrutinizing them for tears or stains.

"Now you have no more excuses," she said, handing one to each daughter-in-law. She looked up then at Robert, her face glowing with an added joy. "Oh, so you're finally home. I'm glad you came. I see you've been introduced. Now Robert, could I prevail upon you to bring a couple more folding chairs from the basement? And Don, would you mash the potatoes? Supper won't be long."

She seemed to almost skip back to the kitchen followed by Katie,

Cassie, and three of her little girls. Faced with these loving marriages, Robert had begun to keenly sense his single status, so he was grateful to Anna for making him feel right at home with a job to do.

Robert got a preview of the meal as he went through the kitchen. A quick count of the five colourful salads and vegetable dishes alone set his stomach to rumbling. And he spied pies.

Anna had one small granddaughter on a chair beside her, another sitting on the counter on her other side "helping" pour gravy into a china dish. Don wore the littlest one on his shoulders as he mashed vigorously.

In the basement, a leggy young girl with cinnamon braids lay on the floor reading beside the glowing embers in the woodstove. On the couch, a gawky teenage boy sat engrossed in a game on his phone. The boy's cowlick kept the hair out of his eyes in a way Robert envied. He couldn't catch the eyes of either one, so he checked around on his own for the chairs Anna needed. If this basement was laid out like his, the door on the right led to a utility room. Opening it, he found Jesse beside the freezer. Robert had never seen him move so fast, and he couldn't help smiling. The young man was furtively stuffing something into his mouth, pastry crumbs on his lips and one hand behind his back.

"Are you supposed to be eating those, Jesse?" Robert asked.

"I fink so," Jesse said with his mouth full. He slipped by Robert and out the door with the contraband still held behind his back, now in plain sight.

Robert snickered, found the chairs, and followed the trail of crumbs Jesse left as he ate his second butter tart.

Jesse stopped at the couch and tugged on the shirt sleeve of Cowlick Boy. Waiting for his preoccupied young relative to answer him, Jesse looked up at Robert and motioned to the debris on the floor.

"You should clean that up," Jesse told him, then returned to his insistent shaking of the absorbed youth. "C'mon, Caleb. Play UNO with me." Unresponsive, Caleb remained mesmerized by his screen.

"Caleb. C'mon."

If Robert's hands hadn't been full of chairs, he would have prodded the kid. But Burk came down the stairs and seemed to instantly size up the situation. He whispered something in Caleb's ear.

Robert heard, "Aww, Dad..."

"Jesse used to play Ring Around the Rosy with you for hours when you were little," Burk said in a low tone. "Sabrina, you too."

The girl on the floor rose and walked over to a game table without moving the book from in front of her eyes.

Caleb pocketed the phone. "Okay, *Uncle* Jesse. Put me where you want me."

Jesse pulled him over to the table.

Robert brought the chairs upstairs to the now doubled-in-length dining room table. Another family was arriving.

From the melee came Don's voice, "Aaaaand... it's Baby Sister!"

A young woman with unruly blond curls and Anna's blue eyes carried a sleepy miniature of herself in her arms. Burk introduced Robert to Beth and Steve, the sturdy dark husband who followed her, carrying two-year-old twins, Tori and Viv. The girls clutched his collar, looking gravely at the crowd of greeters who had assembled. Hugging ensued and Robert distanced himself to stand near the bookshelf.

It was a marked contrast to his own reunion with family, Robert couldn't help noticing. He'd let himself into his parents' large brick home and, to be fair, this time at least half of the family had directed a nod at him before carrying on their discussion of stock market vagaries. With them it was always as though he were invisible. Just like any repayment from his youngest stepsister of the loan he'd made her eight years ago.

Anna, flitting about, seemed to be everywhere. Food appeared on the table and more on the sideboard. Everyone gathered to sit at the table and Robert was pulled in by Don to sit between him and Anna. A lull signalled Burk to rise.

"Family, food, a bond in Christ—this is as good as it gets, isn't it?" He grinned, his deep-set, hooded eyes, taking in each one in turn. There were murmurs of assent.

"Almost," Robert heard Anna whisper.

Burk turned to her. "Yeah, you're right Mom. We're missing Dad... and David. Let's thank God for what we do have."

When Burk's prayer got around to his brother, he was literally begging God to change David's heart, open his eyes, and bring him back to them.

He prays like he's talking to someone right here in the room. But what's with David?

By the sound of Burk's prayer, the missing brother was refusing to speak to the family and there was a hint of some legal trouble. Robert realized he knew almost nothing of Anna's family and personal life.

When Burk finished and the stir of dinnertime resumed, Anna turned to Robert as she passed the platter of turkey and ham. "You've got a little competition at this meal, eh, Robert?"

"Mom said you've been over here quite a bit this fall," Don said, taking the bowl of glazed carrots from him.

"I clean forgot the stuffing," Anna said, smacking both hands on the table. She sprang up and raced out of the room.

"Spring-loaded, I've always said," Steve remarked, nodding after his mother-in-law. He worked at cutting meat for his girls. One of the twins was persistent in her desire to do her own cutting. With an angry frown and a guttural roar, she snatched the knife away from her father with a swinging motion, and narrowly missed slashing her little brother's cheek. Beth gasped, quickly checking the unscathed baby.

Then she stood abruptly, set him down on Steve's lap, picked up the young knife assassin, and marched purposefully toward the stairs. The startled baby began to cry.

Little Miss Stabber, too, opened her mouth wide and began to wail loudly. "A WAH OU AY WAH EEEE—"

Her howls followed her up the stairs.

"I think that translates into 'Pray for me!'" Steve commented with a wry smile. A wave of heartless laughter erupted around the table.

"Glad the days of spankings are over for us," Burk said

But Jesse suddenly gave vent to a suppressed sob. He hung his head so low it almost touched his plate while his round shoulders heaved with emotion. Katie put her arm around him, murmuring comfort in his ear.

"Jesse is distraught whenever the little ones have to be disciplined," Anna whispered to Robert.

Burk winked at Robert from across the table. "So we were talking about your visits here with Mom. Has she been trying to mend things for you, too?"

Next to Burk, Caleb burst out, "Ha ha, like my jeans, Dad. Remember that?" He shook his head as he plopped a huge mound of mashed potatoes on his already-loaded plate.

"Caleb came to stay here for a month last July," Burk began.

"And," the young lad interrupted, "I always slit my skinny jeans a bit at the bottom so they fit over my shoes. So one day, Oma hands me my stack of laundry and I go to put on the jeans and I'm pulling and pulling. Can't get them on. I look close and there she's sewed up the slits."

"All beautifully done, I might add," said Katie, smiling. "The stitching so neat you can barely see it."

"Mending is good," Steve said with a sly look at his wife who had just returned to the table with the perpetrator, now smiling and good-natured.

Beth lightly backhanded her husband's shoulder. "I'll get to it. Just don't let Mom hear you say that or she'll be over with her sewing machine."

"What about my sewing machine?" Anna came in carrying a large bowl, sage-tinged steam wafting from it.

"Just some snide comments about your mending fetish," said Don. "Is there a spoon for this Jell-O?"

"Oh, I forgot that, too. Be right back," his mom said, rising again.

Cassie pressed Anna back down in her chair. "Oh, no you don't. I'll get it."

"Thank you, dear." Anna looked up at Robert beside her. "What are my kids filling your head with?"

"Apparently you have a reputation for mending. They were wondering if you'd done any for me." He grinned at her as they exchanged glances.

Anna looked away with a knowing smile. "I did ask another neighbour over for supper. I just hope we didn't miss a knock at the door with all this chatter."

"Actually, I thought I did hear something earlier," Burk said. "Do I need to go somewhere and make a personal invitation or something?"

"Oh dear. I'll call Joan and see if she was here already." Anna jumped up and went to the phone. "In the meantime, think of whether you'd like dessert before or after the program you're going to give me."

Robert looked down at Anna's barely touched plate of food, the cost of her caring for others. In this same way she had selflessly served and cared for him through the past five months. Her family seemed to accept their mother with such easy equanimity, but he did not treat lightly the wonder of being seated beside the numinous.

"I'm gonna say it," Jesse announced, taking a plunge into the conversation. He looked around at his brothers and sisters, his eyes bright and glittering.

"What's that, Jesse?" Steve asked.

"We should play games affer supper—all of us." He worked his tongue, managing the long sentence. "We should play UNO."

"A game is a great idea, Jesse. There's one we learned recently that'll be fun for a big group like this," Katie said. Her bracelets tinkled with her bird-like movements as she explained a variation of charades she and her daughter had planned.

"It's called Layers, kind of a combination of Taboo and charades, and you keep taking away more and more clues—"

There was a loud knock at the door. Anna came through from the kitchen to answer it.

Neighbour Joan walked in, scanning the crowd rising from the table, a grim set to her mouth. Beneath her coat, she wore a festive red sweater with matching earrings and carried a thick manila envelope under her arm.

"You said you'd like to see these sometime," Joan said, handing the envelope to Anna, who peeked inside.

Looking up, Anna told the family, "Joan brought some snapshots of her sculptures to share with us." She turned back to her neighbour. "Let me get you a plate of food and you can eat while we pass them around."

She hurried to the kitchen for a plate and Don went to the basement for an extra chair. Sabrina offered to take the twins and their two young cousins downstairs to play.

Uncharacteristically subdued, Joan correctly named each of Anna's children. They introduced their mates and children.

"It's *Dr.* Burk Fawcett now, isn't it? Congratulations." She shook his hand, smiling her rusty smile. Robert wondered who this stranger was and what she had done with his neighbour.

"Ah, someone does read our Christmas newsletter after all," Burk said. "Well, it's still pending, but I finally completed my dissertation."

Joan seated herself and carefully examined the steaming plate Anna had heated for her, using her fork to extract something unwanted from the stuffing. She looked up at Anna. "You know I don't eat anything green," she said, then turned toward Burk. "And what was this dissertation about?"

"It was a bit more involved than we might want to get into right now, but the Cliff's Notes version—Cole's Notes for you Canucks—is that it's a theological study of the role of repetition in the building of bias."

Robert made a mental note to follow up on that with Burk. He couldn't imagine what it had to do with theology, but he'd certainly come up against bias, thinking of his Uncle Stan. And Pat Siggleady.

Joan stared at Burk. "I'll take your word for it." She motioned to the packet she'd brought. "Go ahead and have a look at those."

While the younger women cleared the table and insisted Anna sit and visit, she opened the envelope and exclaimed over the photos it contained. "I haven't seen these before. Oh, Joan, they're amazing! What exquisite detail! Tiny dishes, and even a lace tablecloth."

Arms laden with stacks of plates, Cassie's eyes opened wide as she peeked over her mother-in-law's shoulder. "Like fairy houses. How do you do it with such depth?" she said, nudging Katie's sleeve as she went by. "Look at these."

Taking one of the photos, Robert saw a single log, its bark largely intact. But some of it was cut away to portray the interior of a tiny furnished cottage, intricately carved to the minutest detail. There was, indeed, a lacy relief in wood draped over the small table.

"These are true works of art," he said with admiration to Joan, who glowed with satisfaction. She straightened in her chair, the beginning of a smile softening her face.

"What have you done with these? Were you selling them?"

Before Joan could swallow to answer, Jesse said, "C'mon, le's play a game!"

Robert distinctly heard Joan utter a disgusted "tsk."

"Not yet, Jesse." Anna held up her hand. "Not before I get my program."

They were all drawn toward the living room as Caleb began playing softly on the ancient piano. Anna settled herself on the couch next to him.

Joan, refusing Anna's urging to join the family in the living room, finished eating alone at the table, chary and aloof. As the family jostled for seating, settling little ones, Katie and Sabrina began unpacking their instruments and tuning up. Caleb sat poised and ready. When Burk beckoned Joan over, she stood grudgingly, planting her feet beside the end of the couch, her arms folded.

Robert sat in a rocker next to Joan as Cassie lined up three of her girls and Beth gathered the twins. In ragged unison, they lisped a surprisingly long Bible passage about the birth of Jesus. One of the twins kept eyeing Robert and jerking her head down whenever he smiled at her. But still he could see the deep dimple in one of her cheeks. Little practiced with children, he was buoyed by his success with her. They finished with an earnest rendition of "Away in a Manger."

As the girls scampered to their seats on the floor, Anna prodded Jesse and he stood. With a wide grin almost obscuring his words at times, he recited a Christmas poem.

"Wha' can I give 'im? I'll give 'im my heart." Jesse finished to enthusiastic applause, then bowed deeply. When everyone laughed, he bowed several times more.

"Okay, Jesse. We don't want you getting the big head. C'mere and sit down." Don grabbed his brother around the neck, rubbing the buzzed head with his knuckles.

"Is there anything you have to share with us, Burk?" Anna asked.

Burk reached for a worn leather bag. "I won't lay the whole sermon on you, but there have been a couple of ideas I've been impressed with this season from the account of Christ's birth."

Out of the corner of his eye, Robert noticed Joan's sudden agitation, her hands and feet skittish as a cat. He, too, felt inexplicably unsettled at Burk's mention of that name, but he sternly reminded himself to remain tolerant.

From his bag Burk pulled not a Bible but his lime green laptop. He opened it and scanned the screen, then said, "Luke, the Greek physician—a fellow biologist perhaps," he nodded at Robert, "records that a huge crowd of angelic beings sang, 'Glory to God in the highest, and on earth peace, goodwill toward men.' That's usually taken to mean we ought to treat each other nicely at this time of year, the Christmas spirit and all that. But the word order is no accident. It's important to remember what comes first. 'Glory to God in the highest.' Only when God is honoured and given his rightful place will there be peace on earth. So far, all we've got is God's goodwill toward men in the gift of his Son Jesus to us undeserving sinners. It's up to each one of us to honour God and receive what he offers."

"And what's that?" Joan rasped with heavy skepticism.

Burk looked over at her and smiled. "I was getting to that, Mrs. Klug. What he offers is peace with him if we recognize our failure to meet his standard and if we acknowledge that Jesus has paid the penalty we deserved."

"Hmph," said Joan, taking a step back from the couch she stood beside.

There were a few moments of silence.

Don cleared his throat softly, staring into space. "I wish I could get that across to some of the folks I have to deal with every day. They're usually so full of turmoil and seem to have no clue why."

In the quiet. Robert considered the turmoil of his own life and wondered if he fully knew the reasons for it. He felt an inexplicable inner nudging, but toward what he didn't know, and the sensation made him uncomfortable.

Finally, Anna patted Burk's knee. "Thank you, son. Every year the Christmas story teaches me something new."

There was a rustling at the loveseat near the piano as Katie stood, her violin protected under her arm, now bare of bracelets. "Sabrina and I played this piece for our church Christmas concert. It's an arrangement excerpted from Gloria in Excelsis Deo."

"Tha' means glory to God in the highes'!" Jesse called out.

"You got it," Sabrina said, smiling and tapping her uncle's shoulder with the tip of her bow.

"So, we give you Bach's Gloria in Excelsis Deo," Katie said softly, tucking the violin under her chin.

The moment she and Sabrina touched the strings with their bows, Robert was transported by the swirling harmonies. Golden arching contours of the violin line contrasted with the warm, darker countermelodies of Sabrina's viola.

Watching Anna's face as the mellow sounds of the duet swelled and fell with Caleb's unexpectedly gentle accompaniment, he saw tears clinging to her lashes.

"So beautiful," murmured Cassie when the music finished, leaning on her husband's shoulder, her youngest asleep on her lap.

"Whoa, I guess I should have brought my accordion," Don said, earning himself a sleepy swat from his wife.

"Now games," Jesse said.

"All right, Jesse. Now you kids can play games," Anna said. "I've got to deal with this turkey." She got up and offered Joan her chair, but the woman gave a tight and rapid shake of her head.

"I'm fine here," she said.

Anna brought the poultry carcass out to the table and began removing the meat.

Katie and Sabrina put their instruments away and passed out pencils and papers, explaining the rules.

Jesse was clearly in his element. Looking around at his family, he bounced on the edge of a chair, arms snaking back and forth, wrists flapping, his grin broad.

"Settle down, Jesse," his mother said to him, *sotto voce.*

"I can't settle down!" Jesse said loudly, bouncing harder and giggling long.

From his place on the floor, arms wrapped around Beth in front of him, Steve asked, "Why not?"

"*You* know," Jesse said, looking around at everyone. "Down syndrome!" He glowed as everyone laughed.

As the game progressed, Robert watched Joan as though watching his own alter ego. Both of them, he knew, were tempted to give in to the sheer contrary pull of withdrawing from the group. There was comparative safety on the outside of it, in contrast to the vulnerability of participation. Burk's gently mocking play-by-play made it all the more intimidating.

Sabrina, the first to act, gave an expert performance of her title, "Have Yourself a Merry Little Christmas."

"Miss Sabrina stunned her admiring public with her perceptive interpretation—"

"Da—ad!" Sabrina said.

Don's turn followed, miming, "We Three Kings."

"Officer Fawcett gave a spirited but unconvincing performance..." Burk's commentary was stifled by a cushion to the ear.

"Not in the house, boys," Anna called from the table.

"Still got eyes in the back of your head, eh, Mom?"

"Never forget it, Donald. Never forget it."

Beside Joan, Cassie disentangled herself from her two youngest girls to stand before the family. She made motions indicating there were three words in the title.

"Oh, I won't be doing this, I can tell you." Joan had their full attention as she stalked back to the table and began to gather up her pictures.

"You could just sit and watch if you'd rather, Joan." Wiping her hands on her apron, Anna rose to help her. "And do stay long enough for some dessert."

"No," Joan said, tight-lipped. "Thank you. If you'll just tell me where you've put my coat, I've got to get back to my cats."

Steve went upstairs for the coat while the others stood to say goodbye. Joan nodded at their repeated praises of her art.

"Good night," she said, and added stiffly, "Oh, and thank you for supper."

The door closed against the fast-fallen December night. Anna leaned on the door, looking around at the rest of them and gave a helpless shrug.

"I don't suppose anyone is interested in pie?" she asked.

The living room was abandoned in an immediate rush to the table. Robert had purposed to see the Layers game through despite dreading his turn. He refused to draw attention to himself the way Joan had. But when the little ones were put to bed and Sabrina pulled Anna back to the dining room to fulfill her promise of a game of Scrabble, he tagged along to the table.

Sitting there nibbling a second piece of pumpkin pie, arranging and rearranging his bothersome vowel collection, Robert gleaned soundbites of the living room conversation. There were Stanley Cup predictions and fond reminiscences of a large tribe of guinea pigs from days gone by. When Steve asked about something called "openness of God" theology, Robert was mystified by the fervency of Burk's rebuttal. Robert was asked his opinion about climate change and his answer was listened to thoughtfully. There were toilet-training mishaps recounted, Don's dramatic stories of police life, and tender memories of their father. Steve and Don checked with Robert to settle a dispute about the relative size of grizzly bears.

At the Scrabble board, Anna helped Sabrina find a triple word score for "cap," added to Robert's previous "able." It amused him the way she kept helping her granddaughter, whose score was rapidly outpacing even his own.

The bowls of oranges and nuts diminished down to the dregs. Everyone, including Robert, was blamed for eating *all* the Turtles and leaving *all* the ribbon candy. Anna was scolded for buying hard candy since no one liked it. Someone strongly suspected that the same stuff was reappearing year after year in the interests of frugality.

Anna lifted her chin and replied tartly that if the federal finance minister ran the country the way she ran her home budget, Canada would be carrying no national debt whatsoever.

When Robert finally pushed open his own door at half-past eleven, he was satiated with more than just turkey and chocolate truffles. When he looked in his bathroom mirror, the smile he'd worn most of the evening was still on his face. This evening he'd had a first-hand view of love and constancy, faith and nurturing, warmth and stability. A longing sprang up in him, and with it a sort of unfamiliar goodwill toward men. Then he remembered Burk's admonition that peace with God preceded true goodwill. He didn't know what it meant, but the natural aversion he felt toward the idea puzzled him.

CHAPTER 35

Sole Eve, associate sole, to me beyond Compare above all living creatures dear!
—John Milton, *Paradise Lost, Book IX*

The next day, Robert took a deep breath and opened the research document on his computer. Energized by the stimulation and surge of hope he'd experienced yesterday at the Fawcetts' Christmas celebration, he was determined to sort out the maze of notes and data. If he could ever organize this mess of findings into a respectable research paper, it would be a major achievement toward tenure.

Discovering a colony of Dracula ants so far inland had to be his best prospect yet. Well, it wasn't technically a discovery. For the past three summers he'd studied the colony of these ants that another biologist had discovered on Cortes Island off the coast of British Columbia. It was surprising to find them as far north as Canada. The beginnings of another colony in the western foothills of Alberta was bound to be viewed as astounding serendipity. Of course, he'd helped it along a little. It was easier to watch the colony's progress when he could make frequent visits. But he'd been slowed these last months by pangs of professional doubt. It wasn't kosher, strictly speaking, to plant one's "evidence." Yet the colony was thriving. That was the important part.

Now, however, he was plagued by doubts about the standard

practice of tracking an organism's evolutionary backstory. Was that approach, in fact, begging the question? Anna's questions were getting to him.

But it was high time he made some progress. He could at least be the first to document the phenomenon.

Robert riffled through his notes and in two hours had formed an outline. What was that maxim Anna had tossed out to Jesse when he was balking at having to scrub the pots? "Well-begun is half done." He sat back in his squeaky black office chair. Now he was well-begun. But time was running out in this academic year.

Robert leaned forward again to begin writing and only got the first page done before he quit typing. The trouble with getting down to writing the paper was all the extraneous images the data conjured in his memory. Queen Dracula ants became muddled in his memory with late evening beach trysts. Shiny insect bodies would become eclipsed by the moonlit gleam of his wife's smooth brown thighs until he was mad with throbbing ache for her. It was supposed to have been a working trip, that idyllic coastal retreat last May. She had agreed to accompany him at the last minute. But the rhythm of the surf and sun-induced drowsiness did its age-old work on them. They came together, deadlines forgotten, financial pressures evaporated, perpetual pettiness dissolved. She walked beside him through the dappled forest paths behind their cabin, holding his hand. Small-framed and glossy-haired, smelling of cocoa butter, she dreamed aloud softly as she hadn't done in years.

He'd told her, then, of his constant void. Of course she'd always known of the accident that killed his mother when he was a year old, but now it was a deeper loss he confided: the missing piece in his life that accounted for so much of his striving. She seemed to hear the very longing and loss of his heart and answered it with her own.

"Oh Bobby, Bobby," she'd said, holding his head against her chest, stroking his hair.

Flat on their bellies, they'd watched for long stretches the industrious habits of the ants. The insects would find their favourite food—centipedes—paralyze them and feed them to their larvae. When the adult ants pierced their own larva again and again until they found the soft life-juice they loved to drink, she and Robert stared at each other. He was familiar with these insects' habits, knowing the young would be scarred but unharmed by the practice. But he saw she was horrified, and he knew the memory it brought to mind. They didn't talk of that one stain from their past that would always lie buried between them.

Robert swiped his face with both hands and shook his head. Back to the matter at hand. But a rogue question came to mind. Why *would* the practice of larvae-sucking have begun? It would seem to go against all principles of propagating one's species. A sort of species suicide. After all, that first ant, eons ago, couldn't have known the outcome of doing such a thing.

Taking a deep breath, he vowed to make serious progress in the week before classes resumed.

By noon the next day, he had the skeleton of his first draft written. It was still very rough—there were large gaps to fill in with hard data—but as he leaned back and stretched, his chair squawking loudly, he had squelched the pangs of conscience and felt satisfied.

When he heard shouts outside, he glanced out the window and saw the Fawcett males on the driveway with hockey sticks. A moment later his doorbell rang. It was Burk wanting to know if Robert would come out to even up the teams in a round of street hockey.

Images of junior high Phys. Ed. classes popped into Robert's mind. He reminded himself this wasn't stiff competition, and he didn't have to prove anything. He'd also grown up a bit since those days of being the smallest and scrawniest.

As he watched Jesse trotting behind Don, who was stick handling toward the opposite goal, he said, "Sure, I'll be right out."

When Robert emerged in running shoes, Caleb tossed him an extra stick. Jesse pulled on Robert's sleeve to claim him for his team with Don. Burk, Caleb, and Steve formed the opposition. It wasn't long before jackets and even hoodies were tossed on Anna's brown lawn alongside Steve's baby monitor as they sweated and loped up and down the driveway. On one play, Robert shot wide to the right, but the ball bounced off Jesse's stick right into the net where he stood in position beside it. Whoops of disbelief followed.

"What a fluke!"

"You couldn't do that again if you tried!"

Jesse beamed with pleasure, taking full credit as they slapped his back and tousled his hair.

"You guys were only scoring because of the slope down toward our end," Steve complained with a laugh as they all stopped for a breather. Jesse's face was scarlet and he was puffing loudly.

"Anyone else need a drink?" Robert asked. Everyone nodded and followed him to his place.

He handed out ginger ales and the others, politely leaving the lone kitchen chair, leaned against the counters.

"Drink ginger ale much?" Steve nodded toward the large collection of green cans stacked in a long pyramid down one counter. Robert grinned.

"Good game," Don said, raising his can of pop. There were murmurs of agreement and chuckles.

"I should probably go. Dusty'll be waking up any minute," Steve thanked Robert and headed out the door, baby monitor in hand.

"Yeah, thanks for that," Don said. "I promised I'd pick up my womenfolk from the Ginger Tea Room by 2:30, so I'll see ya later. Wanna come, Jesse?"

The brothers left, arm in arm.

Burk was tipping his drink back for the final drops when Robert said, "I found the idea behind your dissertation intriguing. Something about repetition causing bias?"

"Yeah, a theological study of the role of repetition in the building of bias. I guess you know all about what goes into a dissertation. And then the pressure of defending it." Burk said. "So I take it you've come across your share of bias?"

"Not so much in my academic field."

"No, I wouldn't expect so," said Burk.

The note of irony in his tone puzzled Robert.

"But what was it that resonated with you?" Burk asked.

"There's a character in the neighbourhood here who's convinced the end is near." Robert was conscious of Caleb watching, listening, his drink forgotten. "The guy has a lot of conspiracy theories all jumbled together into a doomsday scenario. The worst of it is, the people he's influencing will get all fearful, waste their money trying to prepare for something that'll never happen, and probably even spread these ideas around."

"According to my research," Burk said, "there's a direct correlation between multiple expressions of an idea and an underlying mindset or set of presuppositions. The more we hear and speak an idea, the more convinced of its truth and importance we become. That's true on an individual level, as well as societally. And while that's fine when the idea is truth, it's a big problem when the idea is mere speculation—or worse, outright falsehood. It's frightening, actually, the speed with which the unthinkable can become thinkable."

Robert nodded, knowingly. "Like racial hatred, as an example?"

"Yes, that. But on other fronts as well," Burk said, hesitating a moment. "It isn't just the ignorant and uneducated who succumb to this, you know."

"Meaning?"

"Bias and unfounded presuppositions are alive and well in academia."

"Give me an example."

"Well," Burk began, carefully setting his pop can on the line-up of other cans. Caleb added his to the stack. "One example I dealt with in my dissertation was the complete turnabout that's occurred in universities regarding belief in God. Just to verify, let me ask you this: do you think belief in a deity is the predominant view at your college, or any of the institutions you're familiar with?"

Robert thought for a moment. "I don't really know what the beliefs of the faculty are."

"Which actually makes my point. So you don't know what their beliefs are on an individual level because—?"

"Because what?" Robert shrugged.

"Why is it you don't know?"

"I suppose because it never comes up. But what do you mean, it makes your point?" Robert cocked his head to one side and folded his arms.

Caleb moved closer to his dad and Burk put his arm around the boy's shoulders.

"Culturally we've come to think of belief in God as a solely private matter—something that ought not to be discussed openly. That's a dramatic difference from the days when such beliefs were a matter for intense public discourse," Burk said. "The topic never comes up, as you said, because it's been relegated to the irrelevant. And yet what a person believes about God has huge ramifications in how they live their life."

"I wouldn't know about that. But how does that have anything to do with 'the role of repetition in the building of bias'?"

"Simply put, for a few generations now, the culture has been told that God is an out-of-bounds topic. It may have begun as a well-intentioned way to avoid conflict in polite society, but it's ended up creating a taboo. What I discovered in the course of my work was that the major universities in Canada and the U.S. were begun as Christian schools, seminaries for training ministers. But over time, those convictions were eroded to the point that at present, there's case after case showing they are now clearly hostile to Christianity."

"Don't you think 'hostile' is a bit melodramatic?"

"Tell you what, why don't you give me your email and I'll send you my work if you like. That's only one of many examples of bias I found, and interestingly, most of them centred on institutes of higher learning." Burk smiled, pulling himself away from the counter. "Great game, though, and thanks for the drink, Robert." He waited while Robert tore a strip off the back of an envelope and scribbled his email address. Taking it, Burk tapped Caleb's shoulder with his knuckle and said, "Let's go, son. We've got some packing up to do before dinner."

CHAPTER 36

―――――― ∾ ――――――

*...to the lookers-in from outside, the inmates, gathered round the
tea-table, absorbed in handiwork, or talking with laughter
and gesture, had each that happy grace which is the last thing the
skilled actor shall capture—the natural grace which goes with
perfect unconsciousness of observation.*
—Kenneth Grahame, *The Wind in the Willows*

"What do you think?" Beth asked as she and her mother walked
Amelia through the sparsely furnished rooms of the home Steve and
Beth had just bought. "Mom's been telling me you have a gift for home
design, so I purposely haven't hung any pictures or unpacked very
much. I wanted your opinion."

Turning around a few times, Amelia surveyed the living room
thoughtfully. From Anna she'd been learning to make use of what one
already had. For a moment she blocked out the navy couch, light oak
tables, and neat stacks of cardboard boxes piled in one corner as she
took stock of the room's fixtures. A stone fireplace was centred in a
cedar-planked wall with high octagonal windows. An adjacent wall
featuring a large expanse of floor-to-ceiling windows partly covered
by dark green and pink floral drapes and rust-coloured carpet formed
the basic skeleton of the room. On the front entry wall opposite the
fireplace, a mirror-tile bullfighter fought his bovine foe on tiptoe.

She turned to Beth. "Tell me what you love about the room."

Beth told her that the windows, with their view of the valley, and the fireplace were their favourite features.

"Then you won't be offended if I suggest removing the drapes and the matador?"

Beth laughed. "If I knew those mirror tiles would come off without destroying the wall, they'd have been gone already. He's giving me nightmares!"

Amelia walked a little closer to the offending tiles. "They might just pop off by prying a bit with a small trowel." She turned back to Beth. "Can you give me an idea of how far you're willing to go with decorating?"

"You mean budget-wise?"

"That, and how much effort you're willing to make, how much disruption you're willing to put up with, how radical you're willing to be in terms of change and innovation..."

Beth grinned at Amelia. "So what are you thinking? Dynamite?"

"No, no. The room actually has good bones. Let me be a little more specific. Have you thought about replacing the carpet?"

Beth nodded vigorously. "We definitely want to put in hardwood floors, but I can't see that happening right away. Maybe not for a couple of years."

"Have you checked underneath the carpet? A house of this age actually might have had hardwood originally."

Beth's eyes brightened. "That'd be great! I'll get Steve to take a look."

"How about paint?"

"Oh, we can paint. No problem with that."

"What about painting the woodwork and the cedar on that wall?"

Beth turned to look at the empty bookshelves on either side of the fireplace and the cedar above them. "Hmmm. Steve liked the wood." She eyed her mother. "This may call for a little of the art of subliminal suggestion, eh, Mom?"

Anna shifted Dusty on her hip, pulling his chubby hand away from her glasses, and smiled at the younger women. "It's very effective."

Amelia looked from one to the other, confused.

"You whisper your idea in your husband's ear a few nights in a row just as he's falling asleep," Beth explained, "and eventually he thinks it's his own idea and suggests it back to you."

Amelia studied Beth's laughing face, incredulous. "And this actually works?"

"Well, it's more of a joke in our family," Anna said. "But it is a playful way to let a man know something you'd like without nagging. You catch more flies with honey than you do with vinegar, dear."

Searching for something to say that wouldn't sound self-pitying or bitter, the lump in Amelia's throat grew. Anna must have noticed her eyes beginning to swim. The older woman engulfed Amelia in an embrace soon shared by Beth.

"I'm always praying for reconciliation between you and your husband, dear," Anna told her, patting her back. Amelia kept silent, fearful of the futility of that prayer.

Dusty squirmed in the midst of them.

"Come on, let's have a cup of tea and you can tell me all the latest from your visits with your midwife," Beth said, leading the way to the kitchen where tangy aromas of maple and tomato came from a crockpot. "Mom, could you put Dusty down for a nap? He may need a change first."

"With pleasure. Shall we go off to Dreamland, little man?" Anna carried the baby down the hall. "Dreamland Express! Chugga, chugga, chugga—choo-choo!"

Baby giggles wafted back to the kitchen.

"The midwife says baby's heart rate is good and strong and I'm measuring just right for my due date. There's certainly a lot of movement in there," Amelia told Beth.

"Sounds great. You might even be a candidate for a home birth."

"Oh, I don't think I'd want to try that for my first birth. The birthing centre Sherry works from gives me the best of both worlds—limited intervention but all the bells and whistles ready in case of an emergency. But hey, if you've got a pen and paper, I'll jot down some ideas for your living room."

Beth directed her to a drawer and Amelia sat down at the table.

"I'd say paint the woodwork a creamy white," Amelia said as she wrote. "If not throughout the house, at least the mantel and the fireplace wall. I'm thinking a soft grey with a blue undertone for the other walls would tie in with your navy couch."

Anna returned to the kitchen and shooed Beth to the table while she finished making the tea.

"Next you could buy an area rug, something you'd want for the longterm. From that you could pull an accent colour. Something like lime-green or orange for cushions and curtains would really pop against the navy and it would be easy to switch out later if you wanted." Amelia looked up to find Beth staring at her, eyes twinkling, mouth open. "What?"

"I thought you were an English teacher. Where did you learn to do this?"

Anna came around from the other side of the counter with a tray of steaming cups of Rooibos tea. She sat down with the younger women, covering Amelia's hand with her own. "Amelia is a woman of many talents."

"It's always been something I loved," Amelia said. "When I was about ten, I desperately wanted a dollhouse. I'd never been allowed to play with dolls, but I figured the house might be okay with my mom since I wouldn't be rocking babies or anything." She noticed identical sad and sympathetic looks on her friends' faces. "I begged and begged my mom and she finally agreed to let me have one. But only if I read through a textbook on architecture. She was hoping I'd find my way into a respectable career that way. The book was way over my head, but I loved the pictures and diagrams, so one thing kind of led to another and I've been reading design and decorating magazines ever since."

Beth took the paper and read it over, shaking her head with a smile. "I can picture it. Yeah, this is great. We can do it." She looked up at Amelia. "What about using both those colours, lime and orange?"

Amelia laughed. "I tend more toward the monochromatic myself, but I think the brights would suit you. And it'd be fun for the kids."

Steve burst through the back door just then, carrying a squealing upside-down twin under each arm. He set them down and began undoing jackets. The pink-cheeked girls were chattering unintelligibly about their walk in the woods.

At dinner later, Amelia was thrilled to feed small Dusty his version of the simple beans and Boston brown bread meal Beth had prepared. She laughed at her own self-consciousness when Steve teased her for her inability to offer the baby a spoonful without opening her own mouth.

When the meal was finished, Beth hovered over the twins who, with miniature hands, delivered plates one at a time to the dishwasher. Steve cleaned Dusty's face and took him to the family room couch, submitting to the moist mauling only a baby can give.

Anna had asked Amelia to drive on the way home, the moonlit winter night enveloping them snugly in the car's warm interior. She carried with her the memory of the beauty of the children, the bright, clear whites of their eyes and their pearly small teeth reminding her of the little Chiclets gum squares she used to buy as a child. Envy rose graspingly as Amelia considered Beth's devoted husband and happy home. With an effort, she fought it down.

"Thanks for inviting me. I'd expected a dismal New Year's Eve, but it's been great. I love your family," she told Anna, quite truthfully.

"I'm glad, Amelia," Anna said quietly. "I am so grateful for them. They are a great comfort to me now that Gerry is gone."

They had ridden in silence a few kilometres when Anna made a suggestion. "Have you ever considered starting a business? Something like private tutoring or home decor consulting?"

Amelia turned to her in surprise. "It never occurred to me."

Anna's look was all encouragement. "That might be a way to stay with your baby but still make an income after your maternity leave is up. You definitely seem to have a talent for design."

As Amelia mulled over the idea, she began to see new possibilities. The chart on her fridge *was* showing progress on her debt repayment—she was, in fact, ahead of schedule. If she could pay it down until her monthly expenses only comprised half of the mortgage payment, her car payment, food, and utilities, then her salary requirements would be considerably less. And there would be time to transition. She could contact furniture stores where they were familiar with her from her frequent solitary meanderings and build a clientele. Perhaps she could start a blog.

Suddenly their headlights revealed the towering figure of a bull moose, looming large and dark on the deserted highway. Amelia slammed on the brakes, throwing both her and Anna hard against their seatbelts. Adrenaline surged through her. She pulled to the right and stopped the vehicle on the shoulder to calm her hammering heart.

Anna's hands were outstretched to the dash.

The moose stood immobile to her left, far above their small car, its dewlap quivering as it turned its unwieldy head and casually strolled off the road.

"Oh, these moose!" Anna said. "They're downright pesky the way they think they own the road"

Tension and the incongruity of calling the huge animal a pest made Amelia laugh nervously. She leaned her head back against the seat and closed her eyes as she exhaled deeply.

Anna patted her arm. "Those critters can do serious damage. Thank the Lord he kept you vigilant and us safe. But I do need to get back before Yanni brings Jesse home from floor hockey."

Seeing headlights coming up behind them, Amelia put the car in gear. As she drove away, she realized, by the trembling of her knees, that the incident had shaken her for more reasons than the obvious. It brought back a similar event that had taken place one spring night four years earlier. Gradually her heart slowed to a normal pace and she was able to tell Anna about it. She and her husband had been coming home from Edmonton and had taken a detour to avoid what looked like a lengthy delay caused by a major accident on the highway ahead.

"If it hadn't been for the grid of these prairie roads, we would have ended up seriously lost. Somewhere out here on a gravel road, a doe sprang up in front of us. We stopped suddenly, just like tonight, only to see a tiny newborn fawn by the edge of the road, still wet. And when the doe turned away, we saw this huge red splash of afterbirth dangling behind her. It was so weird—I couldn't understand why she would start to run away from her own baby. I kept insisting we should do something to help the poor little fawn, but my husband said no, we would just make matters worse if we interfered. You see, opposite the fawn on the other side of the road, he'd seen this pair of glittering green eyes. It was a coyote, and the doe was running away from the fawn to draw it after her."

Amelia lapsed into silence, remembering the sheer vulnerability of the doe's condition, giving birth alone and in danger. She hadn't thought of that night in years. She knew emotional reactions to events like this were common fare in pregnancy, but now it preyed on her mind.

"Amelia?"

"Yes?"

"Remember, you won't be alone when your time comes."

Anna's reassurance was comforting, yet she couldn't help wondering what lay before her. "Seems like a day doesn't go by that I don't think about the life I took and wonder if because of that, this baby's life will be taken from me."

"Mm-mm. That isn't how God works with his beloved ones." Anna reached over and stroked Amelia's arm. "Remember, He doesn't punish us as our sins deserve."

Amelia pondered the depth of that grace, the opposite of the tit-for-tat way she tended to think. "I know, I know. Whenever I start on that path, eventually I hear your voice telling me that He gently leads those who are with young."

CHAPTER 37

⁓

But keep the odds of knowledge in my power...
And render me more equal, and perhaps
A thing not undesirable, sometime Superior; for, inferior, who is free?
—John Milton, *Paradise Lost, Book IX*

The minute Anna opened the door to Joan, her phone rang. "I'll just get that quickly. It may be my daughter-in-law." She hurried out of the room.

It irritated Joan to have her welcome cut short by one of Anna's many phone calls. The woman always seemed to be on the phone. Joan didn't waste time that way. And the daughter-in-law had just spent a week here recently. What more could they possibly have to talk about so soon? Joan had been looking forward to a quiet visit with her friend now that Anna's family had finally left, and she resented being put on hold.

She glanced around the tidy living room. "A clean house is the sign of a small mind," wasn't that what they said? Joan didn't have time for constant cleaning; there were more important things in life. The low winter sunlight streamed through the wide south window, highlighting a couple of streaks on the glass.

Fragments of Anna's phone conversation wafted in from the kitchen.

"...he may not be ready to consider that. There are always two sides to every story, remember... I can understand how you would want to do that, but please dear, never forfeit the important for the urgent... Sometimes the least said is easiest mended."

At that moment, Jesse came down the stairs and attempted to help Joan off with her coat. "No, Jesse, I'll keep my coat on. I won't stay long."

Head hanging, Jesse slunk out of the room.

When Anna bustled back into the living room, Joan asked her who had been on the telephone. Anna halted midstride, her eyes casting about the room and finally returning to Joan's face. "Just someone who needed a shoulder to cry on."

"I never had a shoulder to cry on. Nobody knows all I've been through. People didn't seem to want to listen when *I* had troubles. Someone even told me, 'You know, you could pay someone to listen to your problems.'"

"I'm so sorry to hear that," Anna said, her eyebrows knit up in sympathy.

"I know why that is. It's because I look strong. So I just became a listener for other people. Lots of people have cried on my shoulder over the years, I can tell you." She scrutinized Anna's face closely for her reaction to this.

"That's sometimes the best help you can give them," Anna said simply. "Come sit in the kitchen and I'll make you a cup of coffee. Or would you prefer tea?"

"Not that anyone ever took my advice," Joan added, following her into the next room. She sat on a low-backed stool. "I'll have the coffee."

Anna began filling the coffeemaker with water as Joan took in the multitudinous family photos and grandchildren's drawings on the refrigerator. Joan always wondered how Anna managed to open the fridge with all that paraphernalia hanging on it. On the small kitchen counter were snippets of paper with Bible verses written on them and envelopes bearing return addresses involving the words *Christian* and *Bible*. She shifted her gaze to a plant on the windowsill that looked like it could use some water.

"I see you still haven't finished those curtains you were talking about making," Joan said.

"The curtains? Oh, for the kitchen. No, I haven't even thought about them yet. The fabric's still sitting upstairs in my sewing room."

"Well, it can't be all that complicated. I've been able to finish refurbishing two boxes full of clothes so far this winter. What have you been doing with all your time?"

The bitter-brown aroma of coffee began to mingle with spice as Anna thawed two cinnamon buns in the microwave. "Well, I.... I mean—"

"I had quite the incident last week with my daughter, Doris." Joan interrupted. "She finally called me. It's been months since I heard from her. She and Louise were coming through from Calgary. Of course, Michelle wasn't with them—I'm not speaking to her." Another mopey look from Anna made Joan hurry on. "That's how we do it in my family. When we don't approve of someone's actions, we make sure they know it so they can change. Anyway, Doris and Louise said to meet them at Walmart. So I walked all the way up there—"

"You walked? That's amazing! It's at least six blocks." Anna placed a steaming cup and warm bun in front of Joan and another for herself at the counter.

"Of course I walked. I'm not a rich farmer's wife like you are. Anyway, I get close to them and I see they're watching me and laughing. Then as soon as I get right up to where they are, they stop." She stared at Anna, waiting, while sipping her coffee.

"I don't know what you mean."

"They were laughing *at* me."

"Oh surely not."

"I think I can tell when I'm being made fun of, Anna." Feeling too warm, Joan took off her coat and laid it across the low back of her stool. "They stopped laughing as soon as I got there."

"Could there be any other reason why they'd do that?"

As if Anna would know. "Look, I know my own daughters. I know them well enough to know that's just what they would do. They've never had any respect for me."

She hated to admit it to Anna, whose kids were so perfect, but it was true, and Joan had always been honest to a fault. Yet she was not about to share the rest of the content of her daughters' diatribe against her—some sort of "cathartic confrontation," Louise had called it, along with ridiculous accusations that Joan had never told them she loved them. If feeding them and housing them all those years wasn't enough, nothing was.

"Things are not always as they seem," Anna said. "I have sometimes thought someone intended to offend me and later found out that's not what they meant at all."

Anna never misses a chance to preach. "You've always had it so easy when it comes to kids," Joan said. She was surprised to see tears spring into Anna's eyes. *Oh no, I hope she's not going to start blubbering. I can't cope with that kind of negativity.* Joan surged ahead. "But you have no idea what I've been through with my three."

After a deep breath and a fluttering of eyelids, Anna asked, "Did you have lunch with your daughters? Or shop?"

"I can't stand shopping. All those big businesses with their useless junk, trying to suck the last dollar out of us seniors on fixed incomes. No, the girls wanted to go out for lunch, so they chose the restaurant."

"Well, that was nice of them."

"I didn't say they paid." Joan quaffed her coffee, watching Anna carefully to see if she'd enjoy the little joke. As usual, her neighbour just sat there owl-eyed. The woman really had no sense of humour.

Anna took a long drink and slowly put down her World's Greatest Grandma mug. "It's been wonderfully mild this winter, hasn't it? I'm enjoying just zipping out without getting all bundled up."

"You obviously haven't been out this morning like I have. My daughters didn't even offer me a ride home, so I ended up walking both ways." Joan bit into her warm cinnamon bun. *Not too bad.* "The thermometer sure knows it's winter. I thought the wind would pick me up and carry me across the prairies. We'll probably have a big dump of snow all at once. I remember one year we had all our snow in May. But it's not good for the trees and perennials to be exposed like this all winter. They dry out so bad."

"I've been reading that mulching can help," Anna said.

"It can if you have someone to help you do it. I don't. My daughters never help me with things like that." Joan took another sip of her now lukewarm coffee. "But I guess I'm glad they have their own lives. I raised them to be strong and independent. When I was young, I swore I'd never end up like the women back home—baking bread and taking care of babies. But I'd had all three of the girls before I read *The Feminine Mystique.* That's when I woke up to reality."

"And what reality was that?" Anna looked at Joan intently, carefully unrolling her cinnamon bun.

"That book helped me realize I couldn't stay with that worthless man. That and a lot of other things."

"Such as?"

"Such as, that washing diapers and cooking and cleaning was a waste of my life. That I couldn't teach my daughters that's all there was to a woman's life. So I started saving some money out of the grocery budget so I could leave. Of course before I had the chance, Norm had to go and shoot himself."

Anna's eyes opened wide and the hand holding her teacup froze midway to her mouth.

"I thought I told you about that," Joan said.

"I had understood it to be an accident," Anna said, putting down her cup and placing her hand on Joan's arm. "I'm so very sorry, Joan."

"You have no idea what I've been through." Joan pulled her arm from under Anna's hand. "It was a terrible shock. In the head he did it. It was an awful mess to clean up, I can tell you that much. But it's all water under the bridge at this point. In a few months the initial shock wore off, and I've got to say, I never felt so free. It was the best time of my life. "

"I wonder if your daughters would say the same thing."

Joan glanced at Anna sharply. Her tone had been gentle, but the words stung. "That it was the best time of their lives? Probably not. The stomach aches they used to get. Of course there was no life insurance, you know. Not for a suicide. I figure he did it on purpose just to spite me. See, if Norm had lived, I would have at least had child support. As it was, I got nothing. But I guess all those hard times were good for the girls. They got to learn things about life—how hard it is to make a living, how there's no free lunch, how we've got to pull ourselves up by the bootstraps if we want to survive. And my daughters have never been any man's slave. At least that much I did right." She picked up her jacket.

"The years of raising children go by so quickly, don't they? Even though the days were long at the time. And then we have the quiet of these later years to evaluate our parenting." Anna set down the remaining half of the cinnamon roll. As she did so, an errant raisin in the moist, dark centre fell away, sticking to the edge of her plate precariously. She stared at it, deep in thought. "As memories of my mistakes come to mind, I find myself often begging forgiveness, either from my children or from—"

"Everybody makes mistakes, Anna. There's no point in going over and over them," Joan said, swinging her jacket around her shoulders.

What she didn't need right now was a sermon. "But I really must get back to my babies. They never want me to be away from them for very long. Oh, and the coffee wasn't too bad. It's hard to get a good cup these days."

Anna left the counter and followed Joan to the front door. She must have seen her neighbour wince as she bent to zip her worn winter boots. "Can I help you with those?"

"I've been doing for myself all my life, Anna. I can manage just fine." Joan zipped the second boot and straightened, willing herself not to betray her stiff joints.

She buttoned her jacket tight against the wind. Walking down Anna's driveway to the sidewalk, she was careful not to walk on anyone's grass. She, for one, had some respect for other people's property. Unlike those brats who had lived next door to her and had worn a bare path across her front lawn on their way to school every day. Thank goodness they'd moved out. It had cost her far too much to put up that fence to prevent further damage.

On the way home, Joan found herself buoyed by some intangible inner shifting, like the dissipating pop of steam that lifts the lid of a simmering pot. It was always good to give vent once in a while to some of what percolated within her.

Opening her door, she was greeted by her adoring public, who swarmed around her legs with joyful meows. A blustery day like this was the perfect day to be indoors. And fresh home-made bread would be just the ticket. Yes, she felt expansive enough to bake a couple of nice loaves of multigrain bread. Maybe she'd even bring one over to her old friend Anna.

CHAPTER 38

———~———

How guilt once harbour'd in the conscious breast
Intimidates the brave, degrades the rest.
—Samuel Johnson, *Irene: A Historical Tragedy,* Act IV

On the first January morning of the new semester, Robert arrived early at the college. He had sheared away thick frost on his windshield as his breath came out and hung in opaque white puffs. In the blue of the morning streetlight, every detail was enrobed in a fur of hoar frost. It spiked out from every twig and blade in the dry, prairie cold.

Despite the time he had spent scraping, he was still so early that his feet made the first melted marks in the virgin frost on the sidewalk. At the main entrance, he slid his ID card to unlock the door.

Once inside, he checked his phone and realized that without his glasses this morning he'd misread the time. Robert was encouraged that, like a downward coast to spring, the days would begin to get noticeably longer in just a couple of weeks.

His shoes squeaked loud on the glossy, newly polished corridor floors, emphasizing his aloneness. He began unbuttoning his brown leather jacket. One of the buttons dangled limp. Perhaps Anna could—

Robert was arrested by the vivid, bloody colours of a large poster on the wall just outside the science department's main complex of offices. Assaulted might be a more accurate term. "Choice is..." the poster read, and flaunted a graphic and gruesome photo of an infant, its skin glistening as it lay on a surgical tray. Lying next to forceps and the other steel tools, the tiny body was incomprehensibly perfect with its finely etched eyebrows, intricately coiled ears, and requisite fingers and toes. Yet a red-raw gash violated its abdomen. And one of its arms had been severed, then replaced close to the body.

A wave of revulsion came over him. The picture tugged at something in the recesses of his memory. He stood rooted, eyes locked on the picture, repulsed yet fascinated.

When he heard the distant sound of voices and footfalls, he knew he must act. Furtively, hurriedly, like one caught committing an atrocity, he snatched the top edge of the poster. He seized and pulled at the heavy paper. Again the body of the tiny child was torn. Robert tasted bile. Stubbornly, the corners attached by thick tape remained fixed and he had to pull them off one by one. He crumpled the whole despicable thing into a tight irretrievable ball.

Then he wondered if he should have done so. He may have destroyed evidence, yet he couldn't leave such offensive material for someone vulnerable to discover. Someone like Sarah-Mae. The staccato clip of high heels signalled her approach and Robert opened the Science Cluster door for her, stuffing the crumpled paper under his jacket.

She stopped squarely in front of him, a huge expectant smile on her face.

"You'll never guess, so I'll just have to tell you," she began, peeling off her yellow suede gloves and unwinding her fuzzy matching scarf. She paused for effect, eyes shining. "I met someone during the break!"

Oh no. Not another deadbeat. Robert let go the door and followed her to his office where she leaned in the doorway.

Sarah-Mae held up a hand. "And before you say anything, he's *not* another deadbeat."

She slipped off her coat, hung it on the coat-tree, then turned back toward Robert's office. He stood, still holding the jacket draped over his right hand, and awkwardly set his briefcase on the desk.

"He's my granny's nurse. Gran took a fall and broke her hip on Boxing Day, so a lot of our Christmas was spent in the hospital. That's how I met Glen. He was so kind and gentle with Gran," she said with a half-smile. "We've been out three times and he treats me great."

She twisted her hands together in front of her, raising her shoulders in a girlish shrug.

"Congratulations," Robert said, his jacket still hanging from his arm.

"Thanks." She threw him a wry sidelong glance and started back to the reception desk, then paused. "And that little package you have hiding there under your jacket, Dr. Fielding?"

He started guiltily, but she was smiling.

"Don't worry about it—no need to share. You couldn't tempt me with doughnuts today if you tried. I'm way too excited to eat." She swung back to her desk to start the day.

Robert stuffed the ball of paper into his wastebasket and dropped another crumpled sheet on top.

He'd begun to think he may have averted a crisis when in passing the Student Centre on the way to the lecture theatre for his first class, he heard a kerfuffle. More posters were the centre of attention there. He quickened his pace. It was someone else's worry. He didn't need any more drama today.

But by late afternoon, the worry dropped unbidden into his lap again. He'd been summoned to meet the department head and was just arriving when out of Dr. Baldwyn's office came Phil Thiessen. The lowered brows and tightened corners of his mouth may have said more than Phil intended. Apprehension pressed at Robert's imagination regarding this meeting. Thiessen, uncharacteristically, said nothing as he strode by.

Dr. Baldwyn came right to the point. "You are aware, no doubt, of the dilemma the college faces as a result of certain posters found on display this morning."

Robert nodded.

"This raises a bit of a ticklish problem," the big man said, staring down at his knobby hands spread out on the desk before him.

"Ticklish? How so?"

Dr. Baldwyn studied Robert from under fringed brows.

"Dr. Fielding, think about it. The controversial nature of these posters has already aroused media attention. Were you under the impression that they could simply be removed and tossed in the recycle bin without raising the issue of students' freedom of expression? No, no, something must be done. Which is why I am asking you to step into a recent vacancy on the college ethics committee. Rather than create an adversarial situation, we have need of a voice of moderation."

Waves of relief and then alarm came over him in turn. Phil, he knew, must represent the "recent vacancy." Replacing him would be part of the ticklish situation. It put Robert in a bad way with his friend, certainly. He knew, too, that three women comprised the ethics committee together with Jamie McCoy, a prospect that did nothing to sweeten the appointment for him.

Baldwyn's gaze had not wavered. "I trust you to bring balance and reason to the committee's deliberations." The brows rose in question.

"I'll do my best," Robert answered, doubting his best would be adequate but elevated by Baldwyn's confidence in him. And he felt a prick of conscience at the irony of his appointment to the college ethics committee, given his research project manipulations.

His fears had not been unfounded. After classes, Robert arrived at the office of Fran Dorne, the fiftyish, pinched, and narrow English professor. A cloying, sweet smell overwhelmed him. Every inch of wall space was covered with art prints and photos, feminist posters and slogans. Three pairs of female eyes—Fran, Deb Smythe from Trades, and Business prof Penny Ollender—appraised him briefly. From behind three Earth goddess statuettes and the burning Moonflower candle on her desk, Fran nodded at a chair near the door. Robert shifted a short stack of books and papers from the chair to the floor in order to sit down. He glanced down, waiting for McCoy, and idly turned over the topmost book. *The Vagina Monologues.* He dropped it as though scalded.

Staring at him with one eyebrow raised, Fran turned and whispered something to the well-upholstered young woman beside her, whose corresponding stage whisper was unmistakeable.

"And there's more testosterone coming."

Jamie McCoy swept into the room, rubbing his hands together as though arriving at a potluck. "G'day mates!" he announced. He was impervious to the hostility on Fran's face.

When everyone was settled, Penny, dressed for success in a tan pantsuit, flicked back her shiny black hair, sending a tang of spicy fragrance to compete with the heavily scented candle.

She opened a thin folder on the slim briefcase perched on her lap and without introductions or preliminaries convened the meeting. "I'm entirely unclear as to why this committee has been required to meet in this case." She kept her eyes fixed on the two women across the desk from her. "It seems a rather straightforward matter. The offensive posters have been removed and the students responsible have been caught." She picked up a paper from the folder and scanned it with a frown. "I suppose our role is to recommend an appropriate discipline."

Fran leaned forward. "Immediate suspension. These students have committed an absolutely abhorrent act and we must send a clear message that the college will not be manipulated by what amounts to visual terrorism."

"Deb?" Penny nodded at the younger woman.

Deb's ponytail mimicked her nod. "The posters *were* incredibly disturbing."

The conversation had volleyed between the women as if they were alone in the room, but now McCoy cleared his throat. Fran eyed him with open suspicion.

"These kinds of shock tactics are used when a small vocal minority understands they've lost the ideological battle but they've decided to keep on fighting simply because they're mad about having lost." His words met with grudging acceptance and the women let out a collective breath. "The fact is, there *are* abortions and they're legal, so the losing side will just have to get used to disappointment."

"So what's your recommendation on how to deal with our culprits?" Penny asked him.

"Oh, I'm absolutely in favour of suspension," McCoy said. "Indefinitely. We can't be too strong on this point. The college will not tolerate these subversive acts and there must be consequences for violators."

The word "tolerate" triggered a chafing within Robert. Dr. Baldwyn's expectations of him and his own need for logical consistency urged him to offer another perspective.

He took a breath. "There have been shocking images displayed here before. Amnesty International's presentation on worldwide human rights violations last May would be just one example. That eye-opening lecture resulted in some valuable discussion—"

"That's totally different." snapped Fran, startling Deb who had been listening to Robert with interest.

"Apples and oranges," Penny said.

"Comparing other people's suffering to the life-saving blessing of legal abortion is an insult to the real victims of human rights abuses." Fran said. "Besides, some of the photos on these posters may actually depict natural miscarriages or still births, and others are so old that they date to the days when abortion was illegal."

This scrap of irrationality did nothing to build Robert's confidence in her argument. The hole in her logic was the inescapable fact that, much as he hated to contemplate it, the pictures showed *mutilated, dead human beings.*

"To my knowledge, human biology has not changed in the last hundred years and the results of an abortion then would certainly be the same today," he said with a perverse pleasure in playing the opposition.

"Whose side are you on?" Fran shot him a look that sliced through his calm detachment.

Robert felt again the accustomed futility of trying to talk a thing out. He certainly hadn't intended to sound as though he were on the anti-abortion side. And he had no wish to further incur the wrath of the woman. Placed as he was by Baldwyn to be an advocate of moderation and tolerance for freedom of expression—at least that was how he'd interpreted it—he attempted a change of course.

"If these students are expelled, we make them martyrs for a cause and the college then becomes guilty of suppression of free speech," he said. "Something that won't play well in the media."

Worry sprouted on the women's foreheads, but McCoy was quick to rejoin. "This is an internal matter that I think can be handled quietly and without fanfare."

"But they're activists. Isn't media coverage exactly what they're after?" Penny asked. "They obviously have no fear of publicity, so it's doubtful they'll quietly submit to losing their academic year."

"Expulsion is most definitely what is called for in this case," McCoy said, "and I think the media is generally on our side in the issue, so I doubt there's anything to fear."

"You've got to admire their courage for an unpopular cause," Deb said.

There was a stunned silence. McCoy, Penny, and Fran shot her looks of such contempt, she blushed.

"Look," Fran said, "our role is simply to make recommendations. We can do that in the strongest possible terms, and from there it's up to the disciplinary board to implement them. And I may still have a little influence with at least one of those board members." She gave a tight smile. "We've made our decision, so I'll write up our conclusions and turn them in to the president by tomorrow morning. Now if you'll excuse me, I believe these terrorists have wasted enough of my time."

Disquieted and full of unrest, Robert slowly rose with the others to go their separate ways. He felt sure their collective conclusion had been neither reasoned nor just. Dr. Baldwyn would be displeased. Robert's one excuse was that, as Fran had said, it was the responsibility of the ethics committee to make recommendations, not to implement them. That was small and tawdry comfort, however, when they were all aware that the committee's recommendations were invariably rubberstamped by busy administrators.

What rankled sorely was the one-sided discussion he'd just witnessed. Regardless of the implications for his own pro-choice opinion, there had been a troubling lack of weighing the evidence on both sides of the issue and objective consideration of the respective arguments. He recalled Burk Fawcett's dissertation—that accepting data that only fits a certain favoured paradigm results in confirmation bias. Like wrestling with an inert opponent, he'd found no satisfaction in the mutual bolstering of the sole viewpoint with flaccid argument and flabby polemic. Surely there was no need to resort to the irrational, the fallacious, or the emotional. Freedom of choice and basic women's rights provided a cogent line of reasoning for the pro-choice view. Didn't they?

For a crucial moment he wavered, his soul teetering on the cusp of the unthinkable. Rubbing the back of his tight-muscled neck, he recalled the repugnant poster. What would Phil have said during that meeting?

As Robert plodded back to the science wing, slinging his laptop bag over his shoulder, he dared his mind to venture further and wonder what Anna would have said.

It was half past six by the time he knocked at the Fawcetts' door and Robert hoped he hadn't missed dinner entirely. At the door, Jesse's commodious smile drew him in and then instantly switched to an evil leer. On cue, Robert half-heartedly responded in kind, eliciting an unabridged giggle from the youth.

"Mom's on the phone," Jesse said. Pulling Robert's hand toward the dining room table, Jesse ushered him to a chair. "She said, 'Ea' withou' me.' But I waited for you."

A hand appeared in the kitchen doorway bearing a paper with the hastily scrawled message: "Supper on table. Go ahead w/out me. On phone with young friend—solving probs of world."

Jesse grasped Robert's hand in his dry plump one and closed his eyes. "Dear Father," he began, and Robert was struck with the poignancy of the address. This young man now had no father. "Thank you for beau'ful fros' an' goo' day at the Lodge... an' for this food, an' that Misser Fie'ding could come for supper an' that he's gonna play Lego with me affer supper. Amen."

A chuckle escaped Robert as he considered the irony of being an answer to prayer.

Jesse sat expectantly. Picking up a serving spoon, Robert lifted the lid of the casserole. Shepherd's pie. And coleslaw beside. And butter-glossy bread sticks dotted with coarse salt. He filled their plates. The meat dish could have been warmer, but the filling meal soon settled some of the gnawing in his belly. Some, but not all. Though he was apprehensive at the prospect, he was inexplicably compelled to discuss the day's events with Anna. But she was otherwise occupied, and snatches of her phone conversation continued to drift through to the dining table.

"...yet not even a sparrow falls to the ground apart from God's will..."

Could it be that a fetus has rights equal to an adult?

"...and the very hairs of our head are all numbered..."

As a biologist, Robert had long known the facts of human development from conception on. He had simply concluded that the rights of an adult woman weighed more heavily on the scale of justice than did those of a fetus. What other way was there to determine whose rights took precedence?

"But you know," Anna was saying, "God is the judge of all the terrible things that happen in this world, and just because he doesn't pay all his accounts in fall, like it used to be on the farm, judgment is still coming."

Robert's stomach clenched at the conflict within him.

"Scripture says he works *all* things according to the counsel of his will, so nothing that happens is random," Anna said.

Try as Robert would to reason out the issue by logic alone, there was an undercurrent of emotion that, unbidden, kept boiling up within him. Despite the tight lid he'd kept on it for years. To contemplate any other view on the abortion issue implied that all those who participated in it were accomplices to mur— *No!*

"God allows what he hates to accomplish what he loves," Anna was saying.

Jesse pushed on his arm, shaking Robert out of his thoughts.

"C'mon, le's play wi' Lego," he said, prodding Robert toward the living room coffee table where mounds of the colourful plastic bricks were arrayed. It was the last thing Robert was inclined to do. He sat dumbly while Jesse began to fumble with the blocks, pushing pieces toward him.

Aware that Jesse was shaking his arm, Robert glanced at him.

"I'm your bes' friend," Jesse said with a wide smile.

One look at Jesse's face, a study in joyful anticipation, sealed Robert's course.

They sat on the floor where Robert was gradually caught up in the familiar satisfaction, reminiscent of his own childhood, of constructing houses and vehicles—one plus one equals two, pieces fitting together pleasingly. He would call for "a black six" or "red corner piece" and his sidekick would faithfully rattle through the supplies for the desired pieces. Jesse always, of course, punctuated his discoveries with a facial contortion for Robert's benefit. A community began to take shape—Jesse seemed delighted to recognize their own subdivision with its fence around Joan Klug's home, the road to the college, the local elementary school and convenience store, and the playground on the next block.

Glancing at the dining room clock, Robert was surprised to find two hours had flown by. He was still more surprised that the time with Jesse had soothed and subdued his troubled mind. Murmurs coming from the kitchen indicated that the world's problems had not yet been resolved. He stood with a raucous cracking of ankles and knees. Jesse laughed. Robert submitted to the gentle pressure of a hug from Jesse as he handed over Robert's jacket from the hooks in the front hall.

"G'night," Jesse said. "Tha' was fun!"

"That it was, Jesse. Good night to you, too."

Robert left behind the warm cocoon of Anna's home with an awareness that the simple pleasure of playing with Jesse had been a balm to his angst. A blast of icy west wind against his back as he crossed the driveway and unlocked the door of his duplex stirred again some of his inner turmoil. With a firm, almost physical effort, he pressed it down. Yet he feared sleep could be slow in coming because of the battle still simmering beneath the surface.

CHAPTER 39

The human understanding when it has once adopted an opinion
(either as being the received opinion or as being agreeable to itself)
draws all things else to support and agree with it.
—Francis Bacon, *Novum Organum*, 1620

They were already bowing for the blessing when Robert noticed the tiny cartoon clipping beside his plate. He read it while Anna prayed over the succulent chicken pie and Caesar salad. In the simple drawing, a fish had crept out of the sea onto a deserted beach. Chagrined, it was reading the sign posted there: Evolve at Your Own Risk. He grinned when she looked up.

Anna leaned close and patted his arm, her shoulders hunched, her smiling lips tight, holding back a laugh. "I thought you'd like that," she said.

"I'll have it framed," he said, chuckling again as he put it into his wallet.

Anna began cutting generous wedges of the steaming pie, vented by a chicken-shaped cut-out in the top crust.

Robert closed his eyes and lost himself in the contrast of salty flakes of pastry and tender chunks of chicken, the sprinkle of coarse salt on top bursting on his tongue. He looked up when Anna laughed.

"Robert, I do believe you're moaning."

"It's very, very good," he said.

She again patted his arm. "Open up the lid, Jesse, and it will cool so you don't burn your tongue." Anna helped Jesse pull back the top crust of his piece of pie and the steam rushed out.

"When you didn't show up on Thursday, I was a little afraid you'd been put off by my spending the evening on the phone last Tuesday." A piece of chicken on her fork was suspended midway to her mouth as she looked at him.

"Faculty meeting," he said. "But you have no worries on that score, Anna. I look forward to your cooking and the conversations."

"Good. Then I have another question, if you're up to it."

"I like the direct approach."

"I've been reading about something called irre—irreducible complexity. Tongue twister, that. And I was wondering if you could explain it to me."

Robert glanced sharply at her. Did she know that was a term invented by an antievolutionist? Was she trying to goad him? But Anna's placidly trusting face gave no hint of irony. He took another bite and chewed, gathering his thoughts.

"I believe it has to do with the simplest form in which an organism could possibly survive."

Anna eyed him, lips parted, motionless. He knew she expected more, but he could think of nothing to add that she would understand. He reached for the water jug.

"What I've been reading about," she said, "is this irreducible complexity in relation to something Charles Darwin once stated. He said that if anyone could find an organ, say a wing, or an eye—let me see now..." She reached over to the sideboard for a piece of notepaper covered in delicate handwriting. "Ah yes. If an organ or structure could be found that could *not* have been formed by 'numerous, successive, slight modifications,' then his theory would 'absolutely break down.'"

Really, this quoting of Darwin to him, a biologist, was preposterous. The spiral of water overshot his glass as Robert poured, leaving a spreading puddle on the tablecloth. Anna quickly grabbed a couple of serviettes to mop up the spill.

"Oh, sorry about that," he said, helping her blot up the last of the water with his own napkin.

"I knew you'd be familiar with all of this," she said. "So I was wondering what your answer would be. How could an eye, for example, be formed by many small changes when there would be no useful function of any of the steps along the way? A half-formed eye wouldn't allow fifty percent vision. It wouldn't see anything at all, would it?"

"It's good you asked about all this because there are new scientific discoveries almost every day that have put evolution on a more solid foundation than even the theories of gravity or quantum physics. This idea of irreducible complexity has been proven to be a failed theory. It's been put forward by an antievolutionist, and as so often happens with these types of people, their *a priori* assumptions get in the way of good science." *She may not be able to follow this, but she's the one who asked.*

"How so? And what are *a priori* assumptions??" Anna asked, resting her chin on her hand.

"Basically, presuppositions. So rather than looking further for an explanation for something unknown, these people default to 'We don't know how this could have happened so it must have been God.' But that really says more about the ignorance of the person who gives up on science than it does about the limitations of Darwinian processes."

"That's an interesting perspective. I hadn't thought of it as giving up." She offered him another slice of pie. "You said irre—" she stumbled on the word again, smiling sheepishly. "Not sure why that word's giving me such trouble today. Okay, let me try again. You said

IC is a theory that has failed. Can you explain that to me?"

"I believe the man who coined the phrase thought he found one example—the bacterial flagellum—"

"Oh yes. I read about that. It's the sort of motorized part in a bacterium, right?"

"I suppose very simply, yes. So, he thought the flagellum's individual components didn't have any function by themselves. But that's been proven false. There's a smaller subset of proteins found in the flagellum that are the same as those making up something called the Type III Secretory Apparatus. It works by producing toxins that poison its host—"

"It's hard to unnerstan'," Jesse said.

"You've got that right, son. It is very hard to understand," Anna said, turning to him. "Why don't you go play with your cars and trucks for now, Jesse, while Mr. Fielding helps me understand it."

These distractions from Jesse are unnerving.

The young man pushed his chair back and made his way to the coffee table, spread with cars, but not before furtively snagging a chocolate chip cookie from the plate on the sideboard.

"I saw that, Jesse," Anna said. She passed Robert the plate. "Help yourself. I wouldn't want to reduce you to having to pilfer one for yourself."

He helped himself to one, and then another. "You understand, don't you, that since a simpler form of the flagellum exists and functions, it shows that the flagellum is not irreducibly complex?" Robert said.

Anna craned her neck and raised her eyebrows. "Uh, I may be in a little over my head," she said, laughing. "Or maybe a lot. I think I understand that you're saying the flagellum evolved from the simpler... other thing, whatever that was."

Robert smiled. "The Type III Secretory Apparatus, yes."

Jesse's motor sounds began humming from the adjacent living room where he knelt at the low table. Miniature emergency vehicles and their sirens attended several multicar pileups.

"I read about that, too," said Anna. "Some experts apparently say the Type III thing evolved *from* the flagellum and not the other way around."

"I don't... It doesn't really matter. The data shows that the smaller number of components truly do have a function."

"Would simply having all the parts be enough, though?" Anna asked. "Doesn't the total system have to be built up step-by-step in order for a mechanism to evolve?"

"That's right."

"Well, my reading of IC is that if you took out a part at any stage in the evolutionary process, and the organism or structure couldn't function at that stage, then it's an irreducibly complex system. Like an eye, for example. Or this," Anna said, grabbing a pen and drawing an arch on the backside of her notes. "If I draw an arch—"

"Make two. For McDonald's!" Jesse called from the living room.

Robert and Anna laughed.

"Just one this time, Jesse. So this arch represents a functioning system of a living thing. It's standing on its two legs and they're joined by the curve at the top. Now if I cut it in pieces—" With her pen, she slashed the arch through in several places, leaving a long leg on one side. "And take out even just one of those other pieces, it isn't an arch anymore. It's non-functioning."

Robert pondered the crude diagram for a moment. "Ah, but you see, potentially, the long side still functions, because it's able to stand by itself."

"I see," Anna said, looking deflated as she stared at the drawing.

Robert finished his cookie and wadded up his napkin. He was glad to have been able to put Anna's questions to rest. As he was about to push back from the table, Anna raised her head.

"But not as an arch," she said, looking up at him.

"I beg your pardon?"

"If I understand it correctly, evolution is all about slight, successive changes that are *beneficial,* right?"

This just won't quit. "That's right."

Anna picked up the pen and tapped the paper. "So getting back to our drawing here, would there be any benefit in trying to form a new structure by adding one piece of these parts of the arch to this standing side? As far as I can see, it still wouldn't be an arch and it would make the long side topple over. So even that part wouldn't function. It makes me wonder, where's the benefit?"

Robert sat for a long moment staring at the diagram, his mind racing. Like a couple of Jesse's crazy drivers, the confluence of his thoughts was rushing to a conclusion he instinctively rejected. Yet to reject any line of cogent reasoning by instinct was untrue to his beloved premise: to follow the evidence wherever it leads.

Finally, he stood, thanked Anna for the meal, and hurried to his home and computer. He barely noticed her startled look at his abrupt departure. He would get to the bottom of this.

CHAPTER 40

———⁓———

Alas! What can they teach, and not mislead
Ignorant of themselves, of God much more
And how the World began, and how Man fell.
—John Milton, *Paradise Regained, Book IV*

Energized and already thinking about his first class of the day, Robert scanned the notes he'd made yesterday researching the antievolutionists' camp.

Standing at the kitchen counter, his knife glanced off the cube of hard butter as he tried again to scrape off enough for the toast in which he'd already torn a hole. Finally, he took a large bite of the toast and knifed a chunk of butter into his mouth at the same time. Maybe that study on the spreadability of butter an opposition MP had recently decried wasn't such a waste of federal funds after all.

In the beginning, when he'd begun looking at intelligent design websites, he'd experienced a measure of dismay. He believed it was only fair to examine both sides of an issue. He was unprepared for the scholarly research and carefully documented, peer-reviewed data offered by legitimately educated scientists. Some of the questions they raised had been ones he'd wondered about early in his education, too. An especially obvious problem was how life could come from non-life. Others, like the conundrum of the many finely calibrated conditions required for sustaining life he'd not even given thought to. That was in the beginning, but then he turned to the true science sites, his trusted sources—

That was it! He had his opening statement for today's lecture. He typed it in and added a few more notes, then glanced at the time.

Grabbing his laptop and jacket, Robert tore out the door. Clouds hovered above the eastern skyline, wicking up the juicy colours of sunrise. It was heartening to notice the lengthening days.

He was halfway to the college when he realized he'd left behind his file folder with the midterm tests he'd planned to return to his students. He pounded the steering wheel. Well, they would have to wait another day.

He could barely keep still as students filed in, plopping their books on desks, the bleary-eyed ones choosing seats furthest back in the lecture hall. Waiting those few extra seconds after nine until he could feel all eyes were on him, he began.

"In the beginning there was... hydrogen."

A few students straightened up. The soft scratching of pens and tapping of notetaking began as he followed his outline. He was caught up once again in the grandeur and marvel of how life on earth had arisen.

"Evolution has been seen and demonstrated now so many times and in so many diverse ways that neither anyone in the scientific community nor any thinking lay person has any doubts about it whatsoever. The only doubters are those whose *a priori* faith prevents them from ever looking at serious evidence."

He stopped for a breath and noticed several students exchanging glances, which bolstered his confidence. Fervour warmed him as he checked his notes and continued.

"Evolution is not only true, modern biology and medicine would be absolutely unthinkable in its absence. It is fertile, predictive, and it allows fruitful research. New understandings coming on an almost daily basis are all subject to rigorous repeatability. It has been the guiding light behind almost every single new advance in micro—and macro—biology, medicine, and biotechnology for more than a hundred and fifty years."

After that preamble, Robert carried on with the prescribed lecture. Toward the end of the class hour, he clarified a few of his points in answer to several questions as well as to clear up a bit of confusion on last week's assignment. He assigned the next chapter's reading and sat down as the students filed out. Closing his lecture document and gathering his papers, remnants of student conversation floated down to him.

"Man, when he said 'in the beginning' I thought we were in for a sermon," a youth in skinny red jeans said to his girlfriend.

"Yeah, the whole thing was pretty funny." She hoisted her backpack onto one shoulder and laughed as they walked out the door.

"Not sure what that was about," one young woman said to her friend.

"A bit of a rant, I'd say. Hope that's not on the exam," the other said, laughing.

Funny? A rant? He slumped back in his chair. Evidently he'd failed to convey the wonder he felt at what evolution had created. He scratched absently at his chin, disappointment washing over him.

For the rest of the day, Robert stuck to the script of his lectures, dashing home at lunch to retrieve the test papers. At least that went well, and he returned them to the students as promised.

By three-thirty he was famished, but Dr. Baldwyn had called another meeting and he couldn't leave until 4:45. He was distracted throughout, plagued by second guesses. A rant, the girl had said. A rant! That put him in approximately the same category as the likes of his neighbour Pat Siggleady. A rant was the purview of the defensive.

Driving home, his mind replayed the lecture, and he began to listen to himself. Had evolution truly been *seen* so many times? Did *no one* in the scientific community have doubts? Guiltily, he thought of the bibliography of sceptics of Darwinism Phil had sent him, which he'd scanned only briefly before deleting. How about rigorous repeatability? On a macro scale, that was blatant falsehood and he knew it—had known it when he fervently perused his texts and websites the day before as well as when he'd expounded it this morning in class.

Perhaps the real crux of his presentation was his assertion that modern science would be "absolutely unthinkable" without evolution. What would be the use of any scientific endeavour without a guiding foundational premise? And more practically, wouldn't uprooting that foundation wither the growth of modern science, throwing droves of scientists out of work? Considering that argument in the brutal light of logic, he knew the employability of proponents of a theory did not determine its validity. Of course, there was still the matter of science's reliance on the regularity of natural laws. He should have emphasized that more. But he recalled Phil's assertion that some of the greatest scientific minds of the past had relied on those regularities precisely because of their belief in a deity.

His body stiff with tension, he didn't notice his speed until he saw the flashing blue and red lights behind him. Groaning, he looked down and read the speedometer. Eighty-five in a fifty-kilometre zone. His first speeding ticket ever! He'd been rather proud of his twenty-two-year record. A sigh of misery rushed out his mouth as he hunted in the glovebox for his registration and opened the window for the approaching officer. It was an ignominious end to the day.

At home, he browsed the fridge, ravenous. He pulled out a package of wieners and a ginger ale. Slashing open the wrapping, he downed one cold wiener in three bites. He found some mustard and added a stripe to the next one—and the one after that.

Not too bad considering the contempt *she* used to have for "beaks and feet." Still hungry, he dropped a Pop Tart into the toaster.

CHAPTER 41

—————⁊—————

For thou art, from sin and blame entire
Not diffident of thee do I dissuade
Thy absence from my sight, but to avoid
The attempt itself intended by our Foe.
—John Milton, *Paradise Lost, Book IX*

Robert slammed his fist down on the folder of scribbled notes beside him. The good start he'd made during the Christmas break had remained that—only a start. It was already late January and he should be much further along on the project. His turmoil of the past months made him jumpy, his thoughts scattered. He faced a constant volley of mental argumentation far removed from anything to do with Dracula ants. Leafing through his notes, he tried once again to focus. He reread what he'd written so far, but it was useless. He closed the computer file and opened another window, surfing for something mind-numbing, something to dull the head clamour, some way to lose himself.

Hours later, Robert's head jerked up from his computer screen when he heard a car pull up the shared driveway. 10:34 p.m. He saw the lights dim to park and waited for someone to emerge.

Abruptly he shut down the online images. Why was he so powerless to resist these sites? The thought of squeaky-clean Anna juxtaposed with what he'd been viewing brought a crawling filth to his neck and face. He rose to go to bed when he noticed Anna get out of the vehicle, followed a moment later by a man. Surprised, Robert paused to watch. Not much taller than Anna, the man was powerfully built, her porch light highlighting his shiny pate and ring of grey hair. They disappeared inside.

Robert sat back down. He would sit and keep watch.

But why?

She's an old lady, defenseless and alone.

He looked at his stack of weekly quizzes and lab reports to mark. Might as well make some progress on those. By midnight, he was getting agitated. It occurred to him that so much about Anna brought his grandmother to mind. The veiny hands always concocting treats, the same happy, colourful home full of good smells and intriguing artefacts, each with a story. The same dishes and even the same brand of soap. Lunches with Gran had always been a high point while he was in grade school. Entering her house, he'd loved how the quiet was accented by the loud cadence of her kitchen clock, like a heartbeat above a womb. Above all, he had known he was cherished and important to Gran. She'd had a way, even while scurrying to get a meal on the table, of listening with her eyes, her ears, her whole being. Anna was like that.

Finally, at 12:45, he had begun to imagine the worst and decided to saunter outside and check the license plate. But her door opened just as Robert was about to open his. Her visitor came out, turning to shake Anna's hand—warmly and lingeringly, with his other hand on her arm. She waved, smiling as Mr. Visitor drove away, then looked up and noticed Robert. And gave him a tremulous smile, but it held no trace of embarrassment. She waved at him and started across the driveway, hugging her thick sweater against the winter night.

"You're up late." Her attempt at cheeriness was shaky.

He came out and met her halfway. Looking more closely at her face, he noticed her red-rimmed, watery eyes. "I might say the same of you."

"We had Bible study tonight, and since he had been here for supper, Pastor Tom drove me there and back."

Noticing her shiver, he looked up to the streetlight.

"You'd better get back inside," he told her. "It appears to be starting to snow at long last."

"I wonder if it'll stay this time?" she said, looking up at the feathery flakes sparkling against the streetlight's blue-green glow. "Good night!" She turned to go back into the house.

Only as he lay in bed did he realize his questions about her late-night guest remained unanswered.

CHAPTER 42

---~⌒~---

Because you say, "I... have need of nothing"—and do not know that
you are wretched, miserable...
—Revelation 3:17

Joan awakened abruptly. It may have been the odd bluish half-light bathing her bedroom. Or perhaps the silence. More likely it was the cold. She poked a hand out in the direction where she thought she'd left her robe. It wasn't there, but the extreme chill made her retreat back under her comforter.

She lay there for a long time, drowsing and wondering why it was so cold. She was beginning to feel chilly even under a second comforter. Sitting up, she turned on the lamp, determined to find out. Ah, no power. The alarm clock was black. Now she'd have to read the darn manual again to figure out how to reset it. She swung her feet into slippers and was immediately sorry. Their iciness made her gasp. Pulling on a sweatshirt and wrapping her robe around her, she went to the window and peered out. All she could see was deep blue-white.

The living room window was similarly blocked, and the south-facing kitchen only revealed a stormy swirl of white. Joan hurried to the phone, but there was no dial tone.

"Oh no, oh no, *oh no*." Her voice rose to a thin wail. By this time, the cats were following closely at her heels as she hobbled from one window to the next. Finally, she stepped into boots, grabbed her parka, and tried the back door. Opening the solid door, she saw that her screen door, too, was blocked almost completely by snow. Just a small triangle in the upper left corner showed light. Unfortunately, that was the side opposite where the door opened.

The old woman was overwhelmed with claustrophobic panic. She began to call and scream, pounding on the glass door with her fist. She slumped onto the floor, but the cold quickly drove her back to her feet.

Joan stopped to calm herself. It couldn't be that bad. There had to be a way. She was from pioneer stock, for heaven's sake. She'd lived through plenty of snowstorms growing up on the prairies in the 40s and 50s. The memory of her father came to mind, tying a rope to the door during a similar whiteout to reach the barn so he could do the chores and still find his way back to the house.

But the first thing she'd have to do was layer on some warm clothes. Then find something to dig with. Perhaps if she took out the screen and found an implement to dig herself out... but where could she put all the snow? With the temperature inside, it probably wouldn't melt. Well, she had some buckets. Or it could be stuffed into the bathtub.

She had no one to turn to but herself. It was a good thing she was used to never having anyone to rely on. Her parents and brothers, her no-good husband, her daughters—they had all let her down. And though at the lowest point of her life she had called on God for help, most decidedly he had failed her. Because of that, she'd learned to be resourceful, creative, self-sufficient. She could do this. Doggedly, Joan began to scrape away the thick, sticky snow.

When Robert woke, he reached for his glasses and grabbed his phone. He was alarmed to see 8:30 a.m. Hot breath fogged his glasses as he exhaled. Swiping to the weather app on his phone, he blew out a cloud that hung in the air. What had been predicted as flurries had become the storm of the century. He scrambled into his clothes and pulled on his ski sweater, then added a pair of thick socks. A resonant silence thickened the air. As he checked the windows, their very opaqueness delivered a shiver of isolation.

How was he to get to work through this? The thought of classes carrying on without him left Robert with that uncomfortable feeling of being the outsider again. And then he realized the conditions would likely be citywide. A weight lifted. Everyone would be equally bound. The day suddenly held the promise of an unexpected sabbatical. Except for the cold. He added a toque and his heaviest parka from the back closet.

Robert pulled open the back door and faced his own wide-eyed reflection in the glass of the storm door. Pushing his hardest, he heard only the dull squeak of packed snow. It couldn't possibly be piled all the way to the top of the door, could it? If he could brush away the snow from the upper part of the door, he'd be able to slide a shovel down outside to clear the base. Then he pictured his shovel neatly leaned up against the railing of the back steps.

Groaning, Robert dashed back to the kitchen, pulling open drawers and cupboards for any utensil he could find. He cursed the paucity of kitchen supplies, regretting his reluctance to spend money setting up this house. *She* had almost everything. Suddenly he thought of her, alone in this. Should he call?

He trudged back to the door. Removing the glass could work. He fumbled at the lock buttons with clumsy, stiff fingers. He almost dropped it when the glass panel sprang free first on one side, then the other. And there was the wall of weird blue snow. He smacked snow out and away from a triangular area at the top. A blast of wind blew some back up his sleeve, but he could see daylight.

As he cleared a narrow path through the snow lying deep on the ground, his shovel's motions muffled in the strange white silence, Robert's first thought was to head for Pat Siggleady's. Anyone that consumed with conspiracy theories was bound to be well-stocked for a simple power outage. But first he should dig out Anna.

CHAPTER 43

And clouds arise and tempests blow By order from Thy throne.
—Isaac Watts, "I Sing the Mighty Power of God"

Siggleady, as it turned out, was at Anna's

"I guess I've had my workout for the winter," Rena was telling Anna when Robert got there. She had done almost all the shovelling to get them out and over to the neighbours'.

"It's a lot of work clearing a path through all these 'scattered flurries', isn't it?" Anna smiled.

"I should have bought a snow-blower," Pat rasped.

"Yes," Anna said, "that probably would have prevented this snowfall. Like washing your car is a sure predictor of rain."

Pat eked out a half-smile. Apparently, he had neglected to keep a supply of kerosene for his much-touted, better-than-wood-heat kerosene heater. Anna, on the other hand, had a roaring blaze going in the woodstove in the basement and even the main floor living room was acceptably warm.

"I may run out of firewood here in the house," Anna said. "But perhaps you, Robert, could fetch some more when the supply gets low?"

"I will," Robert said, swelling with the sense of being needed.

It must have been the smell of wood smoke that drew the neighbours, one after another. By ten, they'd all arrived, most having brought bread or cookies or cans of beans and soup. Robert, embarrassed at not having thought of that, ploughed through the deep banks between their two homes to grab what provisions he could find. He waded back with two bags of chips, a case of ginger ale, and half a bag of frozen hot dog buns, no wieners.

They were all gathered there, the Siggleadys, Preng and Yanni, and Joan. Zach and Kaitlyn arrived with their new baby, Celeste, carried in a wrap under Zach's snowboarding jacket, and Hector, the Great Dane, his tail thumping loudly against the door. Joan, worried about her cats' ability to survive the cold, had been insisting Anna should send Jesse to help her catch and bring them over until she turned and caught sight of the dog.

"I suppose size takes precedence," she muttered, eyeing the animal with distaste.

Robert assured her the cats were quite hardy enough, with their luxurious fur coats, to survive even lower temperatures than this.

The Duxburys arrived with their elusive daughters, Kelly, marked by a bad case of acne, and Dalia, a teen of dark-eyed, translucent beauty. Anna hugged them both.

"Always happy to have a day off school without actually being kicked out," Kelly said. Her mother smiled even wider at this. To Robert, it appeared that the woman laboured under the impression that being best friends with her daughters was more important than diligence in education.

Victorene Desjarlais and her kids were the last to come through the door, a dispute between mother and eldest son still simmering. Dakota ignored his older brother's foul mood as Morrigan hung back in the corner of the entry with his jacket on.

"No school today! Freeeeeee-dom!" the six-year-old yelled, dancing in a tight little circle in front of Anna. She ruffled his hair, chuckling.

Anna welcomed each member of the neighbourhood as though it were a long-planned visit. Hanging their coats on hooks and hangers, wet boots puddling in the small entryway, she invited them to the basement where they crowded around the small black stove to warm themselves. Anna even managed to coax the sullen Desjarlais lad down the stairs and Jesse followed, each loaded down with a stack of blankets and well-worn sleeping bags.

Morrigan flopped onto a green easy chair in a funk. His iPhone was already out of battery.

"I'm always telling you to plug it in before you go to bed," his mother told him. "World of Warcraft will just have to wait. It won't kill you to do without it for a couple hours."

The boy's scrawny body stiffened in frustration and he slumped low in the chair.

"Here, Morrigan," Anna said, hurrying to a cupboard and pulling out an assortment of board games. "You might find something to do in here that doesn't need electricity. Maybe you can entice the other kids to play over here at the card table?"

The boy ignored her, tucking his chin and letting his black hair completely cover his face. Anna's arms fell to her sides, her smile fading as she left him. His brother and sister, however, pulled up a couple of chairs as they approached the table. The Duxbury girls sauntered over to them and began opening some of the game boxes.

"Why do these 70s people look so excited about playing a game of Battleship?" Dakota asked his sister, pointing to the picture on the worn box. "This guy looks like he's gonna pee his pants."

The three girls' laughter roused Morrigan enough for him to fling his hair out of his eyes and glance over.

Anna came out of the utility room with a plastic bucket of something frozen and tipped its contents into a large kettle she had placed on top of the woodstove. "All of you must be desperate for a cup of coffee, and maybe hungry, too? Now if I just had some good birch firewood, we could thaw this soup in a jiffy. All I got this year was pine."

"That'll work just fine," Pat said, dwarfed by the shabby brown plaid recliner and comforter that enveloped him. He looked even more grey-faced than he had when Robert had last seen him in September. "It'll just take a little longer, that's all."

"But what to do for coffee?" Anna said. She disappeared up the stairs.

In the circle of neighbours, their usual Thursday routines suspended unexpectedly, a relaxed holiday atmosphere prevailed. Talk turned to the likelihood of regaining power quickly. Pat predicted a prolonged outage, likely leading to a major collapse in services and infrastructure. Joan concurred, adding that most people didn't even know basic survival skills. Jesse sat among the adults, gazing with rapt attention from one to another.

Wayne Duxbury told them it would be back up and running within an hour. "It's this kind of thing that gives us practice in positive thinking," he said with enthusiasm. "Let's just *think* power and we'll *get* power!"

Staring at Wayne for a moment, Jesse said, "I'm gonna *think* about Lego Kingdom Castle 'n then I'll *get* it."

This brought a general round of laughter. Duxbury's smile dimmed a degree.

When the chuckles died down, Zach, an apprentice electrician, said he estimated it would take a few hours for the power companies to get mobile due to the huge snowfall. "But once the weather clears, the ploughs will be out and they'll get on it," he said. "It won't be long. I suspect it's happened because of downed lines from the weight of the snow."

By noon, Anna with the other women's help, had managed to make an inviting lunch. Spread on the extended dining room table upstairs were buns, crackers, and cheese in abundance. Sandwich meats, pickles, and chips filled out the meal and packages of cookies were slated for dessert. In the basement, her kettle was filled with what she called "stone soup," a story she was surprised to find Robert didn't know.

"Just like us, a group of neighbours all contributed whatever they had, and the poor traveller who started it all with only a magic soup stone got his belly filled."

She blessed the food and started ladling soup into Styrofoam bowls and cups as the neighbourhood lined up. Most stayed in the relative warmth of the basement to eat their lunch.

"It's great, isn't it, the way neighbours help each other?" Wayne said, helping himself to another bowl of soup. "It's the goodness in us that just needs a crisis like this to find a way to come out." His wife sat beside him, nodding fervently.

"It certainly does restore your faith in mankind," Rena put in.

Dakota rushed down the stairs just then, reporting that the sun had come out. "You should see all that snow! We can make an awesome snow fort. C'mon Morr, let's go!"

Morrigan, with a kick in the rear from his sister, grudgingly climbed the stairs after his brother. The Duxbury girls followed. Anna prodded Jesse to find his snow-pants and go along with them.

Zach laid the baby in his wife's arms and made for the door too. "Bet we could snowboard off the roof of Pat's shed with all this powder," he said.

Kaitlyn chuckled, nestling farther into her corner of the couch.

They came in an hour and a half later, ruddy and wet, all smiles. Even Morrigan had thawed a little. A trail of drips made the trip up the stairs hazardous for anyone in socks.

"Aw, Mom, you shoulda seen it! Me and Morr and Zach got huge

257

air going off that old shed," Dakota said. Jesse came alongside the boy and threw an arm around his shoulder, beaming, his tiny nose comically red.

"Not just you. We did too," one of the girls said as the others nodded enthusiastically, their faces rosy.

Dakota's mother had lost interest and turned back to her phone, so Dakota turned his eager face to Anna.

"But how ever did you get up there to slide off?" Anna asked, her eyes alight.

"There was this ginormous drift on one side so we could just walk up, and then on the other side it kinda went downhill, like this." Dakota made a sloping motion with one arm.

Jesse mimicked his every move, his cheeks red and glossy as a McIntosh apple.

The spontaneous holiday atmosphere couldn't quell the vague anxiety Robert had about his wife's whereabouts. Surely she wouldn't have gone out in these conditions. Did she know how to cope with a power failure? He tried to keep his mind off the worry by keeping the woodstove fed.

CHAPTER 44

O conscience! Into what abyss of fears
And horrors hast thou driven me;
out of which I find no way,
from deeper to deeper plunged!
—John Milton, *Paradise Lost, Book X*

With the winter's early dusk approaching, Anna had lit some candles and dug out a pair of kerosene lamps which she placed on the two end tables. She had planned a reprise of the noon meal, supplemented by hotdogs roasted in the woodstove. Zach and the children had appetites attesting to an energetic afternoon. Hotdog after hotdog was consumed and most of the bowls of chips on the impromptu folding table soon held only crumbs.

Settled around the stove with the lamps and candles burning, the neighbours bundled or cuddled up and a deep quiet fell. The young people lay on a patchwork of sleeping bags around the perimeter of the seating area, their feet toward the fire. No house sounds of furnace or freezer hummed.

Firelight softened the features of the neighbourly group and drew an intimate ring around them. The Great Dane's snore rumbled under Kaitlyn's feet.

"This reminds me of summer camp bonfires," Anna murmured.

"And ghost stories," Robert said.

Joan's voice cracked a little as she began to speak. She cleared her throat, beginning again. "I remember a storm like this when I was about nine. It came up even faster than this one. It had been a nice fall morning when we came to school, but there was a cold north wind blowing by noon. The teacher saw the clouds coming in and told us we could all go home early that day.

"So me and my younger brother—he would have been about seven at the time— started walking home. We had about two and a half miles to go.

"I was wearing my school dress and only a light sweater. Well, the wind kept blowing harder and it was that much worse for us because we were heading straight into it. I wrapped my sweater tight around me and my brother walked right behind me so he had a little shelter. Sometimes, I remember, I held my honey pail lunch bucket in front of my face. But the wind kept knocking it into my nose.

"By this time there was snow coming down, too, and my bare legs were turning blue with the cold. A little more than halfway home, there was a farm close to the road. We could see the light of their kitchen window from the road.

"My brother was crying and pulling on me to turn in there. It didn't take much persuading, I can tell you that. We both knocked and called as loud as we could, hoping they'd hear us above that screaming wind.

"They took us in and set us right down in front of their cook-stove. I can still recall staring at my bright red face in the shiny trim of that stove. The lady wrapped us each in a Hudson's Bay wool blanket and oh, it felt so good. Then she dished up a bowl of chicken soup for each of us and that started to warm us right through.

"They didn't want to let us go until the storm had died down a bit, but I wanted to get home before dark, so I said we had to leave. I knew my parents would be angry with us for accepting what they would have called charity. My brother wasn't any too happy about leaving.

"I remember the lady knelt down in front of me and tried to give me a coat to wear on the way home. I said no. She kept insisting and I just kept on saying no until she gave up and let us go.

"We finally got home, cold clear through to the bone again, and all I had on was that thin sweater over my dress. I had frostbite on my fingers. To this day they still freeze real easy if I'm not properly covered. I sure learned to bundle up after that. You never know what might happen."

Joan pulled the zipper of her grey fleece jacket a little further up and folded her hands in her lap.

"You've always been so capable and responsible, Joan. And determined," Anna said. "I remember that about you when you'd come help my mom with us kids."

Victorene was staring at the older woman, her phone forgotten for the moment. "Why not take the coat, is what I want to know," she asked Joan. "I mean, she was practically forcing it on you. Why say no?"

"I learned from my parents not to borrow things and never to accept charity," Joan said with a dismissive wave of her hand. "We could look after ourselves. I've had to do it all my life."

Kaitlyn shook her head. "A nine-year-old and a seven-year-old walking two and a half miles alone. Incredible!" she said, gazing down at her infant.

Quiet descended again as they stared into the dancing flames.

"It's amazing what can be accomplished by the force of sheer human willpower," Wayne said, his smile gleaming in the subdued light.

They turned at the sound of Pat clearing his throat. Robert braced himself for another round of conspiracy theories.

"About fifteen years back," the thin man said, "when I was working up in Siberia, we used to have to go out in weather like this." A rasping breath punctuated the start of each sentence. "All kindsa weather. Used to be pretty cold all right. Ya had to wear fur; any of that whatchacall manmade stuff would crack up and fall off ya. And ya wanna talk about snow. We got snowed in all the time. One time, the longest I remember, for three weeks. Makes ya just about squirrelly bein' cooped up with a buncha guys for that long. Most of them didn't even speak English.

"But snow wasn't the only white stuff. Over there we were extracting oil using these forty-foot centrifugal drums. We called 'em 'birds' 'cause the valves 'chirped'." Pat lowered his voice a level. "When we looked into one of them drums at the end of work one day, there was all this dried scum on the inside of it. Some of it was white, whatchacall waste minerals and such. But some of them particles in it glistened and when we chipped off chunks of the stuff, they were real heavy. Well, you can bet every one of us workers there had the same idea." His voice dropped another notch. "Gold!

"So we all started breaking off those chunks and filling our lunchboxes with them. That went on for a couple weeks. Each of us piling up a nice little nest egg in the bunkhouse to take home with us. Price of gold then was about three hundred odd bucks an ounce—nowhere near what it is now. But it was free for the taking and we thought it was a pretty nice deal.

"One day, one of the engineers was around when we were gathering our ore, as we called it. He takes a look at the stuff, puts on his gloves, and takes a sample. Couple weeks later, the lab calls back and tells the chief engineers what's in that scum. Ya wanna talk about panic."

Pat cleared his throat as he leaned forward slowly in his chair. He sat, swallowing hard for a few moments. Robert noticed the young boys sitting up in their sleeping bags, peeking between the arms of the couch and loveseat, listening intently.

"They got everybody outta there pronto! Never knew all that bureaucracy over there could make decisions so fast. The company tore down that shop with all them expensive hoists and lifts, and all that fancy equipment. Only a year later, when I was up there on a different job, I went back to see what they'd done with it. It had all been concreted over. And the engineers still wouldn't park anywhere near there."

"But why?" Zach asked.

Pat craned his head slowly to look down to his left where Zach was sitting on the floor at his girlfriend's feet. "It was hot, that's why."

"Hot? What do you mean 'hot'?" Wayne asked.

"Hot. You know. Whatchacall radium, uranium. Lotsa heavy metals."

"You mean radioactive?" Robert asked, incredulous. "And you men were handling it?"

"That's right," said Pat, bitterness etched in the lines of his mouth. "I've got a lasting souvenir of it, too." He pulled his blanket tighter up under his chin. Tension in the room mingled with pity which drew fidgets among those around the circle. The silence grew deeper.

"What did you do with those rocks?" Wayne asked, his eyes glittering in the firelight.

Pat craned around to frown at the younger man, but merely shook his head.

Wayne looked hopefully at Pat. "If you could start focusing on health, visualize your body's cells—"

Wayne broke off when Anna cleared her throat, rather sharply.

Robert was glad he was not the recipient of the warning frown she shot Wayne. The room grew quiet again.

Finally, Anna asked softly, "Oh Pat, won't you please see a doctor? There may be some help, some treatment or relief they could give you."

But Pat had closed his eyes and leaned back in his chair, a shrunken wisp of a man. He weakly raised one palm and, seeing it, his wife shook her head at Anna. Rena tucked the blanket closely around her husband's frail frame, placing a pillow on her lap and swinging his feet gently up onto it.

Beside Robert, his baby neighbour squeaked and fussed. Kaitlyn pulled her up to her chest, covering the baby and herself with a fuzzy orange blanket. Robert was embarrassed when he realized the muffled gulping and smacking he heard meant she was breastfeeding the infant right beside him. He looked quickly away, then got up to add a few more logs to the fire.

"Whenever there's a power failure, I keep thinking of things I should do," Wendy said in her high-pitched nasal voice. "And I keep ticking them off, realizing I can't do them. I can't use the computer, so I can't do the books for our three home businesses—and the orders have been pouring in." She paused and looked around as if expecting eager new recruits to rush forward. "Can't vacuum, can't bake, can't use the microwave, can't watch TV, can't even exercise 'cause my elliptical won't light up..."

"You could come shovel snow at my place for exercise." Joan's tone was scornful. There was an awkward pause.

"It does make you think about what life would have been like a couple hundred years ago, doesn't it," Zach said. "No wonder they had such large families." Laughter brought back the easy camaraderie of the group.

Anna scurried upstairs and returned with some string. She knotted it into a loop and held out a maze on her hands to the Desjarlais girl.

"Oh, I know this," the girl said, pulling up on two crossed strings with her thumbs and forefingers. The others watched the wall shadows made by their flying fingers as Anna named the shapes they formed together.

"The pioneers used to do this to pass the time on long winter's nights. Jacob's ladder, cat's cradle, candles, soldier's bed—"

"Why'd they give them such weird names?" Brandi asked.

"They probably named them for everyday things they were familiar with. You could give them modern names. Maybe," Anna made the configuration called candles, "cell phone."

"Motorcycle!" Brandi suggested as she formed the cat's cradle.

"I try," said Yanni, who had come up behind them. She took over from Brandi. "Two diamonds." She worked a succession of particularly intricate figures. "Hole in Tree, Lightning. String play very old. My mother, Maq I call her, she teach me." She smiled and passed the string back to Brandi, then returned to sit next to her husband.

"I'm afraid that's all I know," Anna said after a while, letting the string fall limp in Brandi's hands. The girl called Kelsey over and they settled themselves under a sleeping bag against the back of the loveseat to carry on the age-old string tradition.

The Asian couple was seated cross-legged on a pair of large green cushions placed against the arms of the couch and chair. He broke the silence, his smooth voice lulling them with the ease of a practiced storyteller.

"It never snow where I grow up in Kampuchea. This fire reminds me of Pol Pot time. I was nine-year-old when my mother, my grandmother, and my baby sister and me flee our village. The Vietcong were coming—we hear the shelling getting very closer, closer. But my grandmother think they turn toward the north, not come through our village. She not want to leave our home.

"My mother argue and argue with her. Finally one day, I saw troops moving through the jungle not far from our home. I run back and tell Maq. She start gathering up all the food we had. Then she made grandmother move. Yiey grab everything and anything. Maq pull her out the door, our pots and dishes clanging between Yiey's skinny shoulder blades.

"We run with the rest of villagers, most women and children, like us. Maq tore the pots and dishes off Yiey's back, they making so much noise. Then Yiey want my mother to carry them, but she have my baby sister on her back. We leave the pots by the trail, Yiey very crying all the way.

"For months we camp at night, just like this, around the fire. Our food supply soon gone. Our scout lead us through empty villages; all people fled before. Sometimes we found a little rice or a few vegetables in abandon gardens. After that we learn to watch the birds and animals and eat what they ate. Sometimes all we had to eat was rice broth with some leather boil in it. Soup like you make, Anna, 'stone soup'—Oh! If we eat that soup we very love it. I use to dream of noodles and chicken... and always wake up with stomach empty.

"Yiey already old when we start out. Old and skinny. Such little food not help her. Before long, she say she cannot go any farther. I told her, 'Lean on me,' but she did not. She look so weak and ill. Maq so distressed. She scold Yiey and stamp her foot. But my grandmother just lie down under a tree and not move."

Preng sat staring into the woodstove, firelight flickering on his face, his lips taut in a grim line. Yanni pressed her hands together between her raised knees, her eyes luminous, gazing beyond the woodstove into the light of memory.

"Always we afraid the fighting getting closer and now we heard the shells not very far away."

Jesse crept closer to his mother's knee, anxiety written on his face, and she gave a reassuring squeeze to his shoulder.

"Maq always worry," Preng continued, "because we behind our neighbours. They almost disappear ahead of us. She wrap my baby sister on *my* back. Oh, she feel so heavy. Then Maq pick up my grandmother across her back and keep going, stumbling."

The room was very still. Only the snapping of the fire and the even, drowsy breathing of some who had fallen asleep broke the quiet.

"I try to follow. I make it until nightfall. But in the morning, I have fever. I can barely walk and not lift the baby. My mother wrap the baby tightly and lay her between thick roots of a tree there in the jungle. Then she pick up my grandmother and walk on. I very cry and cry. But finally I follow her.

"Three days later, we come to a road where UN trucks meet us. They take us to refugee camp across the Thai border. My mother and grandmother never speak of my sister again." His elbows on his knees, Preng covered his face with his hands. "Only three days. Why I not go on carrying her for three days?"

Robert clamped the bridge of his nose against the ominous prickling he felt there. He'd had a growing shortness of breath as he listened to Preng's story. He straightened up in his chair and exhaled slowly, then shifted once more in the chair.

Anna began to sing softly in a thin voice, "And Jesus said, Come to the waters, stand by My side, I know you are weary, you won't be denied.'" Yanni joined her friend and they finished the brief song together. "'I felt every tear-drop, when in darkness you cried, and I strove to remind you, that for those tears I died.'"

Preng sat up and nodded, eyes glittering.

The horror of Preng's story was made more poignant by Robert's seat next to Kaitlyn and her baby. As he listened, he'd been staring at the child's feathery sweep of lashes on its poreless skin. The tiny, curled ear, the intricate fingers tightly clasping Kaitlyn's finger. Now he was aware of the young woman crying softly. He glanced across the coffee table and caught a glistening in Joan's eyes, too, and on her moist cheeks.

A sluice-gate of emotion cracked ajar within him. Robert opened his mouth and involuntarily, words gushed out. "My wife and I had been married two years when we found out she was pregnant. We had just moved to Montreal so I could start my doctorate, and she was only working sporadically. All I could think about was the ton of student debt we had then and the prospect of lots more to come. We lived in a tiny basement suite with hardly any furniture and we were far from both our families. Not only that but she had been on medication for something unrelated and we found out that could cause birth defects.

"So we decided to terminate. It seemed like the obvious solution. I took her to the clinic and she was in and out in about two hours. We thought we'd solved the problem." Robert swiped his clammy face with trembling hands. "What we never realized was that the date would be burned forever in our memories. It changed everything. We never spoke of it again, but she became depressed and moody. It came between us more than any baby ever could have."

He heaved a ragged sigh. "I said 'we decided to terminate,' but I'd have to admit it was me pushing for it. I think she held it against me all these years..."

Robert glanced around at the staring faces of his neighbours. Anna wore an odd look of dawning recognition that he didn't understand. He was suddenly appalled at what he'd confided.

He shot up from the chair and bolted for the stairs, tripping on one of the teens listening silently behind the couch. Catching hold of the end table, he stepped over the unidentified body and hurried upstairs.

What could have possessed him to spill his entrails in that pitiful way before people he knew so little? He put it down to the relentless pressure he'd felt of recent months, felt it pushing, or pulling him perhaps, to an ineluctable fork in the road. He had never seen so clearly his culpability in the abortion, because he'd never viewed it alongside a true dilemma like the abandonment of Preng's sister. In that case, the mother likely hoped the child would be rescued. In his, he'd ensured there could be no such hope. With this new recognition of his guilt came an overwhelming sense of... of something like betrayal. He recalled Anna's words the first time he'd had dinner with her: "There are so many moral and ethical implications that go along with what we believe about life's beginnings." He could feel the foundations of his worldview cracking, shaking.

What else have I been wrong about?

Robert sat in the thick darkness of Anna's windowless powder room for some while, finding that confession had most decidedly not been good for the soul. It left him with a cloying guilt for which he knew no antidote.

The overhead light flashed on, blinding him momentarily, and there was a groaning rumble from the bowels of the house as the furnace kicked in. When he tried the bathroom faucet, it coughed and sputtered before he could wash his hands. Reluctant to face the neighbourhood again, the lingering cold finally forced him back to the warmth downstairs where he began stoking the fire diligently. His back puckered with the stares and judgment he felt his neighbours must be directing at him.

The others were conferring quietly, trying to decide whether to bed themselves down or go home. It was already ten o'clock. They agreed to wait an hour or so to allow their own homes to warm a bit before they returned. The outside temperature, according to Anna's thermometer and Victorene's dying phone, read about fourteen degrees below freezing. Joan, however, left immediately to attend with the devotion of a mother to her kitties.

CHAPTER 45

―――――*◊*―――――

The wife, where danger or dishonour lurks,
Safest and seemliest by her husband stays,
Who guards her, or with her the worst endures.
—John Milton, *Paradise Lost, Book IX*

Pregnant, Amelia drowsed on the couch in her comfiest sweats, bundled in one of her neighbours, the Holloways' winter camping sleeping bags. Though the rumble of the furnace and the hum of the bar fridge in their wood-panelled rec room had signalled the return of power last night, the Holloways had urged her to stay and she hadn't been hard to convince. Even now she was reluctant to emerge from her cocoon. Besides, for the past few minutes, the baby had been engaged in some impressive gymnastics. Her belly rippled wildly, making her giggle. Again she wished someone else could feel it, enjoying with her the uncontrollable antics of an entirely new person. By now, anyone would certainly be able to see the movements as well.

She sighed. The Holloways had already left the fireside and gone upstairs.

"Ooogh." The inelegant grunt escaped her. There was simply no way to gracefully hoist up her rotund body. Having lain in one position for so long, her hip joints had locked painfully. Gasping, she slung her coat over her arm and took halting steps upstairs.

This must be what it's like to be old. It got cooler the farther up she went.

Doug and Joanne were already busy, checking the fridge, the faucets, rebooting the computer.

Her boots waited at the side door where she'd left them the morning before. "I'll be getting home now. Thanks for everything. You two are lifesavers."

"You haven't looked outside, I take it," Doug said, pointing at the door's sidelight in the entryway where packed snow blocked the daylight almost entirely. "Give me a minute to bundle up and I'll shovel a path to your door. Your place is going to be pretty frigid until the furnace has been going for a while. Jo, wouldja get some hot chocolate ready for when I come in?"

"I'm on it," Joanne called back to him with the water running, cups clattering.

An hour and a half later, Doug returned red-faced and sweating. "Well, it's a beautiful day once you can see it." He was puffing hard, almost as if he could have a heart attack right there on the foyer bench. "But that's the biggest dump of snow I've seen in I don't know how long."

Joanne handed him a cup of cocoa. "A whole winter's worth at once."

"Thanks so much, Doug, for clearing that. And for coming over yesterday morning to get me. I don't think I'd have made it through this storm on my own."

Outside, the blinding sun set everything dazzling. Shielding her eyes from the glare, she looked around at a world transformed. Thick dollops of snow slouched off the eaves of every building, and evergreens and shrubs drooped under impossible weight. She could see why it had taken Doug so long to shovel the fewer than five meters between their doors.

Back at home, she checked to see that everything worked and was glad to hear her own furnace running. It would take hours to bring up the temperature in here. She plugged her phone into the charger. Blooop. Blooop. There were two backlogged text messages.

8:43 a.m. Yesterday's date: "I hope you're all right in this storm. The gas fireplace is not going to work without the electric fan. Maybe you should try to get to the Holloways'?"

4:15 p.m. Same date: "Amelia! Are you all right? Haven't heard from you. Worried about you. And the baby. Stay indoors, wherever you are. Don't try to shovel any snow. Phone battery very low. Wish I could help you."

He said my name! And he's worried about the baby. Well, how do you like that?

CHAPTER 46

───────◦◦───────

She had always known a thousand ways to circle them all around
with what must have seemed like grace.
—Marilynne Robinson, *Housekeeping*[7]

Over the six weeks since the Great Blizzard, the city had sluggishly
risen from beneath the deep blanket of snow and wakened to its
normal life. There had been a settling of the snowpack, and now the
strengthening March sun had been doing its slow and faithful work to
draw rivulets of water out of the shrinking banks.

Yanni slowed her aging Honda to a stop in front of Anna's house
to let Jesse out. He thanked her in his funny way and walked up the
driveway past Anna's light green compact car. Yanni waited, watching
him to be sure he got inside all right. She drummed her fingers on the
steering wheel in an increasing rhythm.

She was eager to get home with the fabric she'd finally bought
today. To get started—laying it out, cutting, watching the beautiful
dress for her daughter, Sareen take shape under her skilled fingers—
it was all pleasure.

She be so excited when she see it. I know Sareen very love this
shiny red material—pretty like her lips.

Finally, Jesse disappeared through his doorway and Yanni drove
around the corner to where her house faced the next street over. She
lugged everything into the house and quickly cleared the breakfast

273

coffee cups and the day's advertising mail off the dining room table. Spreading the fabric out, she fingered the red overlay's light filminess and the lining's sheen. Yanni saved many a dollar on patterns with her ability to make her own for a custom fit.

Ruffles. Many, many ruffles. No lace this time. She designed it in her mind. She would need something to take measurements from, something that was a good fit. Checking the time, Yanni realized she'd need to hurry. There was only an hour and a half until she'd have to put everything away before her daughter came home from school.

Yanni hurried up the stairs to Sareen's bedroom bedecked with posters of singers and photos of friends in silly poses. The bed was made, but haphazardly, and as she went by, Yanni straightened the hot pink comforter she'd sewn for her girl. In one of the dresser drawers, she knew, was a purple shirt that Yanni remembered fit Sareen well. She'd take her measurements from that.

It was the bottom of the third drawer she opened that caused her heart to stop and her stomach to plummet.

It cannot be. No, not my Sareen. My good girl. She not do this thing, this bad thing.

"No, Reen, no!" *Maybe this white paper-twist sticks not that pot stuff.* Yanni smelled the hateful thing. It was. She knew that sweetish smell unmistakably. It brought back hideous memories from the refugee camps in Thailand.

Maybe someone put this in Reen's purse—she not know what to do with it. Yes, that must be it... But the note lying next to the joints told a different story:

Sareen, you said your parents have no clue, so you keep the stuff for now. Don't smoke it all without me!

Oh, what can I do? I have such shame. No one must know. But I must ask someone... I ask Anna. She has son who do bad things. Always she ask in church we pray for him.

Yanni left everything as it had been in the drawer. Slowly, she went back to the dining room. With sorrowful tears, she folded the lovely fabrics, now tainted by her discovery, and put them back into the bag. Her daughter might never know what she had traded for the sake of a bit of rebellious foolishness. Yes, she would talk to her dear neighbour. Anna would tell no one. She would pray with her and comfort her. Anna would help.

Pat Siggleady sat in front of the bluish screen of his computer, his fingers limply grasping the mouse. He'd just come across another sinister scam the World Bank was trying to pull and he was overwhelmed. He shook his head feebly and blinked rapidly trying to clear his blurring vision. If only that would clear his foggy brain as well. Increasingly, his bodily functions seemed to be conspiring against him these days. But he persevered. Someone needed to sound the alarm. And it might as well be him. What, after all, did he have to lose?

The scenario laid out before him was dire indeed. And it was imminent. By late summer or October at the latest, the biggest financial collapse the world had ever seen would be history. It would be an apocalypse to dwarf the crash of 1929. By this autumn, it would be too late for so many. They would come begging then, wishing they had prepared as he had.

Pat mentally ran down his checklist, frustrated by Rena's refusal to allow him to cash out their RRSPs. That woman could be so stubborn. But he had several thousand dollars in cash reserves, withdrawn gradually over the last couple of years in small bills and small amounts at a time. He also had a dozen gold coins. The cash might do initially, but of course it would soon lose its value after a collapse. Hence, the gold. Even if it didn't retain its value at its current historic high, it was still legal tender and would maintain its face value. He couldn't resist taking another look at it.

Pat walked slowly over to his small safe, stopping frequently for breath. It took three tries before his weak and trembling fingers could manage the combination. Then he examined the coins in one ounce and half ounce denominations. They gleamed brilliant yellow under the fluorescent light of his windowless basement office. They were quite pretty with a nice hefty feel in his hand.

He returned them to their hiding place, relocked the safe, and pondered the other supplies he'd laid by. Each week for over a year, he'd made his own list of staples for Rena to add to her grocery list. At least she hadn't balked at that. Now the buckets of beans, grains, pasta, milk powder, and dried vegetables lined an entire wall of this office, floor to ceiling. There were shelves of canned food, too. Enough to feed the neighbourhood. *If* they were sorry they hadn't listened to him. He would have to see about kerosene for the space-heater, but other than that, he thought they were ready for anything.

But were they? What about water? Gasoline?

A faint squeak of running feet on snow froze him. Waiting and listening, he heard nothing more. Which brought him to the inevitable question of ammunition.

This is when he wished he had someone to confer with. His wife was unsympathetic. When he broached his concerns, whether about world conditions or their own preparedness, he sensed her eyes glazing over and her mind tuning him out.

Whenever he phoned one of his children, he could almost hear eye-rolling in their tone of voice and they'd quickly shut him down. Once, his daughter had accused him of "stressing her out" and causing her to have anxiety attacks. It would be a different story when they had to come running home for shelter and food and protection.

He needed to talk to someone. Who could he turn to who would give thoughtful consideration to this information? Someone with an awareness of the world situation? Someone who valued the old ways of making do and doing without? Someone who cared about the neighbourhood?

Anna! He would call Anna. She had practically saved the neighbourhood during the power failure in January. Her life on the farm would have taught her a lot of self-sufficiency skills. And that loaf of bread she'd brought by the other day, why, she might even know how they could set up a communal bake oven. It was true that in the few conversations he'd had with her over the years, he could tell she hadn't always believed everything he told her. She'd kept coming back to the idea of God being in control. But she had always shown him respect. And she had an influential way with people. Yes, he would definitely call her. Anna would listen.

Joan thrust her hands into her armpits, less to warm them than to keep herself from slamming them against the bathroom wall. *This is too much!* A terrible dream and throbbing head had wakened her first thing this morning. Then she heard the tic-a-scritch of her cats up to no good. When she at last hobbled down to the living room, shaking out the kinks in her feet and knees along the way, there they were, tearing apart the Styrofoam packaging from her new toaster. Little clinging balls of the stuff were everywhere.

She had taken one look at the mess, let out a weak moan, and gone straight back to bed. But not before stubbing her toe on the golf club she kept under the bed in case of intruders. Joan groaned loudly, which only hurt her head more. She tried to keep her head perfectly still as she lay down, lest the bowling ball inside it slam into the sides of her skull. Who could have exposed her to this flu or grippe, or whatever it was? Joan was never sick. Not like some people her age who were just walking medical textbooks.

I don't know how some people can stand being sick all the time. This is awful! But just as she got her assortment of time-worn blankets arranged over her again, her insides threatened to explode and she barely made it to the bathroom. When she finished washing her hands, she turned and saw the toilet about to overflow. Another groan, even louder this time. Opening the cabinet under the sink, a small avalanche tumbled out. Joan pawed through it for the plunger she kept there. She sneezed, giving the gust of tickles in her nose full vent. And again. Sniffling, she bent lower to look into the back of the cupboard. *Oh, my head!* An involuntary groan escaped her. The dratted plunger had to be here somewhere. Perhaps the basement? There was nothing to do but make the trek down two flights of stairs. It wouldn't do to leave the toilet full to the brim like this.

From the top of the stairs, it certainly looked a long way down. A fall down these could result in serious injury—especially down the steps to the basement, landing on concrete. Joan pictured herself lying there in her threadbare nightie, perhaps for days or even weeks before anyone found her, slowly dehydrating and starving. She stepped into the bedroom to grab her worn blue robe to cover her tattered night dress. At least they'd find her decently clothed. *Prude descending a staircase. Now that, right there, sounded like something Anna would say.* Joan was too weak to smile.

Having found what she needed in the basement, Joan made her way back, though she had to crawl up the last few steps. Raw grit saw her through the plumbing project, as it had so many crises before. Finally, she could lie down. But the minute she closed her eyes, the shreds of the nightmare that had first wakened her returned, forcing her eyes open. It was her old nemesis again. The strange, indescribable tangle of fear and despair that made no sense. She had tried to write it down: the buttery gloss of mud suddenly, horribly, sprouting up rocks. The smooth, smooth feeling of speed culminating in jagged steel wreckage... It only succeeded in sounding ridiculous. But the recurring dream held such terror for her. And she knew what the real fear was.

It was coming. Inexorably and steadily, Death was coming. Anna herself had said it once: "The death rate is one per person." How could she say it so calmly, glibly almost? Of course, Anna was more than ten years younger. Death had not seemed so imminent to Joan when she was in her sixties either. But Anna did have a quiet confidence, an inner peace, seemingly, that Joan wondered about. What would happen if she asked her neighbour about it?

It's hard to ask advice of someone you've babysat.

Anna was happy-go-lucky by nature, to be sure, but she must think of ultimate realities sometimes.

She heard a knock at the door. *No! It can't be. No one ever comes to my door when I'm well. And now they come?* Maybe it was Anna, bringing something fresh-baked which Joan was in no mood for. But there was no possible way she could answer in her current condition. Another knock, louder. And a dog barking annoyingly nearby.

Now, whose mangy beast could that be? Joan lay still, listening and curious but too weak to move.

There was nothing more.

Shutting her eyes again, the old woman's thoughts drifted back to the spectre she feared. It really was too much. Sewage problems on top of sickness, compounded by nightmares, bound up by all the sorrows of her life, the rejection, the ostracism, never fitting in anywhere... The burden was almost unbearable at times. As much as she prided herself on her self-sufficiency, it was particularly heavy bearing it alone.

Yet she could always talk to Anna. Joan knew she could. Anna would take the time to genuinely hear her. Most of all she would offer love and understanding, the lack of which Joan had suffered sorely all her life. Anna would care.

Kaitlyn finished nursing Celeste and the wee one now lay limp in her arms. All that warm, sleepy heaviness made the young mother wish to close her own eyes for a nap. But it was high time she got busy losing some of this baby fat. Zach had jokingly threatened to tie her behind the car to get her active. The howling winter wind of the last few days had died down and today it seemed the sun would defeat the clouds. Kaitlyn rose from her comfy armchair, wedging Celeste in the back corner of the couch while she went to get dressed for a brisk walk. Hector rose from his rug near the door, wagging his tail in anticipation.

"That's right, boy, we're gonna go for a walk." The tail picked up the pace.

She found the sweet, hand-crocheted strawberry toque and soft pink blanket Anna had given Celeste and carefully bundled the baby, wrapping her in a sling on her chest. She smiled, stepping into some of the most practical pieces of mothering advice she'd received, and it had come from Anna as well: slip-on boots.

Heading out the front door, she turned onto the sidewalk at a brisk pace with Hector in the lead. It was always fun to look into people's houses as she walked along to see how they'd personalized their homes. But, being the middle of the afternoon, it was hard to see into the darkened windows from the white brilliance outside.

Hector stopped just then and barked twice. From between the duplexes and the shared backyards beyond, Kaitlyn caught the sound of distant barking and a glimpse of two dark-clad figures running. Hector strained at the leash in their direction. Maybe that Desjarlais kid, what was his name? Except both these characters seemed bigger. And it was still school hours. Hmmm.

Celeste slept on as Kaitlyn made for the small park at the end of the next block and hoped the bike path was reasonably clear of ice. She stroked her baby's head in the fuzzy cap. She wished she could learn to make stuff like that. What if she were to ask the older woman if she had time to give a few crochet or knitting lessons?

She would teach me. Anna would make the time.!

CHAPTER 47

———————∞———————

Jesus loves me this I know; for the Bible tells me so.
Little ones to Him belong; they are weak but He is strong.
—Anna B. Warner, "Jesus Loves Me"

A reddish-coloured dog barks twice as Jesse comes up the driveway. He doesn't know this dog but he stops near the back door to pet him and the dog smiles up at him, wagging his tail.

Jesse steps inside the slightly open door. He swings his backpack off and hangs it on its hook in the entry. Unzipping the front pocket, he pulls out today's treats. A pretty good haul. The people of the seniors' centre often give him something on his day to volunteer. He puts the loot on the shelf and fingers the packages of candy, counting and sorting through it. There are cherry blasters from Mrs. Halstead, fuzzy peaches from Mrs. Flanders, mini peanut butter cups from Mr. Akins, and some hockey cards from Miss Isaak.

He looks up and notices the backpack is hanging a little crooked, so he pushes up the low side. But it's still crooked. He lifts the loop off the hook a little to straighten it. *Thass better.* He unzips his jacket and hangs it on the next hook over his snow-pants that already hang there. Next, he places his toque on the hook above the jacket, puffing it a little to make it round like a head. Then he slips off his boots and lines them up on the floor exactly under the jacket. He likes it to look like it's a person standing there.

282

Grabbing his stash of treats from the shelf, he straightens and looks around the kitchen.

"Whass for supper, Mom?" he asks. No answer. She must be in the living room. He pads through to the front room. She's not there.

"Mom?" he calls. A little louder, "Mom!"

Jesse stands in the middle of the living room, thinking. Maybe she went to Yanni's. But no, Yanni just dropped him off on her way home from work.

Jesse folds one arm across his chest and taps his temple with the other hand. *Think, think, think. Like Winnie the Pooh.*

Hanky squeaks. Jesse turns toward the cage near the living room window. There's Hanky, asleep inside his toilet paper tube deep in the shavings.

Maybe Mom's upstairs, sewing.

Jesse starts toward the stairs when he hears Hanky squeak again. But it can't be him, because Hanky's sleeping.

Jesse stands listening, undecided.

The sound seems to be coming from the kitchen. He goes back there.

Another squeak. No, not from the kitchen. From the basement. He never looked down when he came in. Jesse doesn't like the look of that dark hole when the lights are off.

He can feel his chest starting to pound. He looks now. And turns on the light.

Jesse freezes at what he sees, his hand still on the light switch. Mom is crumpled up at the bottom of the stairs. There is a big red stain under her head. He feels like a gaping hole has ripped open his chest. Mom's leg is bent forward at the knee like a Barbie doll's. She is the one making the squeaking sound.

Jesse starts down the stairs. Halfway down, his foot crunches on something. It's Mom's glasses twisted up with only one glass in them.

Pieces of the other one are on the steps. A cry wants to come out of him but he clamps his mouth shut tightly, breathing hard through his nose. He edges past her bent leg.

"Mom?" She doesn't answer.

Mom sometimes talks to him about "what ifs?" like this. He knows he has to call for help. He runs back up the stairs and heads straight to the phone above the small desk in the kitchen. He hunches over it. All he seems to be able to take are little breaths. He presses nine, one, one. Waiting for it to ring takes a long, long time.

It seems like he has to give his name and address again and again. He tries hard to "speak with the tongue and the lips" just like Mom always tells him. And the lady asks him who is the person who is hurt. He says, "Mom." He tells the lady, loud, that Mom is old and that there is red—he hates saying that other, scary word— under her head. The lady asks twice if there is anyone else here. No, just Mom, he tells her.

"Can I go back to Mom now?" he loudly asks. He shouldn't yell, but the lady is taking so long.

The lady says yes, he should stay with Mom but not move her. She says the ambulance will be here very soon.

Jesse hangs up the phone and runs back down the stairs to Mom as fast as he can. He sits down beside her. She is shaking a little all over. He gets up quickly and pulls the afghan from the couch. He tucks her in, stretching it across her legs that are bent apart. Stroking her white hair, he waits. And sings a song that Mom sings to him at bedtime.

CHAPTER 48

—⁓—

Be still, my soul—the waves and winds still know His voice
who ruled them while He dwelt below.
—Katharina von Schlegel, "Be Still My Soul"

Robert kicked his office door closed and thumped into his chair, dumping his briefcase on his desk where the contents scattered. In the staff room a few minutes earlier, McCoy had been ragging on Phil again about his emerging beliefs on intelligent design. Phil seemed unfazed by it in a way that amazed Robert. The math prof simply asked questions, troubling questions, and was able to brush off McCoy's belligerence with a shrug and a smile. Robert distanced himself from the debate the minute McCoy included him in his assault.

Thoughts swirled through Robert's head in a way he hated. Not least of his turmoil was the guilt he felt, on the one hand, for being drawn, even fascinated, by Phil's ideas, and on the other hand, his cowardly retreat whenever someone else was around to challenge them. These and other thoughts whirled to an inexorable vortex that he felt helpless to stop. Where was the clarity of the linear pattern of thought he much preferred? Step by step. $a+b=c$. Working to the satisfaction of a nice, logical conclusion.

Robert snapped his laptop shut, zipped his briefcase and stood. He flung on his jacket and strode out of the office.

"Good night," Sarah Mae called after him.

In his grim preoccupation, he barely heard her.

It had only been a year ago, he thought bitterly, that life had been tranquil. His career progressing along swimmingly. Financially, things were afloat, if not perfectly stable. He'd had a wife, two cars, a beautiful home. And then, shipwreck. Robert slid into the seat of his car and started for home.

My poor excuse for a home.

It was bewildering the speed at which he had been inundated by life's storms. Last July he'd come home from vacation to find one of his renters had given notice; the other had simply vanished still owing the month's rent, leaving him shouldering the full payment for the duplex. Two weeks later, his wife announced her pregnancy. He was furious at her carelessness and accused her of plotting it when, he bluntly reminded her, they'd had an agreement.

"She has been unfaithful," he'd told Anna last fall. And he had truly believed that. She had been unfaithful to the picture and plan of their life that had been his vision. *And hers*, his thoughts insisted. Now he recalled the tentative look of suppressed joy on her face as she'd given him the news, the pink strip upheld in one hand. A wave of guilt blindsided him.

In recent weeks he'd had other such thoughts. It was now late in March. He knew she must be close to giving birth, but he'd seen her only once since the day of that last stormy fight when he had moved out. Just that fleeting glimpse in the foyer of the theatre after Jesse's play, when he'd been on the verge of making amends. How could it be that in all that time, they would not have met up even once, as he had expected?

He slammed shut the portal to all such contemplation and turned his mind to the problem of his stalled research paper.

Even that was a muddle. A siren warbled behind him. Ambulance. He pulled over into the right lane with the other northbound traffic.

An RCMP cruiser passed, too, before he could carry on.

His written work was far from publishable in its current condition. The reason for the doldrums, he knew, was not only his growing discomfort about the ethical quagmire he'd landed himself in by manipulating the Dracula ants' ecosystem. It was also the greater battle going on inside him regarding origins. And here was another sea of confusion: Phil had been sending him links to articles on intelligent design or the problems neo-Darwinists were encountering with an old theory in light of new discoveries. Initially he'd read a few but found too stressful the strain of refuting as he read. These days he deleted them unread. But already they had eroded his assurance in what he'd been taught all his academic life. Moreover, doubt was eating away at his ability to confidently teach the curriculum. Robert was beginning to see the evolutionary assumptions in everything he read, even in his own research. The way every piece of data was funnelled into an evolutionary template—was it all built on sand? The question was, could his own work stand without the foundation he'd thought was rock solid? He felt as though he were crowded to the edge of a precipice, yet even to begin exploring the challenges to that foundation was like losing his footing and plunging into the deep. Without a doubt it would mean swimming against the current of scientific consensus. But worse, he was tormented by a deeper question. Was it his belief in pitiless natural selection that had driven him to make the ultimate choice against his own child those many years ago? The thought made him break into a sweat.

He took a deep breath and exhaled, long and slow, to calm his racing mind. Today was Thursday. Dinner at Anna's was one bright spot, anyway. He could feel some of the tension wash away at the thought of a good meal and a kind friend. She was a lifeline of stability with her way of putting things into perspective. Tonight, he needed a good dose of her tranquillity. He'd tell her about this unrest he felt. She always listened. She always heard. Anna would understand.

The lights of EMS vehicles flashed a warning even before he turned onto Magnolia Street. With a surge of adrenaline, he saw they were parked in his own driveway. And they were sliding someone onto a stretcher through the back of the open ambulance doors.

He parked on the opposite side of the street and swung out of the car in one motion. An auburn dog with black-tipped ears and tail barked sharply as Robert ran toward the knot of neighbours who had gathered.

CHAPTER 49

———————∾———————

Teachers are the greatest freaks on earth.
—Anne Frank, *The Diary of Anne Frank*[8]

Amelia really couldn't blame the kids. It was Friday afternoon. Red Deer's snowstorm of the century two months earlier had infected everyone with a bad case of cabin fever and she, too, was about done with school. Her mind was on other things. Like her shortness of breath, her pelvis that felt so fragile it could break with her next movement, and her winter boots that were too tight because of the swelling in her feet and ankles. Her due date was still two weeks away.

But, oh, those kids had tried her patience to the limit this week. One more week of work and she'd be free to focus on her magnum opus. A thrill of anticipation coursed through her. Her last students of the day began straying into the classroom. Sitting up straight in her desk, she took as deep a breath as she could and stood. As she did, she felt a wetness. Could this be—?

There was still one more class to teach. She took small steps to the door. Some of the students were giving her curious looks.

Trying desperately to inject authority into her tremulous voice, she said, "I'll give you this class to catch up on your novel reading. Vice-Principal Goushalak will be down to supervise." *I hope.*

The high school buzz began even before Amelia left the room. She hurried out the door to the nearest girls' washroom, texting Val Goushalak on the way.

Searching her memory about water breaking, she wondered how long she had until active labour began. A conflict of excitement and fear scrambled her thoughts.

As she entered the girls' room, a circle of her Grade Tens turned surprised faces toward her. Staff usually used the washrooms at the teacher's lounge. Something must have been written all over her face because, as one, the girls came toward her and began asking questions, putting arms around her, stroking her hair.

"You're in labour." Kelsey Rivers said. "Danielle, go get Ms. Goushalak. She'll take her to Emerge."

"No, wait. Ms. Gouchalak is taking over my class," Amelia managed. "Let me check. It might be a false alarm." She entered a washroom cubicle.

"Are you kidding?" Kelsey called from outside the stall. "I have three sisters and I've been there every time one of them went into labour. You definitely have the look. Right, girls?"

Amelia heard murmurs of agreement.

There's a look? She came out to find all eyes on her. Amelia looked around at the familiar faces, some smiling, some apprehensive.

"So how many minutes apart are they?" Kelsey asked.

"What? Oh, no contractions. I don't think so, anyway. It's just—"

"Your water's breaking," Kelsey decided. Her disparaging comment last week that "poetry is dumb" was instantly forgiven. The girl was destined for a career in nursing.

"Well, maybe. I'm not sure yet."

"Okay then, was it a gush or a trickle?" The tall, thick-waisted girl's intense stare demanded an answer.

Amelia looked up at her and said, "More of a trickle, really."

"And no contractions?" The other girls' heads snapped back and forth from Kelsey to Amelia like spectators at a ping-pong match. It would have been comical had Amelia been less preoccupied.

"No, not yet. But I still have a class to teach and I'm nervous about walking around in case I leak anymore."

"Forget the class," said Danielle. Six other heads nodded vigorously.

"You can call in sick," Chelsea said. The sisterhood concurred.

"We're supposed to be in Phys. Ed. right now, but I'll talk to Mrs. Rondeau later and let her know what's happened," Kelsey said. "C'mon girls, we'll carry her."

They slung purses toward their backs, flung back long hair, and grasped wrists to create a living chair.

"Oh no," Amelia said. "I don't want everyone staring."

"Anybody stares, I'll smack 'em upside the head," said Kelsey.

"But what if she leaks on us," Janessa whispered.

"Hilary, go get a wad of paper towels."

Hilary dashed over to the dispenser, pulled out multiple sheets, rushed back, and covered the human armchair.

Emma and Toni hoisted Amelia up into the other girls' lowered arms, then held open the washroom door.

Peeking out down the hallway, Toni said, "Coast is clear."

Amelia gave a weak giggle hanging onto Kelsey's and Danielle's shoulders as they carried her down the empty corridors.

"You okay to drive?" Kelsey asked when they got her to her car. "'Cause I have my learner's and I could take you."

Seven faces crowded close to peer through the driver's window.

"Then how would you get home?" Amelia asked, buckling her seatbelt. "No, I'll be fine. But girls, thanks for the 'ride'!"

"We'll miss you!"

"Good luck!"

"Bring the baby to school so we can see her."

"Him," Kelsey said. "She's carrying low. It's definitely a boy."

When they backed away from the car, Amelia pointed it toward home, her mind on autopilot. What she really wanted was to talk to Anna.

At home, she tugged and kicked off her tight boots, dropped her coat onto the back of the couch, and on her way to the bathroom speed-dialled Anna. Uncharacteristically leaving her clothes on the floor, Amelia quickly changed into her robe. *Ahhh, sweet relief.*

There was no answer at Anna's. *Maybe she's in the basement or upstairs and couldn't get to the phone in time.* She left a garbled message. Amelia knew Jesse avoided the phone, preferring instead to call out nonchalantly whenever it rang, "Mom, you better get that."

She tried again. *Come on, Anna, please be home! You said you'd be there for me when the time came.*

No answer.

Amelia tried Beth's number, thinking Anna might be with her. Anxiety rose in her like a clinging vine. Repeated rings, then voicemail. Amelia left another message.

The trickle of fluid had become a thin stream now. She called Anna's number again, setting her phone on the edge of the sink. With each ring, the vine of worry took a stronger hold. The plan had been to remain at home as long as possible to stay in the comfort of familiar surroundings and avoid unnecessary interventions in the natural birth process. Anna, as Amelia's doula, would drive her to the birthing centre only when labour was rhythmic and actively progressing.

Breathing deeply, Amelia went to the bedroom and lay down on her side. She closed her eyes, trying to settle her scattered thoughts.

First, the baby was still moving around strongly. That was good.

Second, no contractions so far. *What was it I read about a dry birth? That's bad, isn't it? Stop it, Amelia!*

Third, first babies don't usually come very quickly. Maybe she should sleep for a while to conserve her strength. She tried to shut off her racing mind. Hopefully, Val had gotten her text and had been able to cover for her last class of the day. What a pack of unsupervised sixteen-year-olds with winter cabin fever would do for fifty minutes was frightening to contemplate.

When would be the right time to call the midwife? Oh! The overnight bag. She'd have to finish packing it with the last things: toothbrush, toothpaste, robe, slippers...

Nope. Sleep was not going to happen. But it did feel good to lie there, unrestricted by clothing. The quiet greys of the bedroom were a blank slate for contemplation after the busy surroundings of school. Except for that jarring patch of white wall marking the absence of one dresser. It had been the easy way to paint last year, but back then she'd never have foreseen that he would leave. Or stay away so long. She knew now why she'd never painted it to match the rest of the room. Always hoping he'd come back, change his mind, embrace the baby.

Her belly began to tighten ever so gradually, a girdle of muscle pulling together. *So that's what contractions are like.* Amelia realized she had held her breath throughout. Absolutely the wrong thing to do. From what she'd read and heard, she knew the contractions wouldn't all be as mild as that.

She reached for her journal and pen on the nightstand and began to record the times. Then she called Anna again. She thought of those diehard feminists who had given birth alone. How could they? The helpless vulnerability she now felt was fogging her mind, obliterating competence or any sense of being equal to this monumental task. The image of the doe she'd seen that spring night four years ago came vividly, violently to mind. That memory of the crimson afterbirth streaking down behind the animal raised Amelia's level of alarm.

Another contraction gripped her.

Would she, like her namesake Amelia Earhart, die an uncharted death, alone? She could almost hear her husband's response to such an idea: *Don't be melodramatic.* But had her mother destined her to such a fate by giving her the name?

I cannot do this alone! She needed a soothing touch, an encouraging word. Above all, she needed to share this epochal event with someone who loved her. And the baby.

In a rush, words of promise and comfort flooded her mind: *He gently leads those who are with young. I am with you. I will never leave you.*

After another contraction, she tried Anna's number. Again, no answer.

Should I call the midwife now?

But with contractions so erratic and no closer than nine minutes apart, it seemed a shame to bother her. Yet Amelia could at least warn Sherry that labour had begun. Reluctantly she punched in Sherry's number. What she really wanted was Anna! She needed Anna. It came to her then that Anna had not actually promised to be with her. What she'd said was, "You will not be alone when your time comes."

Before she could grasp the significance of that, the next contraction began. Tighter, harder, like being clamped in a vice, the pressure made Amelia gasp. This one was much stronger. Focusing intently, she began exhaling slowly.

"Born Free Birthing Centre, Sherry speaking," the voice on the line said. "Hello?"

Amelia couldn't respond, still in the midst of a long breath.

"Hello?"

Finally, she was able to tell Sherry what was happening. The midwife assured her everything sounded fine and instructed Amelia to keep in contact. She told her that things generally move slowly in a first birth and that Amelia should come in with her labour coach when the contractions were about five minutes apart. As she finished the call, another hard contraction squeezed her.

Breathe out. Long and slow. Okay, that's starting to hurt.

Released from its grip, Amelia got up to dress and gather her purse and bag of baby essentials. There was nothing to do but call a taxi and get herself to the centre. And it had better be soon, while she could still manage it. She was opening the bag to run her hand across the sweet soft blanket when another wave of pressure caught her. Head down, she grasped the edge of the dresser tightly with both hands, breathing slowly. But the contraction built and built. She began to moan softly.

"Oohhhh, uunnnnhhh." She tried to keep her voice low, like Sherry had advised. This one seemed to be lasting longer. Interminably.

Oohhhhh, Bobby, where are you when I need you?

CHAPTER 50

Be still, my soul—thy God doth undertake
To guide the future as He has the past;
Thy hope, thy confidence let nothing shake—
All now mysterious shall be bright at last.
—Katharina von Schlegel, "Be Still My Soul"

Robert had been in a state of agitation all day at the thought of what had happened to Anna yesterday. He'd called the nurses' station for an update at his first break late in the morning, but they would give no details since he wasn't family. Not family! By calling again later, introducing himself as Dr. Fielding, he did manage to squeeze out of the cheerful, glib nurse that Anna was in stable condition. When he was finally free to leave the college at 3:30, he headed straight for the hospital.

Coming out of the elevator, he met Don and Cassie, each carrying a large coffee from the hospital's Tim Horton's.

"What's the latest?" he asked them.

"We just got in from Calgary airport a bit ago," Don said. "She's going to be all right, but it'll be a long recovery. The doc told us she's dealing with a broken kneecap, three cracked ribs, and on top of all that, a myocardial infarction. They'll be taking her for angioplasty tomorrow."

"What about all the blood on the floor in the basement?"

"That would have been from the laceration on her head," Cassie said. "They said the cut wasn't very big, but head wounds always bleed a lot even if they're not very serious. She must have cracked it on the stairs when she fell. Or was pushed, I should say." Her eyes were troubled and bitterness tinged her words. "I can't stand seeing her in so much pain."

Tight-lipped, Don drew in a sharp breath. He looked at Robert intently. "I've been talking to the officers who first arrived on the scene. They don't have any suspects yet, but I heard them say something about this looking like a gang initiation. A first for Red Deer, apparently."

"Gang initiation. What, they just beat up old ladies for fun?"

"Random violence against someone helpless initiates them by reducing inhibitions to further crime. It shows their commitment to the gang and binds them to it as part of a criminal element."

"Incredible!"

"It's clear they didn't break in or even come in past the doorway," Don continued. "Nothing was stolen—one of the indicators of an initiation. Mom must have just answered the door, they came in, roughed her up, and threw her down the stairs." He swiped at his nose with his free hand and shook his head. "I'm going to do some checking around. I've already talked to a few of the neighbours. But I've been wondering who made the 911 call. It wasn't you, was it?"

"No, not me. Maybe one of the neighbours."

"Easy enough to find out from the emergency call records," Don said, glancing down the hall. Pulling Cassie with him, he stepped closer to Robert to make room for a couple of orderlies pushing a gurney. "So when did you get there?"

"By the time I got home yesterday, they already had her on a stretcher and were putting her into the ambulance," Robert told him. "At first the police wouldn't let me in the house, but they were having trouble moving Jesse. When I heard him screaming, I managed to convince the officer outside that I knew him and might be able to help."

"He was screaming?" Cassie and Don asked, almost in unison, their eyes wide.

Robert nodded. "Well, more like a series of squawks. I found him hiding in the utility room in the basement with his face in a corner. I figured it was the police officer making him nervous, so I asked him to leave. No problem after that. As soon as Jesse saw me, he turned to me and held on tight. But his whole body was trembling violently and he was sobbing. I've never seen him so worked up. I took him to my place to wait until Beth arrived. He wouldn't let go of me."

"Well, it's a good thing you're here now to see Mom," Don said. "She's been asking for you."

Robert followed them to her room. In the second bed, curtained off, Robert found chairs full of Fawcetts. A gush of them, he thought, knowing Anna would have appreciated the pun. They turned to look at him and nodded as he pushed the curtain aside a bit.

Burk sat holding Anna's hand with his daughter perched on one of his knees. With his other hand he held Katie's. Next came Caleb, his eyes watery. Opposite them sat Steve, his arm around Jesse, who sat shrinking back from the hospital bed, his head down as far as it could go. And holding Anna's other hand was a tall, thin young man, tattooed and pierced. His gaunt face, fixed on his mother's, showed a turmoil of emotion.

David.

Anna lay in the midst, small and betubed, a large bruise purpling the delicate skin on one side of her face. Pity flooded through him, and with it a dark rage at those who had done this violence to an innocent.

Beth was on the phone but hung up when she saw Robert.

"Oh, here he is right now, Mom," she said, turning toward Robert.

"My mom had a message on her voicemail this afternoon, and she wanted to—" Anna was plucking at her daughter's sleeve.

Irresistibly Robert took the hand that David had just released. Despite the ravages done to her, there was a luminous, fragile beauty in Anna's face against the white pillow. Her eyes fluttered and she whispered something.

"I'm sorry," he said. He couldn't hear for the beeping of the monitor and the scraping of chairs as some of the family left the room. She waited, putting weak pressure on his hand.

"...need you to do a favour," she croaked.

"Whatever I can do," he assured her, his heart full.

"My friend called my home. Beth brought message... having a baby—" Anna winced, exhaled slowly. Robert waited, wishing desperately to ease her pain.

"I was supposed to... drive her." A gasp. "Can you take her—"

"To the hospital?"

"No." Anna shook her head too hard and the tube in her nose was displaced. He put it back with trembling hands.

"No. To birthing centre... I was supposed to... on corner of... here..." She fumbled for a piece of paper on the bedside table. It fell to the floor and wafted under the bed where Robert retrieved it.

"Oh, Mom, I could have driven her," Beth said.

Anna's voice croaked and she tried again. "No... Robert."

This was unexpected. And well beyond his comfort level. His mind flooded with scenes of screams and blood and panic. But he shoved the address in his pocket and said, "Yes, of course. I'll look after it. You just rest and get better."

"Go right away!" Anna whispered hoarsely, staring intently into his eyes.

Squeezing her hand, he read volumes in that look. It seemed to be full of more meaning than the errand itself. *Go right away* meant he needed to stop wading and dive in, embrace the search for truth wherever it would lead him, no matter what. It meant he must have the courage to face censure, ridicule, or loss along the way. It meant reconciliation, restitution, and maybe, just maybe, restoration. Those deep blue eyes gazing relentlessly at him called him to a surrender deeper than he'd ever dared contemplate before.

For now, though, they called him to do as she'd asked. This strange and simple request. On the way to the parking lot, he began to lose his nerve and question the whole escapade. What was he to do? Arrive at a stranger's door and say, "I'm your ride to the birthing centre"? What if the woman was in the throes of hard labour and couldn't walk? And where in the world was the woman's husband anyway? It was just too weird. However, he'd promised—and the power of her look compelled him. But he couldn't help shaking his head with a doubtful grimace. Anna had certainly plunged him into it this time.

Driving out of the parking lot, he fumbled in his pocket for the scrap of paper marked with the addresses of the centre and the woman's home.

CHAPTER 51

————⟋⟍————

That ye may live, which will be many days
Both in one faith unanimous, though sad
With cause for evils past, yet much more cheered
With meditation on the happy end.
—John Milton, *Paradise Lost, Book XII*

"Nine eleven something," he muttered. Hmmm. Upside-down. "Okay. One sixteen, Wells Crescent." *What? It can't be!*

He braked hard for the yellow light and studied the note in his shaking fingers.

It was an address too familiar. His left knee began a rhythm and sweat beaded his forehead. Overcome with surges of emotion, he *knew*. But would she want him? The thought of his high-handed abandonment of her last summer filled him with bitter regret.

It was time to make a brave step forward—no more cowardly retreats. It was also time to see what his high performance car could do.

"C'mon, c'mon, *c'mon!*" His voice rose at the hapless traffic light.

Robert pushed the limits of the law, weaving his way through the Friday traffic on the way home. Home!

He parked at the curb, leaving the car idling and the door open. Dashing to the house, he yanked the door open.

"Amelia!"

He rounded the corner and found her bent over in the hallway, clutching her overnight bag, one arm in the sleeve of her coat. Robert grasped her shoulders and stooped to meet her face. Seeing it creased in pain pierced his tumultuous heart.

Amelia opened her eyes to look into his. "You came!" She wanted him!

With more effort than it used to take, he gathered wife and belly, coat and tote, into his arms and carried her out of the house.

"My precious Amelia." His voice was husky with feeling. "It's time for us to meet our baby."

ENDNOTES

1. C.S. Lewis, *The Horse and His Boy* (New York, NY: Harper Collins, 1954), 176.

2. C.S. Lewis, *Mere Christianity* (Glasgow, UK: William Collins Sons and Co. Ltd., 1952), 101.

3. Dr. Seuss, *The Cat in the Hat* (Boston, MA: Houghton Mills, 1957), 50.

4. Lewis, *Mere Christianity*, 109.

5. C.S. Lewis, *The Four Loves* (Glasgow, UK: William Collins Sons & Co. Ltd., 1960), 83.

6. Eric Hoffer, *The Passionate State of Mind: And Other Aphorisms* (New York, NY: Harper & Row, 1955), Aphorism 113.

7. Marilynne Robinson, *Housekeeping* (New York, NY: Farrar, Straus & Giroux, 1980), 10.

8. Anne Frank, *The Diary of Anne Frank* (New York, NY: Doubleday & Co., 1952), 6.

ACKNOWLEDGMENTS

It is a risky thing to place a raw manuscript into the hands of discerning readers. I'm especially grateful to those who cared enough to tell the truth. Deb Elkink, Becky Hurst, Becky Magill, Barbara Penner, Sheila Webster, Janell Wojtowicz – your insights are priceless to me.

Thank you to Dr. Mike Matthews for the doctoral dissertation title, to the parents of Down syndrome sons and daughters who shared anecdotes with me, and to those who encouraged me and believed in this book.

And to my husband Mike, who supports me as I write and rejoiced with me over every surge in word count – you have my heartfelt love and gratitude always.

ABOUT THE AUTHOR

In a fit of optimism at age eleven, ELEANOR BERTIN began her first novel by numbering a stack of 100 pages. Two of them got filled with words. Lifelines, her first completed novel, was published in 2016, followed by Pall of Silence in 2017, a memoir about her late son Paul.

She holds a college diploma in Communications and worked in agriculture journalism until the birth of her first child. The family eventually grew to include one daughter and six sons (the youngest with Down syndrome) whom she home-educated for 25 years.

Eleanor grew up on a Manitoba farm, spent 20 years in cities and towns, and in the past 16 years has come full circle to embrace country life again. She lives with her husband and youngest son, Timothy, amidst the ongoing renovation of a century home in central Alberta where she reads, writes, sweeps up construction rubble and blogs about a sometimes elusive contentment at jewelofcontentment.wordpress.com.

Please visit Eleanor's website for more of her books
and to subscribe to her newsletter:
www.eleanorbertinauthor.com

TITLES BY ELEANOR BERTIN

THE MOSAIC COLLECTION

Love and Unexpected Stress Responses

(a short story in *A Star Will Rise: A Mosaic Christmas Anthology II*)

Tethered

Unbound

Grounded

(a short story in *Before Summer's End: A Mosaic Summer Anthology*)

Like Wool

(a short story in *Hope is Born: A Mosaic Christmas Anthology*)

TIES THAT BIND

Lifelines

Unbound

Tethered

Pall of Silence

(a memoir)

Coming soon to

THE MOSAIC COLLECTION

The Third Grace by Deb Elkink

The past casts a long shadow—especially when it points to a woman's first love.

Fifteen years ago, Mary Grace fell for the French exchange student visiting her family's Nebraska farm. François renamed her "Aglaia"—after the beautiful Third Grace of Greek mythology—and set the seventeen-year-old girl longing for something more than her parents' simplistic life and faith.

Nowadays Aglaia works as a costume designer in Denver. Her budding success in the city's posh arts scene convinces her she's left the country bumpkin far behind. But "Mary Grace" has deep roots, as Aglaia learns during a business trip to Paris. Her discovery of sensual notes François jotted into a Bible during that long-ago fling, a silly errand imposed by her mother, and the scheming of her sophisticated mentor conspire to create a thirst in her soul that neither evocative daydreams nor professional success can quench.

Will her dual journey across oceans and time in her search for self satisfy her cravings?